What readers are saying:

'Wow! What a journey this is… a complex weaving of space, engineering, Luna, and most of all, humanity.'

(Top 500 reviewer)

'Edge of the seat stuff pretty well for the whole book.'

'The best scfi book I've read in ages!'

'Amazing. Really enjoyed reading this book as much as I have all of Kilby's books'

'…kicks into overdrive to the point where it is nearly impossible to put down'

'Very well written, fantastically created, and quite believable. Very hard to put down. Can't wait for the next book in the series.'

'This is a clever and fascinating take on Moon survival after a massive solar storm hits Earth. Good solid characters, and fast moving pace........it's a ripper of a yarn.'

'One of those books you can't put down.'

BY GERALD M. KILBY

RESOURCE CONTROL

MOON BASE DELTA
BOOK 2

GERALD M. KILBY

OUTER PLANET
MEDIA

For notifications on upcoming books and access to my FREE starter library please join my Readers Group at geraldmkilby.com.

CONTENTS

CHAPTER 1
PERSONAL DEMONS

Hunger gnawed at Renton, seeping into every crevice of his consciousness, draining his vitality, and rendering him incapable of concentrating on anything other than relentless thoughts of food. These thoughts took on strange shapes, akin to hallucinations, all orbiting around the notion of nourishment in its myriad forms. Most of these visions, however, regressed to the cherished meals of his youth, lovingly prepared by his parents—rich, hearty, and soul-satisfying fare.

Selene's assertion that Moon Base Delta could support thousands of souls was not unfounded, but it was marred by a single shortcoming: utter lifelessness. Yes, the base possessed the infrastructure to generate an abundance of food for its inhabitants, but none of it could be revived without a foundational stock: seeds for the grow-houses, cell cultures for synthesizing meat analogues, eggs and fry for the aqua-ponds.

Even the stores of the gases necessary for initiating the process, primarily carbon dioxide and nitrogen, were all sadly lacking.

The base had been designed as a closed-loop ecosystem, its biome's inputs and outputs, including those of the human occupants, all contributing to its perpetuation. Restarting even a fraction of this intricate web was proving to be a Herculean feat.

Luck had allowed them to activate one food synthesizer using a strain of microbes that had endured a decade of cryogenic hibernation. Yet, efforts to accelerate production foundered, as the majority of the required reactants were either inert or contaminated.

Matteo had assumed responsibility for this mission, his fixation bordering on obsession. He now dedicated every waking moment to the biolab, striving to increase production. But despite Matteo's unwavering dedication, the production of synthesized food covered a mere fifth of their caloric needs. They couldn't survive on this meager supply alone. Although production was slowly increasing, the pace was glacial. It would take months, perhaps years, to reach a point where they could subsist on the synthesized food. Furthermore, it wouldn't provide all the essential nutrients. They would eventually succumb to deficiencies, not unlike the scurvy-ridden sailors of old, dying from a lack of vitamin C.

Renton and the others had eventually resigned themselves to leaving him to his task, as their presence only served to exasperate Matteo to the brink of anger. Eventually, one by one, they retreated. Renton seldom saw Matteo now, and when he did, his colleague appeared gaunt and haggard, his visage a tapestry of anxiety. Matteo spoke only of obscure chemical reactions, the language of which went far above Renton's comprehension. It was a side of Matteo that Renton had never witnessed before, verging on obsessive-compulsive. Then again, how well did any of them truly know each other? They had been together only a brief while before the catastrophe of the solar storm, and their fight for survival had only just begun. None could be immune to the strain. So, they left him to his task, checking in periodically to ensure he hadn't entirely lost his grip on reality.

With Matteo essentially out of commission, Renton, Alice, and Yuna shifted their focus to scavenging the base for any supplies they could uncover—primarily food. They found precious little that could be consumed with any certainty that it wasn't tainted. While the lunar surface might be a sterile environment, the warm, damp atmosphere of a previously densely populated human colony fostered the proliferation of bacteria—some of which could be fatal if ingested, such as E. coli, Listeria, Salmonella, or worse, Botulism. Although irradiation might render their discoveries theoretically safe, none were willing to be the first to sample the offerings. As their hunger intensified, however, it was only a matter of time before one of them might succumb to the temptation.

The vastness of the base and the offline, inaccessible areas impeded their search, necessitating the use of EVA suits. Consequently, they turned their attention to the auxiliary structures surrounding the base, some of which, like the maintenance area they had utilized to access the primary facility, had been operational until the solar storm. These sites proved more fruitful, and they managed to secure packaged food supplies that were, more or less, still within their expiration dates. Their exterior excursions even included a return trip to the emergency shelter they had sought refuge in after the shuttle crash. However, the rewards were meager compared to the effort expended, as they had already depleted most of its resources a few weeks prior.

When their scavenger hunt reached its conclusion, and no more areas were worth searching, they pooled their accumulated supplies along with the meager bounty from the biolab, and with the aid of DOA, the AI managing Moon Base Delta, they calculated their projected survival time.

DOA took note of these nutritional limitations and generated a series of dietary plans that ranged from a complete nutritional and caloric intake, which would deplete their supplies within weeks, to a severely restricted diet that would last many times longer but demand extraordinary willpower. In the end, they settled on a compromise, although it was still extremely austere.

And so, the arguments began.

Initially, Alice and Yuna were pissed off that DOA had calculated a higher caloric allowance for Renton and Matteo due to their larger biological mass. But they ultimately acquiesced when the AI assured them it was necessary to ensure that all of them reached the brink of starvation simultaneously. In other words, they would all die at more or less the same time.

Disputes then arose over their next steps and long-term survival plans. Selene, still stranded on the luxury Axial Luxor Hotel, reported that the situation on the wider lunar surface had evolved into a struggle for individual survival. Few people were willing or able to render aid to them, as doing so might jeopardize their own chances. This entrenchment unfolded against the backdrop of a cautious consolidation by the two remaining power blocs—SINO and Xilinex. Neither had made overt moves for control, but everyone knew it was only a matter of time before a full-blown war erupted between them. In short, no one was coming to their rescue. Moon Base Delta might be vast and virtually impregnable, but it was too remote from the primary population concentrations in Shackleton and Amundsen Craters. Therefore, most people calculated it was better to stay put and conserve resources.

This assessment of the broader lunar situation did nothing to alleviate their immediate concerns; worse still, it only served to heighten their awareness of the precariousness of their predicament. Survival was firmly in their own hands, and they desperately needed to devise a way forward.

Renton suggested restoring a rover to operational status so they could venture further afield, possibly to another outpost where abandoned supplies might be found. However, the nearest unaffiliated outpost was hundreds of kilometers away—a risky endeavor with no guarantee of success.

Yuna argued that the base had not yet been fully explored and insisted they should complete that task first. Why risk venturing too far from the base? Alice initially supported Yuna's proposal to thoroughly search the base, but she preferred using robots over embarking on extended EVA suit excursions. Renton countered that regardless of whether they employed robots or physical exploration, they were unlikely to discover any more than what existed in the operational sectors. He didn't think it was worth the effort. Matteo, of course, was solely focused on the biolab, and it was impossible to engage him in any other conversation, so they didn't bother trying.

Ultimately, they agreed that Alice would work on the robots while Yuna identified potential sectors to investigate. Meanwhile, Renton would attempt to restore a rover to working condition. There wasn't much else they could do.

It was at this point that they all began to drift apart, opting to spend time alone, each absorbed in their own pet project—much like Matteo and his obsession with the biolab. Perhaps they had simply grown weary of each other, or perhaps they needed to withdraw and regroup. It could be that they were all grappling with the accumulated effects of trauma. Regardless of the reason, Renton found himself preferring his own company, channeling his dwindling reserves of energy between repairing a suitable rover and studying lunar topography maps to identify potential outposts that might hold the key to their survival.

As days turned into weeks, the situation in Moon Base Delta became increasingly dire. The crew's bodies grew gaunt, their faces etched with the pain of perpetual hunger. The base, once a symbol of humanity's ambition and ingenuity, now stood as a stark reminder of the fine line between life and death.

Renton's efforts to repair the rover were arduous, but he clung to the hope that their salvation lay just beyond the horizon. Alice and Yuna worked tirelessly to expand their knowledge of the base, unearthing hidden secrets and long-forgotten areas that hinted at the possible potential for survival.

Matteo, meanwhile, remained holed up in the biolab, his once-brilliant mind deteriorating under the weight of his single-minded pursuit. He had become a husk of his former self, a pale specter driven by the desperate need to crack the code that would unlock their salvation.

As the days wore on and their circumstances grew ever more precarious, the four wayward souls clung to their individual obsessions, not realizing that their greatest strength —cooperation and unity—had been lost along the way. In the cold, unforgiving environment of the moon, the survival of Renton, Alice, Yuna, and Matteo would ultimately depend on their ability to overcome their personal demons, rediscover their shared purpose, and reignite the spark of hope that had succeeded in getting them this far.

CHAPTER 2
THE OUTSIDE CLOSES IN

The shrill, high-pitched squawk of a proximity alert shattered Han Sundar's nighttime slumber, catapulting him bolt upright in bed. He checked the time on a small digital monitor located on the bedside table—3:45 AM. This was the fourth alert this week, but the first to invade his sleep.

Beside him, Sheneese turned and lifted her head from the pillow. "What is it?" Her voice was a combination of concern and annoyance.

"Something's triggered a motion sensor," he replied in a hushed tone, doing his best not to disturb the quiet any further. "It could just be another animal, perhaps a deer or a coyote that's wandered too close to the perimeter wall." He reluctantly slid out of the warm bed and navigated his way downstairs, padding across the cold stone floor to a bank of monitors that served as the epicenter of their security system. He silenced the alarm and then studied the readout, searching for any indication of what had triggered the warning. Behind him, he heard Sheneese follow him down, then the familiar clunk-click of a round being chambered into a bolt-action sniper rifle, Sheneese's weapon of choice, her preferred method of negotiation these days. She joined him by the array of monitors, the weapon cradled securely in her arms.

"There's movement on the road leading to the main gate," Han spoke in hushed tones, his finger pointing at an aerial map of the observatory compound where a red marker blinked a short distance from the entrance, indicating the location of the activated motion sensor.

"Let's hope you're right, that it's nothing more than a large animal, and not another desperate soul searching for food supplies," Sheneese offered, her tone suggesting she wasn't fully convinced.

The frequency of these attempted intrusions had risen sharply, particularly over the course of the past few weeks. The situation beyond the observatory's protective walls had deteriorated at an alarming rate ever since the local food distribution center had been besieged and overtaken by armed militia groups. With the National Guard having effectively abandoned the region, the populace was left to fend for themselves, pitted against the unchecked violence of opportunistic gangs.

Three days prior, their local radio station, which had been providing them with regular updates and news from the outside world, had fallen ominously silent. Now they were left with only sporadic broadcasts from much further afield. These painted a grim picture of the current state of affairs, chronicling the rapid fracturing of society into the hunter and the hunted. All were desperate to find sanctuary from the increasing numbers of militia groups that now roamed the countryside, plundering what they could from whomever was weakest.

They had already fought off two attempts. These were small, disorganized groups numbering no more than a handful of opportunists who probably just happened upon the observatory compound in their relentless search for sustenance. Perhaps they had been ordinary decent folk before the solar storm: the local mechanic, the baker, or even the guy who delivered your pizza. Now they roamed in well-armed packs, seeking to take advantage of any opportunity to stock up on supplies.

But these groups were getting bolder. Just a few short weeks ago, firing a couple of rounds of buckshot into the air had been more than enough to send them scattering in all directions. Back then, the prospect of sustaining life-threatening injuries far outweighed the meager prize of a bag of rice. But now, with the food distribution center gone and rumors of the sanctuary cities in the east closing themselves off to newcomers, there was a growing sense of desperation among the local populace.

Han and Sheneese both recognized the reality of their situation: it wouldn't be long before knowledge of their location spread among these increasingly desperate groups, and it was only a matter of time before one of them tried to mount a serious attempt to seize control of their refuge. Just the previous week, they had spotted a drone buzzing over the forest canopy, venturing past the mountain's protective barrier and making its way toward the valley. The presence of the drone could only signify one unnerving possibility: someone was conducting reconnaissance of the area, meticulously scouting and gathering intelligence. They monitored the drone's progress throughout that afternoon as it methodically zigzagged across the treetops, its flight path betraying its determined search for information. At one particular moment, the drone ventured close to the observatory, placing it well within a range where it could examine the compound's layout and defensive measures.

Han's eyes now turned to the feed from their own security drones, which were ceaselessly patrolling the skies above the observatory. He entered a new set of instructions to one of the machines, guiding it to a position directly above the winding track that led to the entrance gate of the compound. The night-vision image that appeared on the screen glowed with an eerie, otherworldly green hue, but the resolution was good enough for Han to discern a large off-road vehicle stationed about three hundred meters from the compound's entrance, its imposing bulk partially concealed by the embrace of the tree canopy.

"It's not an animal. Do you see that truck down there?" Han gestured at the screen.

Sheneese leaned in. "I see it. And it looks like it's had a radical Mad Max upgrade," she responded, concern growing in her voice.

Han switched the display from standard night vision to infrared. Almost immediately, four distinct reddish shapes emerged from the velvety darkness—four individuals on the move. They split into pairs, each advancing on either side of the narrow track, steadily and purposefully making their way toward the compound's entrance gate.

Han switched the feedback to standard night vision, now that he had a bead on them, and zoomed in.

"They don't look like a bunch of yokels. They're well-armed, wearing tactical equipment," he said, casting a glance at Sheneese, whose face betrayed her escalating fear. "And judging by their movements and hand signals, they might be former military personnel."

Han bit his lip at the realization of what was about to unfold. "You'd best get to the Crow's Nest."

Sheneese grasped the rifle and prepared to ascend.

"But wait for me to activate the lights; you'll have a clearer target." He tossed her a small walkie-talkie.

She acknowledged with a nod, pocketed the compact radio, and proceeded up the stairs to the observatory's uppermost level at the apex of the Equatorial room. From there, a somewhat precarious metallic ladder would lead her to a makeshift perch nestled atop the ancient dome, aptly dubbed the Crow's Nest. From this vantage point, she had an unobstructed, panoramic view of the surrounding area, its protection further enhanced by the addition of thick steel plates welded to the railing. However, Sheneese's shooting abilities were hindered by the lack of a night-sight on the rifle, rendering her unable to effectively discern targets until the compound was illuminated.

Han studied the movement of the four figures who had now reached the gates and assumed positions flush against the wall, two on either side. He maximized the zoom on the drone feed to gain as much detail as possible without jeopardizing its stealth, wary of maneuvering the drone any closer and inadvertently revealing its presence through the telltale hum of its rotors.

The two assailants on the right side of the gate were preparing to climb over. One stood with his back braced against the wall, his hands cupped together, offering a boost up for his buddy.

This is the moment, thought Han. The moment when he would find out if all that work he and Sheneese had put into perimeter security would pay off. The compound already had a solid brick wall that circumscribed the exterior. It was old-school industrial, almost Victorian in design and material, around twelve-feet high with a stone capping. Nevertheless, it would present few challenges for a pair of determined climbers with the right skills. To address this vulnerability, over the course of several weekends, Han and Sheneese had painstakingly added an unassuming, yet deceptively effective, wire railing along the top of the wall. Comprised of three parallel cables separated by the width of an average human hand, this seemingly innocuous railing concealed a potentially lethal secret—one Han now fervently hoped would prove to be an effective barrier.

A hand grabbed the stone capping as one of the men began to pull himself up. Han held his breath as the intruder then reached for the cable.

There was a sudden blinding flash, coupled with an explosion of sparks as 20,000 volts instantly discharged from a bank of ultra-capacitors through the body of the unsuspecting intruder. He flew backward through the air and slammed hard onto the ground a good thirty feet away. He didn't get up again.

His associates rushed to their stricken comrade. Han waited and hoped that this high-voltage demonstration would be enough for them to hightail it out of there. His fear was that they would try again and discover that the fence was now dead, as it would take a good five minutes for the capacitors to fully recharge.

To his immense relief, they appeared to reluctantly retreat, slowly retracing their steps down the winding track, leaving behind their incapacitated comrade. One by one, they all clambered back inside their armored truck. For a brief moment, Han pondered the nature of such individuals who would abandon a dead or dying comrade to become nothing more than lunch for some woodland scavenger or carrion bird. He thumbed the talk button on the walkie-talkie. "It worked. They're leaving."

Sheneese replied instantly. "Thank God for that." The radio's poor fidelity was still sufficient to convey the weight of relief in Sheneese's voice.

But they weren't leaving. Not just yet.

The truck started up with a rumble and began advancing toward the gate, picking up speed as it progressed, dust and dirt flying out behind it as the tires tried to gain purchase on the loose ground.

"Shit. They're going to ram the gates," Han shouted into the walkie-talkie.

He flicked on the perimeter halogens, flooding the entire compound with harsh electric light.

"Take out that driver, Sheneese, take him out!"

He bounded up the stairs to the first floor, where his

shotgun sat loaded and ready, nestled atop a mound of sandbags below a small window that faced out to the front of the building. From there, he would have fire control over most of the area inside the gates.

He had just flung open the window when he heard the crack from the sniper rifle. At the same time, the truck barreled through the old iron gates, separating them from their hinges and sending them cartwheeling through the air. He heard a second shot, then a third. One of them must have hit its mark, as the truck swerved violently, teetering on the brink of overturning before slamming into the base of an ancient spruce with a bone-jarring thud.

For a moment, time ceased to exist. Nothing moved save for a wisp of steam gently rising up from the truck's hood. Han aimed his shotgun at the battered machine and fired off a blast, not that it would do much damage, as the truck was well armored with plate steel crudely welded along its sides. But it was good to let them know there was more than one weapon trained on them.

The driver's side door suddenly flew open and a body was tossed out. The truck then shuddered back to life, reversing at speed out from the base of the tree, spinning around to face the wide-open gate. Then it took off back out through the opening, down along the track, and disappeared into the night. Presumably, the assailants had decided that the fight was too much for them.

Han hunkered down behind the sandbags, his breath ragged, his heart pounding as he took in the scene of the blood-soaked carnage out front. Two men lay motionless, probably dead, victims simply of their own desperate hunger. He couldn't help but shake his head at the sheer insanity of it all. *Is this what humanity has been reduced to?* he thought.

"I think I've just killed a man," a voice behind him whispered.

Startled, Han turned to find Sheneese standing behind him, her face a mask of anguish, her eyes wide and wild, like a feral creature.

"We both have." He stood up and brought her into a tight embrace. "Best not dwell on it too much." He broke off the embrace and locked eyes with her. "We need to get the compound secured in case they decide to come back."

"Jesus, you think there's more of them?" She shivered with the thought.

"I don't know. But we need to stay sharp. I'll go and sort out the mess down there. You stay here at the window, keep me covered. I don't want to get caught out in the open if they come back up the track again."

She squeezed his arm. "Be quick. I'm running on adrenaline, and I'm not sure how long I can keep it together."

"Trust me, I'm not hanging around any longer than I have to out there." He shouldered the shotgun, grabbed the walkie-talkie, and headed back down the stairs, out through the front door—which he considered might need a lot more reinforcing. But that was for another time.

Outside, the courtyard in front of the building was flooded with light from the halogens. He was conscious of how much power was being drained from the batteries while these lights were on. He needed to be quick. His first priority was to secure the gateway, then he'd check on the two bodies.

He headed for the garage at the side of the main building, swung open the big wooden doors, and hopped into his pickup. He started it up and drove the short distance to the main gate, bringing it to a halt just inside. He got out and walked back up to check on the body that had been shoved out of the attackers' truck earlier.

He prodded it with the muzzle of the shotgun. When he got no response, he reached down and rolled the body over onto its back. There was a neat, bloodied hole in its forehead right above two cold, dead eyes.

He glanced back up at the window where Sheneese kept watch. His walkie-talkie crackled.

"Is he dead?"

"As a doornail. Nice shot, by the way."

There was a pause before Sheneese replied. "Not quite the same as shooting at targets."

"No, that's for sure." He stood up and gestured toward the gate. "I'm going to check on the other guy. Stay sharp."

He pocketed the walkie-talkie and headed out the gate and over to where the second body lay face up in the dirt. Again, cold dead eyes stared back up at him.

Han recognized him. He was pretty sure that this was the same guy who used to work in the local 3D print store in town. He probably worked on some of the jobs that Han had sent their way. But, like he had said to Sheneese a little earlier, it was probably best not to dwell on that too much.

He shouldered the shotgun, grabbed the body by the straps on his tactical vest, and dragged him all the way back to where the other body lay. He would deal with them both later. He then got back into the truck and parked it sideways across the gateway entrance. After that, he unloaded a long roll of cable from the bed and set to work connecting it to his makeshift electric fence. He unspooled as much as possible, laying a big ball of tangled wire across the top of the truck. It wasn't pretty, but it would do the job, as the dead body in the courtyard would testify.

He moved back to the bodies. Both had sidearms that he took, along with some ammunition stowed in various pouches. He brought it all back into the observatory, switched off the floodlights, reset the fence, and then poured both himself and Sheneese a stiff drink.

They sat for a while, gazing at the camera feeds from the two security drones that patrolled overhead, expecting, at any moment, to see movement along the track or around the perimeter. But there was none.

"Why don't you get some sleep," Han finally said after a time. "I'll keep watch for a few hours, then maybe we can swap."

Sheneese sighed. "Is this our new normal? Keeping watch in shifts, waiting for the next attack?"

Han was too exhausted to answer.

"How long can we continue like this?" she wondered aloud, her voice fraught with fear. "How long before we're the ones sprawled lifeless in the courtyard?"

Han's gaze remained steady, despite the turmoil within. "Get some sleep. Now's not the time for those questions."

She gave a slow nod, her tense muscles easing ever so slightly. "You're right. Now's not the time. We both need rest." She rose to her feet and moved toward the stairs. Pausing, she looked back at him. "Will you be okay?"

He nodded. "Yeah, I can manage another three or four hours. I'll wake you then."

"Okay." Her head dipped, and she ascended the stairs toward the bedroom.

Alone now, in the dimly lit room, Han allowed his thoughts to wander. Sheneese was right—the chaos of the world beyond their sanctuary was encroaching. How much longer could they hold out in their fragile haven? Not very long, he suspected. He couldn't shake the feeling that their time was running out.

CHAPTER 3
WANDERERS

Selene Mene heaved herself out of the hotel swimming pool, beads of water rippling down her body as she turned to sit on the edge. She had completed ten lengths of the modest twenty-five-meter pool so far this morning, but her sights were set on chalking up another twenty before making her way to the weekly meeting, soon to kick off in the operations center. She needed her mind sharp and focused, ready to tackle and subdue any potential chaos that threatened to erupt among the various factions vying for control of the diminishing resources of the Axial Luxor Hotel.

At the outset, when they began to pick up the pieces in the aftermath of the dock explosion, everybody pulled together, helped each other out, and did whatever they could to keep the ship afloat. It was fortunate, in a way, that a fair percentage of the stranded personnel were hotel staff with built-in knowledge and an established hierarchy. But then there were others who found it difficult to adapt to their new circumstances—hotel guests who had been accustomed to the luxury of having their every need catered to, now faced the stark reality of having to roll up their sleeves and contribute to the collective effort of survival.

It was during this initial period that Selene had stepped up, assuming the role of leader because of her unique skill set and her ability to make decisions under pressure. She had been instrumental in organizing the rescue of those trapped in the dock after the devastating explosion. They had followed her leadership without hesitation, and thus far, she had not let them down.

Yet, the one hundred and twenty-seven individuals trapped within the confines of the luxury orbital found themselves facing a grim reality: there was no way off the station, and it was beginning to wear on all of them. A creeping sense of anxiety coupled with the insidious spread of boredom was taking its toll, creating a potentially corrosive mix that could fracture the finely balanced harmony.

Whispers of doubt and unease had begun to spread through the ranks, as certain people started to question the authority that had been bestowed upon Selene Mene. Who elected her? Why should she tell people what to do? It was a tricky situation.

She slipped back into the pool and began thrashing through the water for another twenty lengths.

. . .

When she finally arrived at the operations center, she found the meeting had already started, presided over by Jeff Bodega, the most seasoned hotel staff member left behind after the calamitous evacuation. She acknowledged everyone with a subtle nod as she settled into a chair around the elongated, boardroom-style table. Jeff, his eyes briefly meeting Selene's, returned the acknowledgment before continuing his detailed assessment of the rationing system, which, to everyone's relief, seemed to be functioning smoothly and efficiently. With a stockpile of food sufficient to last approximately six months, there was, as of yet, no reason for the group to worry about hunger or malnutrition.

However, one potential problem loomed on the horizon— the increasingly rampant consumption of alcohol. Some people had resorted to excessive drinking, perhaps as a means to stave off the dull ache of boredom, or perhaps as an attempt to numb the crippling weight of depression that threatened to engulf them. Yet, the group could not reach an agreement on how best to address or resolve the situation, so they decided, for the time being, to set it aside and revisit it later. And so, the meeting trudged on in this vein for another tedious hour, as they discussed the minutiae of their day-to-day existence, stranded in a luxurious hotel parked in lunar orbit.

Eventually, the discussions turned to focus on the other isolated colonist groups, down on the lunar surface.

"The prevailing mood is one of entrenchment," Selene announced with an air of authority. "Both the Xilinex Corporation and SINO have turned their attention to reinforcing their respective areas of control. They've initiated a process of seizing and repurposing abandoned assets while simultaneously assimilating any colonists they encounter within their expanding territories. That's got the remaining independent sectors all jittery. They've adopted a more cautious approach, hunkering down, regulating their resources. For now, it seems, no one is inclined to make any impulsive moves."

Professor Henriksen, who, much like Selene, had waited too long during the evacuation and subsequently found himself also marooned on the orbital, chimed in, "It's hardly surprising, given the circumstances."

Selene nodded in agreement, adding, "True, but it means that the more populous lunar sectors, such as Shackleton and Amundsen, are reluctant to send a ship up here to help us out. Especially if they think one of the two big powers is just going to step in and seize control."

"So, they're all adopting a wait-and-see strategy," he surmised.

"Exactly. And that position becomes more entrenched as each day passes."

Gabriel Grando, who had originally attended the New Lunar Accord conference as a representative of the Non-Spacefaring Nations, proposed an alternative explanation from his perch at the far end of the table, where he and his group of allies had staked a claim. "Perhaps," he mused, "it's merely a failure to communicate."

"Give it a rest, Gabriel. That's not going to help us. Unless, of course, you'd like to take a shot at resolving the issue?"

Grando raised his hands in a placating gesture, "I'm merely expressing a viewpoint—participating in the discussion."

"The crux of the matter," Selene continued, undeterred, "is that everyone is anticipating open conflict between Xilinex and SINO. They're all convinced it's coming, and that's got everyone spooked and hunkered down."

"It would appear to me that our most prudent course of action would be to allow the Xilinex Corporation to assume control of this orbital," ventured Grando. "However, our... unofficial leader here seems unwilling to entertain that idea."

Selene leaned in across the edge of the table, focusing her attention on Grando and his cohort of allies, "Don't go deluding yourselves into believing life under Xilinex's rule will be a utopia filled with rainbows and ice cream. They're a ruthless corporate force, and rest assured, they will extract every ounce of value from us, one way or another." She paused and sat back. "Besides, they're not even concerned with us at the moment. Reading between the lines, it's clear that Xilinex intends to target the more vulnerable and accessible assets first. Since we're not going anywhere, they'll likely bide their time until we're desperate, and then seize the opportunity to take control."

"Well, the sooner the better," Grando replied with an emphatic nod, then seeing the exasperated looks from the others around the table, opened his hands in a gesture of conciliation. "In my humble opinion."

"Your position on the Xilinex Corporation is duly noted, Gabriel. But our consensus is to try to remain as an independent entity." Selene knew Grando didn't have the support yet to mount a meaningful challenge to her authority. But any slip-ups could tip the balance. She needed to tread carefully.

"Any update on getting a comms link back up and running with Earth?" Jeff Bodega asked, moving the agenda along.

"Moon Base Delta will be joining us on screen in a minute, so we can ask them how that's going," said Deejay Bale, the young tech.

"This is a waste of time. Earth can't help us now." Grando waved a hand in the air like he was swatting away a fly. "I'd say they've got bigger problems on their hands now that the entire orbital network has been destroyed."

"Even so, they must be doing analysis on the debris cloud. We could get some definitive answers on how long it will take to clear."

"Delta's online," said Deejay as the main screen in the operations center flickered to life.

The four former crew members of the FISA maintenance vessel Aurora appeared demoralized, a shadow of their former selves. Emaciated, disheveled, and drained of energy, they slumped in their seats within their operations center, each focused on consuming a substance that bore a passing resemblance to food.

"How are you all faring?" Selene ventured cautiously.

"Still alive, I guess," Renton managed between mouthfuls.

"Any indication of a supply mission on the horizon?" Alice inquired, her gaze fixed on her meal, too preoccupied to meet the camera.

"Everyone on Luna's in preservation mode, hoarding their resources. And... well, Moon Base Delta is all the way up in Tranquility, too far for anyone in Shackleton or Amundsen to risk. But rest assured, we're doing everything we can," Selene tried to sound optimistic.

The crew, however, remained impassive to her reassurances. Their attention was solely focused on savoring each morsel of their meager meal.

"Oh, DOA has a request." Renton gestured vaguely in the air.

"Sure. What is it?" Selene was used to the AI being included in these communications with Moon Base Delta. And in many ways, she found it to be far more engaging and informative than any of the crew.

"Greetings, Selene. I trust you are well?" The AI asked in its usual pleasant tone.

"Thank you. So what's the request?"

"As you are aware, my systems have been dormant for over fifteen years, and during this period, much has evolved. I am now confronted with substantial gaps in my knowledge base, which hinder my ability to adequately support the current inhabitants of Moon Base Delta. Acquiring an up-to-date lunar surface map that encompasses all infrastructure developments from the past fifteen years would be of immense value."

"We should have good topographical maps here," said Professor Henriksen. "We can transmit an update to you, which should cover the majority of publicly available data. Just be aware that some information about the SINO facilities is speculative, as they are notoriously tight-lipped about divulging specifics."

"Thank you. That will undoubtedly aid us in pinpointing potential areas for exploration," DOA responded gratefully.

"Exploration?" Selene arched an eyebrow. To her knowledge, the crew was effectively trapped within the confines of the base.

"Eh, yeah. I managed to resurrect one of the old rovers," Renton revealed.

Deejay brought up a map of Tranquility on a separate screen, which the crew couldn't yet see, and started panning around. Data points began to populate the map. "There's definitely some potential places around you. What's your range?"

"During the lunar day, theoretically unlimited, we can charge as we go. But it's lunar night for the next fourteen days, so..." Renton paused for some quick mental calculations. "Four hundred kilometers, tops, and that's a round trip. So maximum distance for safety would be around one-fifty."

"You're planning on leaving?" Selene asked, a note of anxiety in her voice.

"In case you haven't noticed, we're all starving to death here," Alice answered, gesturing at her fellow crew. "Our supplies are running low and only because Matteo managed to get one of the bioreactors working are we not in far worse shape. We have to find food. And soon." She emphasized the last word.

"I understand," Selene acknowledged. "We all have to do whatever we can to survive. We'll send you the chart data as soon as possible."

"One more thing," Renton lifted a finger, gesturing skyward. "The FISA satellite network, LunaSat. We need access. DOA's currently relying on some archaic system for its data comms.

With LunaSat, it could significantly expand its knowledge base, and that would be immensely helpful."

Selene glanced at the Professor. "Unfortunately, we don't possess the necessary access codes. That's under the jurisdiction of Space Division. We can ask them, but we'd need Earth comms for that. Which brings me to my next question. How is that progressing?"

"It's not our main priority, Selene," Renton sighed.

"Just transmit the map data—everything you have," Yuna interjected. "Our primary concern is locating supplies."

Selene nodded. "Understood."

The communication ended.

Sometime later, the meeting adjourned without any further discord from Gabriel Grando, and Selene took solace in the fact that, at the very least, unity had prevailed. Then her thoughts turned to her nephew, Renton, and the beleaguered crew at Moon Base Delta. Were they contemplating forsaking the base to become wanderers, roaming from outpost to outpost in search of food? Possibly.

No doubt many others on the lunar surface were entertaining similar thoughts out of sheer necessity. Soon there would be caravans of desperate people, ceaselessly searching for a better existence until they were inevitably ensnared by the Xilinex Corporation or SINO, or became unintended casualties in the looming territorial conflict. Was this the fate that awaited them all?

CHAPTER 4
DEPARTURE

Renton manipulated the augmented reality projection emanating from his comms unit, ensuring that it seamlessly melded with the motor control interface he was trying to repair on this ancient relic of a rover. If he could just pinpoint and resolve the elusive glitch, then the antiquated machine would be a step closer to rolling out onto the surface of the Moon once more.

Contrary to what he had told Selene during the comms hook-up with the Axial, the rover was nowhere near operational, at least not yet. But he was reasonably confident that between himself and Yuna—who had given up on her quest to search the entirety of Moon Base Delta—they would soon get it working again.

After the meeting, Matteo returned to the sanctuary of the biolab, immersing himself in his passion project, even though Renton tried to persuade him to come and help with the rover.

Matteo's technical skill would have been invaluable, but there was more to it than that; Renton missed the camaraderie, his sense of humor, the way things used to be.

It wasn't quite the same working with Yuna, whom Renton still couldn't quite fathom. While he admired her steely stoicism, she seemed cold and distant most of the time. Perhaps this was just her way of dealing with the situation they all faced.

She was currently inside the cockpit running diagnostic routines, identifying and cataloging all the errors still ongoing with the rover's subsystems—it was an extensive list.

"Renton?" DOA's voice resonated inside his head.

"Yes, what is it?"

"I've just received the map data from Professor Henriksen on board the Axial Luxor and have identified several potential targets for exploration. Would you like to review it? I can display it on the holo-table in the operations center."

"Absolutely. Be right there. Have you informed the others?

"Of course. They have all been informed."

"Okay."

Renton turned to find Yuna standing beside him, which was a little unsettling, as he had not heard her approach.

"DOA's got the map data," Yuna said, her expression emotionless. "We should go check it out. I've contacted Alice, and she's already on her way to the operations center."

"Uh, yes, of course." Renton set down his tools and wiped his hands on his jumpsuit before tapping his comms unit. "Matteo?"

"Yeah?" came an irritated reply.

"DOA's received the map data from the Axial and identified some prospects for us, wants us all in the op-center."

"I know. I got the message," Matteo replied with a slight pause. "Look, I'm kind of in the middle of something right now."

"Matteo, could you possibly park it for a while? We need your input on this. We don't want to make decisions without you there."

Silence.

"Please, Matteo, this is critical," Renton added, hoping to persuade him.

"Oh, all right, but let's not drag it out longer than we have to." Matteo relented.

Renton ended the comms, looked at Yuna, and rolled his eyes.

"Is he coming?"

"Yeah, reluctantly."

They arrived at the operations center to find Alice already there. She glanced over, giving them an exhausted smile of acknowledgment, then gestured at the 3D topographical map that bloomed out from the surface of the holo-table. "DOA's identified all the infrastructure that exists around Tranquility, out to a radius of around four hundred kilometers from the base."

Matteo arrived, looking irritated and distracted.

"Hey, thanks for coming," Renton said, then gestured at the projection. "DOA's got some prospects for us."

He approached the holo-table.

"What's this place?" Alice asked, pointing at a sizable structure to the east of Tranquility.

The map rotated and zoomed to focus on an illuminated 3D rendering of an industrial facility.

"That's Secchi," said DOA. "A mining outpost owned and operated by the Hamamatsu Corporation affiliated with the JAXA-KARI agency. It had a pre-storm population of approximately five hundred. This has reduced to less than thirty, comprising mainly a group of machine operators that failed to return to base in time for evacuation. According to the data provided by the team on the Axial, they would appear to have considerable food supplies on site, as they were fully restocked three Earth days before the storm."

"How far away is that?" Alice leaned in across the holo-table, studying the 3D rendering, her hands on the edge for support.

"Too far," Renton said before DOA had a chance to answer. "The rover doesn't have the range to get there and back."

"Do we want to come back?" Yuna asked the question none of them wanted to hear.

"What?" Matteo seemed affronted by the mere suggestion of vacating the place. "We've got a huge, sophisticated base here. Defensible and potentially self-sufficient."

"Except, it isn't... self-sufficient, is it?" Yuna shot back.

Renton raised a hand. "Let's not argue. Instead, try to focus on finding a potential site to investigate."

"What are these other markers?" Alice pointed to two small illuminated tags, some distance apart.

"Seismic monitoring facilities," DOA replied. "Scientific installations, with no permanent staff. However, according to the data, they maintained a small stock of supplies for technicians doing periodic routine maintenance."

"Then we should check out one of these first." Renton adjusted the 3D map to zoom in on the closest of the two. "It looks to be around seventy-five kilometers due east of here. The rover could manage that, no problem."

Alice, Yuna, and Matteo all took a moment to focus in on this potential source of salvation.

"If it has power, then we could recharge the rover and head south to check out that other installation." Renton pointed at the secondary marker.

"It sounds like a no-brainer," said Yuna finally. "So, who wants to go check it out?"

"You and Renton should do it," Alice offered. "You've both been working on the rover, so you must know it inside out by now. And anyway, you're the best at navigating, Yuna."

Nobody objected to this proposal.

"Any possibility that either of those two facilities was growing their own food?" Matteo asked tentatively.

"None," answered DOA. "They were occupied only for very brief periods."

"Pity. What we really need is fresh bio-stock," Matteo sighed. "I just don't know enough about the reaction process to get any more out of our current setup."

"My apologies, Matteo, that I cannot provide you with better information on the bioreactors." DOA's voice seemed to take on a more sympathetic tone. "They introduced these systems after they took me offline, so I do not possess any meaningful data as to their operation."

"That's okay, DOA," Matteo responded. "We understand that there are sizable gaps in your knowledge base."

"However," the AI continued, "it may be possible to acquire this missing knowledge. In which case, I could greatly assist in optimizing production."

This got Matteo's attention. "Really? How?"

"By connecting to the LunaSat satellite constellation, then I could access a vast array of data repositories housed within the numerous existing FISA facilities," DOA explained. "Many of which have food production facilities similar to the systems that were set up here at Moon Base Delta."

"We've already made the request," Alice chimed in, "but it turns out we need access codes from Space Division, and that can only come from Earth."

"Which means trying to get the ancient X-Band communications system working again," Renton added. He had planned to look at it sometime, but it was way down on his list of priorities—communicating with Earth wouldn't put food on the table, so to speak. There were more important issues. But if DOA could use that network to harvest data from existing FISA lunar facilities, then that could be a game changer—in a whole bunch of ways, not just food production.

"Matteo?" Renton looked over at his old friend. "Can you do it? Get the comms working again? Drop the... uh, obsession with the bioreactor for a while?"

Matteo thought about this for a moment, seemingly not overly enthusiastic about the prospect.

"The supplies we pick up from those outposts should compensate for any loss of production," prompted Renton. "It would be worth it if we can get DOA connected to LunaSat."

Matteo screwed up his mouth. "The bioreactor is finely balanced, needing constant attention. Taking my eye off it, even for a few hours, could risk a reaction failure. If that were to happen, then it's game over. We'll never get it started again."

"I could do it," Alice announced with a renewed vigor in her voice. "If you help me, Matteo, point me in the right direction, and be at the end of comms when I need it. You know more about these old telecommunication systems than any of us. And you'd still be able to devote most of your time to the bioreactor."

Matteo gave a slow nod. "I suppose I could do that."

"Okay then," Renton said. "Yuna and I will take the rover and check out these outposts. In the meantime, you guys try to get the Earth–Moon comms system working. If we find anything, we'll let you know as soon as possible."

"Just a word of caution, if I may," said DOA. "Heading east will bring you closer to SINO territory. There may be activity out there as SINO pushes further out in their quest for territorial control. Unfortunately, I cannot track surface movements using the current FISA satellite. Hence, I cannot give you an advance warning."

Renton nodded. "Don't worry, we'll be careful."

CHAPTER 5

YOUR COUNTRY NEEDS YOU

Han brought the two plates of food he had prepared over to the table where Sheneese had set out glasses and utensils for breakfast. It consisted of tinned corned beef, canned cannelloni beans, tinned sauerkraut, and a scattering of black olives—also from a tin.

"Last of the sauerkraut, I'm afraid," he announced as he sat down to eat.

"Can't say I'm disappointed to see the back of pickled cabbage." She examined her food. "It's an acquired taste—one that I've not been able to acquire."

Their supplies were dwindling, and they knew the time would come when they would need to devise a plan to replenish their stocks. That moment hadn't arrived just yet, but the longer they put off addressing the issue, the more difficult it would become.

In the beginning, Han thought that all they needed to do

was hunker down and wait until some order was reestablished. But the retreat of the National Guard from this area back to their primary compound in the city, the loss of the local food distribution center, and the most recent attack on the observatory made him realize that things were not going to improve anytime soon; they were only getting worse.

The assault on the compound two nights ago had rattled them both. It underscored their vulnerability, emphasizing how isolated they were. It was a stark reminder of the fragility of their situation. Fortunately, their assailants didn't return that night, nor on the days that followed. And so, with great effort, they managed to hoist the battered gates back into position using a block and tackle connected to the tow-bar of their trusty truck. Han also electrified it so that anyone touching it would be welcomed by an invigorating 20,000 volts.

They alternated shifts, keeping a watchful eye on the bank of monitors that displayed real-time information from the perimeter cameras, overhead drones, and an assortment of infrared and microwave motion detectors. But the constant vigilance was taking a physical and mental toll on them. Han found himself questioning how much longer they could endure this exhausting routine.

"Any news?" Han nodded over at the radio desk where Sheneese had been spending time scanning through various frequencies in search of updates.

"Some folks are making their way to the sanctuary cities while they still can, before they seal themselves off from the world. But outside of the cities, the countryside is descending into lawlessness. It's the same news I'm hearing from everyone who's still broadcasting—and they're beginning to thin out. Doug Bannister over in Dale Farm has dropped off the airwaves, as has LeQuint over in Ricksville." She directed another forkful of sauerkraut into her mouth.

"Do you think we should try to make a run for the city?"

"I'm getting mixed reports. Official broadcasts are saying to stay put until order has been restored. It's dangerous to go traveling right now. Others say get to the cities before they're closed off."

Han nodded. There was no point in pushing it now. But the time to make a decision would come soon enough.

An alert screeched from the motion detectors. Han jumped up and ran over to the bank of monitors.

"Oh shit." Sheneese's voice was edged with fear.

"Movement along the track, coming up the hill." He directed the overhead drones to take a look. There was still plenty of daylight, so they should get a good view of whatever was approaching.

He heard Sheneese behind him, gathering her rifle. "Don't tell me they're back?"

More motion sensors screeched alerts. Whatever was coming up that track was big, maybe even a convoy. Han's heart raced. He could feel it thumping in his chest.

Sheneese came up behind him and gripped his shoulder as she leaned in to track the camera feed from the drones. A large four-wheeled vehicle emerged from beneath the tree canopy. It had a sophisticated military look to it, not just a ramshackle beater with a few steel plates welded to it. Behind it, an even larger six-wheeled infantry fighting vehicle, an IFV, now emerged from under the canopy. Its gun turret bristled with weaponry.

"Jesus, they've got a tank," Sheneese's grip on his shoulder tightened.

"And drones. Look." He pointed to the edge of the feed where two huge military drones hovered in parallel with the advancing convoy—big enough to be carrying weapons systems.

"I'll get up to the Crow's Nest," said Sheneese, her voice reluctant.

"No wait." Han reached out to stop her.

"But..."

"We can't fight this." He gestured at the feed, shaking his head. "They'd just blast you out of it in one shot from that tank."

Sheneese didn't argue. She knew the truth of the situation. They simply watched as the convoy arrived at the front gate. The two drones split off, reconnoitering the compound.

From the back of the IFV, six well-armed military personnel emerged and took up firing positions around the group. One cautiously approached the gate pillar... and pressed the intercom. Both he and Sheneese almost jumped out of their skins when the buzzer sounded on the monitor desk. They exchanged a look of incredulity, then Han reached down and pressed the intercom button.

"Hello?" His voice sounded hollow. "Dr. Han Sundar?"

Again, he exchanged a look with his wife. "Yes, this is he."

"And Professor Sheneese Richmond?"

"That's me," Sheneese called out.

"Am I correct in assuming you've got weapons pointed in our direction at the moment?"

Han wasn't sure how to respond. Should he admit the truth and say no?

"Uh... you assume correctly." He decided to err on the side of caution.

"Then please request all parties to stay calm while I hand over. We do not want any accidents. Can you confirm you have done this?"

Han looked at his wife, his eyebrows reaching peak elevation.

"Uh, I can confirm we will... hold fire."

"Very good. Please stand by." The soldier moved away from the intercom, taking up a position close by.

"What the hell is going on?"

"Damned if I know," said Han. "But these guys are seriously professional. I'll give them that."

Two gull-winged doors on the smaller four-wheeled vehicle opened. They swung up, revealing a black-clad figure on either side. One male, one female, both armed with sophisticated-looking sidearms. Han suspected they might be plasma weapons. Clearly, these people, whoever they were, weren't some rag-tag militia. One of the drones dropped lower in the air, providing cover for these two individuals as they approached the intercom on the gate pillar. It buzzed again.

Han pushed the comms button. "And who might you be?"

"We are here to talk to you both. May we enter? It will be just the two of us. The others will remain outside your... impressive compound."

"Well, we're talking now." Han felt like pushing back, to see how they would react.

"Indeed. But the conversation we wish to have is best concluded face-to-face."

Han surveyed the impressive array of weaponry on display, then turned to Sheneese and shrugged. "I don't think we have a choice here. I'll go down and open the side gate. You keep me covered from up here."

She nodded back and hefted the sniper rifle.

He picked up the walkie-talkie, shoved it into a pocket, and made his way downstairs. His heart was pounding, and he took a moment to calm himself down before he unlocked the front door and stepped out into the courtyard. He glanced up at the window where Sheneese would be but couldn't see her. She was keeping herself hidden in the shadows.

He walked across the yard to the small, pedestrian doorway at the side of the main gate. This was thick steel, securely mounted into the wall. He took another deep breath before reaching out to unlock and unbolt it. He hesitated. Was he making a very stupid move here? But curiosity got the better of him. He heaved the door open, its massive hinges creaking from lack of use.

The two black-clad figures stood a few meters back from the gate, hands by their sides, showing that they had removed their weapons. They smiled, and the male figure slowly raised a hand to wave. "Hello, Dr. Sundar. It's a pleasure to meet you. I am Captain Ethan Johnson and this is my associate, Lieutenant Emily Taylor. We have an important mission that we would like to discuss with you."

For a moment, Han tried to figure out what trick was being played on him. But his mind found it hard to focus on anything other than the surreal nature of this encounter.

"Uh, sure." Almost as a reflex, he stepped aside and gestured with his hand. "Please, come inside."

They smiled again, nodded, and walked slowly through the gate.

"What's all this about?" Han asked as they walked toward the house, glancing up at the window to signal Sheneese that everything was okay.

"All will be revealed. This concerns both you and Professor Sheneese Richmond. We can discuss more inside."

They entered the building, climbed the stairs, and made their way into the main room. Han called ahead to alert his wife that they were coming up. She was positioned at the far end of the room when they entered.

"Professor Richmond, pleased to meet you. While I understand the need for a good weapon in these challenging times, if you don't mind, could you point it at the ground?" He gave a broad, disarming smile.

Sheneese complied.

"So, are you going to tell us what all this is about?" Han asked again.

"We're part of a special government operation," Lieutenant Taylor now took up the narrative. "We're part of a task force that's being set up to try to chart a way forward out of this chaos." She gestured vaguely in the general direction of the outside. "To put it bluntly, we're here because your country needs you."

CHAPTER 6
SEISMIC TESTING STATION

They meticulously ran through the final checks on the newly refurbished rover, with the majority of their attention focused on core systems such as propulsion, life-support, hull integrity, navigation, and communications. Yet, despite their best efforts, there were a significant number of minor issues with the machine. The energy storage system was only operating at a mere forty-seven percent of its potential capacity. Then there was the suspension system, which had clearly seen better days. Also, the interior had been stripped back to its bare metal framework—not a major issue, but it did make for a very noisy ride. Regardless of these drawbacks, Renton was confident that the rover was structurally sound and capable of getting the job done. With each passing moment, as he and the rest of the crew grew ever hungrier, he worried less about the lack of creature comforts.

DOA had updated the rover's outdated fifteen-year-old

navigation charts, so at least Renton and Yuna had a clear sense of where they were headed, and it would enable Yuna to determine the most efficient route to take.

Both Alice and Matteo had come to see them off and assist with the EVA suits, diligently running checks to ensure that they were fully supplied and functioning as intended.

Matteo handed Renton a small bag of provisions, saying, "Here you go. Don't forget this. It should keep you going for a day or so, in case there's an emergency. But let's face it, with all the supplies you're going to find at that outpost, you're not going to need it." He grinned as he spoke, and Renton was glad to see a glimmer of the old Matteo, even if it was only for a brief moment. Renton accepted the bag with a simple, "Thanks."

"One last thing," Alice chimed in. "I've brought you a robot friend." She stepped aside to reveal a four-legged robot, a quadruped, approximately the size of a very large dog. "Its name is Oryx." The robot, responding to her cue, moved up to stand beside her.

Yuna bent down to examine the machine. "Is this what you've been working on all this time?"

Alice nodded affirmatively, casting a satisfied glance at the robot. "Yeah, it's semi-autonomous, and you can control it from your comms unit. There should be a new control interface that DOA just added."

Yuna tapped her comms and then stared off into the distance, asking, "Same procedure as before?"

"Yes, but with a few updates and a smoother transition. I managed to iron out most of the bugs," Alice replied.

"Awesome. Can't wait to take it for a spin." Yuna seemed

genuinely excited by the prospect of having this robotic sidekick accompany them. She looked down at the machine, gestured, and Oryx promptly began to move toward the rover, climbing in through the side-door hatch.

As they prepared to depart, Matteo reached over and patted Renton on the shoulder. "Good luck, buddy."

Renton nodded back, feeling a surge of emotion that he found embarrassing, considering they weren't embarking on a mission to Mars. In reality, this was just a quick trip to the store and back. However, after everything they had been through, this was the first time in quite a while when they had actively tried to take control of their destiny and attempt to do something other than starve to death.

Alice glided over and stood in front of Renton. They locked eyes for a moment before she reached out and wrapped him in a tight embrace. It was all Renton could do to keep his emotions in check and not collapse into a blubbering mess.

"If we're all finished with the hug-a-thon," Yuna said, sticking her head out from the side hatch on the rover, "can we hit the road before I faint from hunger?"

With some reluctance, Renton disentangled himself from Alice's embrace, climbed into the rover, and strapped himself into the passenger seat beside Yuna. She cast him a glance, then busied herself flipping switches, powering up the rover, and pressurizing the cabin.

"Okay, here we go," she finally said, and the machine began to move gracefully across the maintenance yard toward the open airlock.

"I would just like to extend my best wishes for success in

your upcoming endeavor," DOA's voice echoed in the cockpit cabin.

"Thanks," said Renton, thinking that even the AI seemed to be getting a little emotional.

They exited the airlock into a long tunnel. Yuna maintained a slow, steady pace, as both of them continuously monitored the status of the rover's systems, alert to any glitches that might appear. The tunnel forked, one side leading to the maintenance sector where they had originally entered the base, the other leading to yet another airlock. This one finally released them out onto the lunar surface, into the darkness of the lunar night —fourteen Earth days without sunlight. They had another ten to go.

Yuna took it slow. The outpost was approximately eighty kilometers away, so there was no need for her to push the rover. However, as the kilometers went by and no alerts popped up on the cockpit console, she began to increase the speed—as much as the rickety suspension would allow. By the time they had covered sixty kilometers, Renton had relaxed considerably. The machine was performing well, and their objective was nearly in sight. That's when an unexpected blip materialized on the radar.

Renton was the first to spot it. He leaned forward in his seat, scrutinizing the radar screen. "There's somebody else out here. Looks like they're about twenty kilometers to the north of us."

Yuna glanced at the screen. "Shuttle?"

"Don't think so, it's moving too slowly for that."

Yuna upped the pace of the rover. Renton kept a watch on the blip, expecting it to change direction at any moment and track toward them. But it stayed true to its course, never deviating. Eventually, it moved out of range, and both Renton and Yuna breathed a little easier.

"There." Yuna pointed ahead. In the distance, Renton could make out the faint pulse of a navigation beacon.

Soon, they began to discern the outline of the outpost, consisting of several squat mounds of lunar regolith, with various antennae and communication dishes poking up from its peaks.

"That looks like the docking bay over there." Yuna pointed at a long tunnel-like structure with a number of umbilical airlocks. "If it's still functioning, then I could reverse in and hook the rover directly into the facility. It would mean not having to EVA."

"Alright, let's give this a try. Just keep in mind, this rover is almost an antique, so some of its systems might have changed spec," Renton cautioned.

Yuna maneuvered the rover in at a crawl, carefully ensuring that the rear airlock was precisely aligned with the docking port on the outpost. As the two systems met, a dull thump echoed through the vehicle, followed by the hum of motors as the docking mechanism engaged and locked them into place.

They exchanged a glance. "I think it worked," Renton said, a hint of relief in his voice. "Come on. Let's go take a look." He stood up from his seat, closing the visor on his EVA suit to activate its systems. Despite the convenience of the umbilical airlock, he wasn't willing to take any risks until they had thoroughly inspected the internal atmosphere.

Yuna then gestured to their robotic companion, Oryx, signaling it to follow.

Together, they cycled through the airlock and stepped out into the outpost's docking tunnel. As they entered, lights flickered on, revealing a stark gray corridor leading them into a common area designed for visiting scientific teams and maintenance crews.

"The atmosphere seems to be okay," Yuna's voice echoed through Renton's helmet. She reached up, flipped open her visor, and took a tentative breath. Her face suddenly contorted. "Ugh, what is that smell? Something must have died in here."

Renton lifted his own visor and was immediately hit with the same fetid odor. "Oh yeah, that's pretty foul," he agreed, grimacing as he removed his helmet. "Okay, let's go find the galley and see what we can scrounge up."

"I think we just need to follow the smell." Yuna sniffed the air.

Locating the galley only took them a moment as it was situated just off the common area. Inside, they found a long table strewn with half-eaten meals, many of which seemed to be cultivating new life-forms. "They must have left in a hurry," Renton mused, surveying the disarray.

Yuna suddenly let out a startled gasp as she opened a locker door and froze, her eyes locked on its contents. Renton rushed over, fearing she had discovered something horrific.

However, he needn't have worried, as the locker was filled to the brim with snack bars—dense, carbohydrate-rich blocks packed with wholesome nutrition. Yuna eagerly snatched one, tore off its packaging, and began eating, with Renton following suit.

It was the tastiest food Renton had ever experienced. He couldn't help but grab another, and then another. He could feel his body reacting to the sudden surge of sugar. It might have been his imagination, but he was certain he could sense a burst of energy coursing through his veins.

In the midst of this chomp-fest, he abruptly froze, then slowly reached out to grab Yuna's arm, drawing her attention. She looked at him, alarmed. "What's wrong?" she whispered.

Renton swallowed the semi-chewed morsel of snack bar in his mouth and placed a finger to his lips. "Listen," he whispered back.

The sound they heard was unmistakable to anyone who had spent time in space. It was the telltale noise of an airlock cycling through its compression sequence. Someone else was entering the outpost.

CHAPTER 7
NEWCOMERS

Renton inched silently toward the galley door, pulling out his rail gun as he went. He was on the verge of pushing the door open a crack to risk a look into the common room area when Yuna grabbed his arm. She gestured toward the robot, Oryx, and then to her comms unit. He immediately understood her intention.

Under Yuna's deft control, Oryx maneuvered its way quietly out the door, across the common room floor, and discreetly positioned itself at one side of a long bench. It sat down on its haunches and remained completely still, blending into its surroundings—just another item of tech. The location offered it an unobstructed view of anyone entering from the direction of the docking tunnel. Renton and Yuna both received a direct audiovisual feed from the robot's camera system as an augmented reality projection from their comms units.

Footsteps, originating from the docking tunnel, intensified

as two figures cautiously entered the area—a man and a woman, both attired in similar dark, ragged, and nondescript jumpsuits, and both armed. The man's head was wrapped with a bandage, a dark red stain over his right eye. They didn't seem that bothered that there might be someone else here, considering they must have seen the other rover when they arrived at the dock. And they hadn't noticed Oryx, presumably assuming it was just some industrial robot used by visiting scientists.

"Haruki?" the man called out. "How'd you manage to get here before us?"

Renton glanced over at Yuna, then slowly pushed the door open with one hand and stepped out. He kept his other hand tightly on his rail gun, just in case.

The two interlopers reacted by taking a step back and reaching for their own weapons. Renton slowly raised his free hand. "Stay cool. Nobody's looking for trouble."

This seemed to settle them down slightly as hands moved away from weapons. "Who are you? Where's Haruki?" asked the man with the bandaged head.

"I'm Renton Hicks." He then gestured behind him as Yuna stepped through the door. "This here's Yuna Djinn." Lastly, he swept a hand over toward the robot. "And that's Oryx." This startled them a little, as clearly they hadn't noticed it. "We don't know any Haruki," Renton confirmed with a shake of his head. "We came here from Moon Base Delta looking for food."

Their eyes widened at the mention of the base, exchanging glances. "I told you," said the woman. "Didn't I say there were people there? I told you."

"So, who are you guys?" Yuna asked.

"Saito Yuuta," the bandage man held a hand to his chest. "Kimura Aoi." The woman waved before continuing. "We've come from Secchi, the big mining facility, over to the east. We're trying to find hydrogen fuel for our rover." She jerked a thumb over her shoulder. "When we saw the other machine docked outside, we thought Haruki might have made it out—although, it did look pretty ancient for a Hamamatsu Corporation machine."

"Secchi?" At the mention of the mining facility, Renton's curiosity was thoroughly piqued. The same place that supposedly housed a massive stockpile of provisions.

"Yeah," Saito confirmed, then raised a hand. "Look, as much as we'd like to sit down and chat with you all day, we have a SINO patrol hot on our heels. We need to locate some hydro quickly and get out of here as fast as we can. I'd suggest you do the same unless you like getting caught up in a firefight."

At the mention of SINO, Yuna seized Renton's arm, urging him into action. "Come on, let's gather whatever supplies we can find and get moving."

They began ransacking the galley and storerooms, with a renewed sense of urgency, gathering anything that looked like it might be edible into storage crates, then enlisted Oryx's help to transport it all back to the rover. Once they were satisfied that they had scavenged everything they could, they made their way back down the docking tunnel, only to encounter a frantic Saito and Kimura. The two newcomers had been diligently searching the outpost for hydrogen fuel packs to refuel their own rover.

"We can't find any hydro here," said Saito, waving his arms around. "And our rover is already running on fumes."

"Yeah. And we got another problem," Kimura chimed in. "We've spotted that SINO rover heading this way, fifteen klicks out."

Renton considered the situation for a beat, doing battle with his better nature—which didn't want to leave these people stranded here. "Come with us, then. We've got room."

"To Moon Base Delta?" Kimura's face beheld a look of incredulity. As if Renton had just offered to take her to some magical fairyland.

"Yeah, where else?"

She grabbed her colleague's arm and pulled him around. "Let's go. You know we can't fight a full squad of SINO operatives. Forget Shackleton."

Saito's face took on a pained expression. "Uh, but what about Haruki?"

"Forget Haruki too. He and his crew might never have even made it out of Secchi." She ran off toward the access hatch for their rover. "I'll get Tanaka," she called back as she went.

"Tanaka?" asked Yuna.

Saito gave an apologetic smile. "The third member of our... crack team."

"If you want to join us, then you'd better get your skates on," Renton gestured down along the docking tunnel. "Grab all the food supplies you have and get everyone into our rover. Do it now, because we're not waiting around."

Renton ran ahead to get the machine powered up, jumping into the co-pilot seat in the cockpit, while Yuna and Oryx finished storing the scavenged supplies. The dashboard console flickered to life as the rover's systems came online. His gaze immediately went to the radar screen. Just as Kimura had said, a blip appeared due south of their position, approximately twelve kilometers away. It was moving at a leisurely pace, yet it was undeniably advancing in their direction.

Yuna leaned in to take a look. Renton pointed at the blip. "It's coming from the other side of the outpost, so they can't see us yet. They probably don't know we're here. The rover will just look like part of the outpost structure." He then pointed out the front window of the rover, off into the distance. "If we could get to that rocky ridge we passed on the way here, park up behind it, then hopefully we won't show up on their sensors, we could wait it out for a while."

"It's as good a plan as any, I suppose," said Yuna. "We sure as hell can't outrun them in this bucket, not with all the extra weight."

Saito entered, followed by Kimura and an older man, all carrying weapons and supplies. "Seal the airlock hatch," Renton called back to them. "And grab a seat on the floor... this might get bumpy."

The umbilical docking port detached, and the rover lurched forward. Yuna had only taken it less than a hundred meters away from the outpost when Renton shouted out. "Wait, stop. I've got an idea."

Yuna looked at him with an expression of equal parts exasperation and alarm. "Seriously? You want me to stop?"

"Yes, stop." Renton then rose from his seat and pointed at Oryx. "We send the robot back to hide and wait for SINO. Once they're inside the facility, it can disable the rover... somehow. Prevent them from following us."

Yuna hesitated for a moment, slowing the rover down while at the same time thinking over Renton's crazy proposal. "Okay." She slammed on the brakes, and the machine came to a skidding halt. She glanced down at the radar screen. The blip was getting closer. "Better hurry."

Renton tapped his comms unit, and Oryx rose from its sitting position at the rear of the rover cabin. "Open the inner airlock door," he called back to the others. "I'm letting the robot out."

Kimura pulled the door open to let the robot into the airlock, then closed it again to set it running through its depressurization cycle.

Once Oryx was safely outside, Yuna started up the rover again and pushed it hard toward the concealment of the ridge. A few moments later, she swerved into a wide, gaping crevice and came to a halt.

Renton sat down again, adopting a thousand-yard stare as he operated the robot through his comms unit, gesturing in mid-air as he manipulated the machine. "Okay, I've got it hidden under the abandoned rover," he finally said, glancing over at Yuna. "I suppose all we do now is wait."

"I see them coming." Renton jerked upright in the seat. "I think they're going to dock. Here, let me share the feed."

Through the robot's camera feed, Renton watched as the SINO rover reversed into one of the docking ports. Along the side of the machine, he could clearly see an exterior weapons bulge—the type used to house a plasma weapon. It wasn't so

GERALD M. KILBY

much a rover as it was a military vehicle. He could now see why
Saito and Kimura were in such a panic.

"Any ideas on how to disable it?" asked Yuna, who was
getting the same visual feed from Oryx.

"That's basically a tank, so it's a bit tricky," said Renton. "It's
hydrogen powered... maybe the fuel lines or simply jam the
robot into the drive train."

"I don't think Alice will be happy if you destroy her robot,"
said Yuna. "She's become rather attached to it."

"Fuel lines then." Renton gestured to instruct Oryx to move
out of its hiding position. He began by cycling through the
robot's visual sensor array until he got an infrared feed with
which he could see a much colder patch to the rear of the
machine, indicating the location of the hydrogen cryogenic
storage tank. Unlike the clunky old rover that Yuna was driving,
which used electric energy storage, or the more modern one
that Saito and Kimura were forced to leave behind, which used
sealed replaceable fuel packs, this beast could hold a massive
reserve of hydrogen fuel, giving it an enormous range and more
than enough energy to power plasma weapons.

Renton cautiously moved Oryx over to the machine and
began examining the side paneling. It didn't take him long to
find what he was looking for: the refueling port, the weakest
part of the tank enclosure. He maneuvered the robot into
position and began using its powerful gripper to flex the port,
back and forth, to weaken the joint. If he could put a crack in it,
then the liquid hydrogen would boil off into the lunar vacuum.

After a brief moment of this mechanical pressure, he saw a
fine mist beginning to escape from a split in a weld. The robot

kept flexing the joint, and the volume of escaping gas increased. He was about to call it done when he gave it one more wrench. The port came away in the robot's gripper, and gas began to gush out of the gaping hole.

By now, anyone inside the SINO rover would be subjected to a comprehensive array of screeching alerts. "That should do it," said Renton. "It won't take long for all that fuel to boil off. Time to get Oryx out of there."

The robot dropped the broken nozzle, turned, and raced back across the lunar surface, just as two SINO operatives exited out through the rover's rear airlock. Presumably, they were investigating why the machine had suddenly sprung a fuel leak. One spotted Oryx and instantly started firing at it. Small explosions of dust kicked up all around the robot as it moved. Some might even have hit the machine, but rail-gun slugs would have little impact on its tough steel hide.

More SINO operatives came pouring out of the rover. Some began remedial work on the leak, trying to stem the boil-off. Others started after Oryx on foot, bounding across the surface at a rapid pace.

"We've got company heading our way on foot," Renton called out to the others. "Be ready to close that airlock as soon as I get Oryx back inside." A moment later, they felt a thump from the rear of the rover. "It's in," Renton shouted. "Close it."

"Closed," Kimura shouted back.

Yuna moved the rover out of its hiding place and applied maximum throttle. The machine lurched forward, its heavy-duty wheels scattering fountains of dust behind them. They bounced around for a moment or two until Yuna found optimal traction control, and they began accelerating away.

"That was intense," said Renton, slumping back down in his seat.

"What happened back there?" Saito called out from the rover cabin. "Can they follow us?"

"I don't think they can follow. We should be good," Renton assured them. Nevertheless, both he and Yuna kept a close eye on the radar. But there was no movement from the base, and eventually, both began to relax a little as they moved further and further out of range.

After around a half-hour of uneventful travel, the old guy, Tanaka, shuffled up into the cockpit, hoping perhaps to catch an early glimpse of the fabled Moon Base Delta. "Just stretching my legs. Hope you don't mind." He wedged himself in beside one of the side windows, craning his neck to look out at the unfolding lunar landscape.

"No, that's okay," replied Yuna. "But it'll be a while yet before you'll catch sight of the base."

"So what happened back in Secchi?" Renton asked, keen to get some intel on the mining outpost. "What made you guys want to get out in such a hurry?"

Tanaka took a long, slow, deep breath, as if the process of remembering was a challenge he'd rather not endure. "There were around fifty of us left behind after the evacuation," he began, "mostly people working outside of the base who didn't get back in time. Anyway, we got ourselves organized, and things were kinda looking okay for a while until SINO arrived and took over the outpost. They said they were rescuing us, but they were really there for the food supplies. See, we just had a supply drop, enough food for five hundred hungry miners for a month. So they knew we were well stocked.

As soon as they had control, they locked down all the supplies and started rationing. That didn't go down well. That was our food... and they just stole it. So, one thing led to another, some people started getting angry and decided to take it back." He lowered his head and rubbed his forehead. "That didn't work out so good—it was a complete disaster. Their attempt failed, SINO cornered them all and just shot them... one-by-one. We realized then what life was going to be like under SINO. That's when a bunch of us decided to get out, try to make it down to Shackleton Crater."

"Shackleton?" Renton was shocked. "That's a couple of thousand kilometers away? How were you hoping to make it that far?"

"By stopping along the way," Saito shouted out from the cabin, obviously listening in on the story. "We reckoned we'd commandeer two of the smaller rovers that used those self-contained fuel packs, very common. We could pick some up at various outposts along the way. We had it all mapped out."

"Didn't work out so well, did it?" said Kimura.

"No, I suppose it didn't," Saito replied, a little sheepishly. "And no sign of Haruki either. Who knows where he and his group are? Maybe they didn't even make it out."

"I see it," Tanaka announced excitedly, pointing out the side window.

Saito and Kimura now moved forward and squeezed into the cockpit, hoping to get their first glimpse of the base.

Ahead, Renton could see the flashing beacons atop the central core.

"Wow, it's big, isn't it?" Saito said, moving his head from side-to-side to get a better look.

"What you see above the surface is only a fraction of what's underground," offered Renton. "The place is really huge."

"We'll be safe once we're inside," said Yuna. "And now that we've got some supplies, we should be okay for a while."

Renton then turned around to face this motley group of travelers. "For what it's worth, it will be good to have a few new people around."

The old man gave a nod in return. "Appreciate it. Good to know there's some decency still left on this godforsaken rock."

CHAPTER 8
NEW LIFE

Han shifted in his seat, trying to restore blood circulation to his right buttock, which had become increasingly numb from sitting in the same position, in the back of a barebones military vehicle, for the last few hours.

His immobility was, for the most part, self-inflicted. It was due to Sheneese dozing off and using his shoulder as a makeshift pillow. Han was reluctant to disturb her, knowing that she desperately needed the sleep.

Earlier that day, back at the observatory, the two officers had presented them with a choice—of sorts. They could either remain in their observatory compound and likely face death from starvation or violence or join the new government task force, do some good, and ultimately increase their chances of surviving past the next year.

Even though this unexpected get-out-of-jail card was a stroke of very good fortune, both he and Sheneese still felt reluctant to leave the sanctuary of the observatory. It was their castle, after all, and it was hard to abandon it. But there was no question of them staying, no matter how they felt about the place. As the two officers were at pains to point out, they would, in all likelihood, be dead within a month. Therefore, Han and Sheneese hastily packed the bare necessities they were allowed and clambered into the back of the four-wheeled military transport, along with the officers, and departed for a future that would, they hoped, be considerably less precarious.

Outside, the natural world sped past, its beauty marred every so often by the ravages of desperate people seeking out a path to survival. Abandoned cars and trucks dotted the roadside, burned-out farmhouses peppered the horizon, they passed villages that seemed completely deserted, as well as small towns bristling with makeshift barricades and lookout posts—twitchy residents with equally twitchy fingers, all trying to protect a way of life in terminal decline.

As Han had feared, his desire for renewed blood flow had woken Sheneese. She lifted her head from his shoulder and glared bleary-eyed around the cabin. "Where are we?" she asked, through a half-muffled yawn.

He pointed out the small side window, its thick bulletproof glass reinforced with a protective wire grill. "We're inside the city. We passed through the western gate half an hour ago."

This got Sheneese's attention. She sat up and leaned across to get a better look at this strange new world. Outside, the streets were deserted, stores were all shuttered, and the only movement was from military vehicles and personnel. Here and there, bodies could be seen slumped on sidewalks. Maybe they were sleeping or maybe they were dead—it was hard to tell.

"Where are you taking us?" Sheneese asked the same basic question Han had been asking since the outset of the journey, with no satisfactory answer. She directed this at Captain Johnson and his associate, Lieutenant Taylor, who were strapped into a pair of seats opposite.

"Airport," the Captain replied, matter-of-factly. It was the most illuminating response he had uttered since the start of the trip.

Han, sensing that the two officers had relaxed a little since entering the city, and seeing as how Sheneese managed to get something out of them, decided to keep probing.

"You haven't said where you're ultimately taking us. What's our final destination?" He shifted in his seat again, a more pronounced movement, now that he wasn't constrained by having to be a pillow.

"We're heading east." The Lieutenant smiled.

"How far?" Han ventured.

"Far enough that we'll be taking a military flight from the airport here. It'll be a few more hours travel. But then you can get settled in and have a long, well-earned rest."

This was as much as Han could extract from the official duo. All subsequent questions were met with polite evasive answers.

The journey, so far, had given Han plenty of time to think. Sheneese had been asleep, and the two officers remained exceedingly tight-lipped, leaving him with little else to occupy his thoughts. Consequently, he began to ponder the purpose of this task force and its possible objectives.

Sheneese's expertise as a physicist was quite versatile. As a generalist, she had a skill set with broad appeal, making her valuable for a variety of scientific research endeavors. Han, in contrast, possessed a highly specialized skill set, refined through years of work at MASTERM. He began to consider the possibility that their mission might be to establish a new debris tracking system, which would map the chaotic mass currently orbiting Earth. If that was the case, only a limited number of locations would be equipped with the necessary infrastructure to support such an endeavor.

So when the Lieutenant had mentioned that they were heading east, Han consulted his mental map of astronomical institutes in that part of the country that had the necessary scientific infrastructure to probe the depths of the debris cloud. A few came to mind, but then again, the times being what they were, the best facility would be the one with the best security. That narrowed it down to just one military installation, built into the side of a mountain.

"The only secure astronomical facility out east that I know of is Strawstack Mountain. Is that where we're going?"

No answer. Blank faces.

That has to be where they're taking us, he thought.

Their convoy passed through several layers of perimeter airport security unhindered, then progressed across the concrete apron, finally coming to a halt beside a waiting military VTOL aircraft. Han, Sheneese, and the two officers all clambered out, and Han took a moment to stretch his limbs and alleviate the stiffness from the journey, at the same time surveying the scene around him. There were no civilians, that he could see. The entire airport was now under the control of the military. Civilian aircraft were all parked up at one end of the runway, leaving the rest to be occupied by these big VTOL machines, which didn't need a runway to take off.

They accessed the craft via a ramp at the rear, which led them into an empty cargo hold. From there, they passed through a bulkhead doorway and into a rudimentary passenger compartment. Han felt like he was in a movie and half expected to be greeted by a group of diverse scientists and academics who, like Han and Sheneese, had been plucked from various hidden locations and safe havens, and recruited into this top-secret mission. He might even know some of them, or come face-to-face with an academic adversary just to spice up the plot. But no, this flight was exclusively for them.

They were no sooner strapped into the seats when the aircraft's powerful engines roared to life, and the VTOL began to lift off the ground. With no windows available to allow Han a view of the world below, he found himself quickly succumbing to sleep, his head coming to rest on Sheneese's shoulder—his turn to use his partner as a pillow.

Sometime later, he awoke to a noticeable change in the tone of the craft's engines. He lifted his head from Sheneese's shoulder, sat upright, and began massaging his neck just as a judder reverberated through the machine as it landed at their destination.

"We're here," offered Captain Johnson, who was sitting opposite.

"Where's here?" Han asked, while still massaging his neck.

"Strawstack Mountain. You were correct in your assumption."

As they stepped out of the craft, he could see the silhouette of several large astronomical dishes nestled high up along the ridge. Around the edges of the landing pad were high concrete walls topped with coils of barbed wire, and lookout posts. In the distance, a road dipped down along a rut cut into the mountain, with sheer walls rising up on either side.

They were shepherded across the pad and through heavy steel doors set into what looked like a concrete bunker. Here, they transferred into a wide industrial elevator that took them down a few levels and spat them out into a long, brightly lit corridor. They followed this route, negotiating a few turns, and eventually were ushered into a huge open-plan area which was abuzz with activity. It reminded Han of MASTERM, the same type of people, the same hyper-technological working environment.

Out from the midst of this cacophony of activity strode none other than Ted Norton, Han's old colleague from MASTERM. Here was a person he thought he would never see again.

"Han." Ted glided over, two other executive types in his wake. He offered a hand and a big smile.

Han shook it.

"And Sheneese. It's great they found you both alive and well." He turned to the two officers that had brought them here.

"Great work, Captain Johnson, Lieutenant Taylor. We'll take it from here."

The two officers gave a sharp, almost synchronous salute and retreated back out through the door.

"So we have you to thank for our... rescue?" Sheneese inquired.

"Yes, you're too valuable to leave out in the wild, fending for yourselves." He gave another big smile.

"How did you find us?" Han's mind was awash with questions, but this seemed like the most obvious one to start with.

"Oh, it wasn't that difficult. I knew you loved that old observatory, and so I reckoned that was the most likely place you'd head for. But, come, come. You must be exhausted. Let's get you quickly up to speed and then you can rest for a while."

He brought them through the crowd of people, down along some more corridors, and into a well-lit, spacious, well-appointed office. They sat down on a large sofa. Ted Norton sat opposite, his two colleagues to one side.

"Introductions," he began. "Sam here is Operations, and Olivia will be your liaison with the brass." He pointed at the ceiling. "This is a military facility, so they have different ideas on how things should be run. Anyway, I'll be quick, as I'm sure you're tired after your journey." He paused for a beat, gathering his thoughts. "We're reestablishing MASTERM, right here. We're hoping to build a new model of what's actually happening in Earth orbit, with the ultimate goal of finding a way through it."

Han pursed his lips, nodding. "I suspected that's what this

was all about. Quite a challenge. Do we have the infrastructure? The computing power?"

Ted gave a shrug. "Not nearly enough, things are a bit chaotic, as you can imagine. But it's our task to try to find a way. And that starts by getting a better picture of what's up there. Once we do that, then we can build some models, develop some hypotheticals."

Han began to think, running some numbers in his head. "That's a tall order. Even if we had all the facilities that MASTERM had, we'd still only be able to track a fraction of the orbital chaos." He paused for a moment, his mind running ahead. "Am I correct in assuming that no Helium-3 capsules have been sent from the Moon since the storm?"

Ted nodded. "I'm afraid so. We believe there have been some attempts by SINO, none successful. But it's hard to know what's going on up there as we have no comms operation, as yet." He glanced over the top of his glasses. "That's one of the items on our list. Establish comms. Anyway, I don't need to tell you about the gravity of the situation we are facing—if I can use that word. If we don't get a supply system back operating again, then the lights start going out. It's bad enough as it is, what with no data network, but with no energy to power industry—" He shook his head. "Things are going to get medieval very quickly."

"What about other sources of power, other technologies?" Sheneese asked.

"Yeah, sure, there are some. But it will take a very long time to ramp up for industry, and we don't have that time. We've all gotten so dependent on cheap fusion power. No doubt, there are probably many other facilities just like this one, buried deep in a mountain in another country, with a bunch of people just like us tasked with solving the very same problem."

"Which is?" Han asked with raised eyebrows.

"Find a way to get a supply capsule through that debris cloud." Norton sighed, then sat up and clapped his hands to signal the end of the debrief. "But put all that aside for now, I'm sure you're exhausted. Go get some rest and we'll see you in the morning." He stood up. "Sam will show you to your accommodation."

They shook hands again, leaving Han and Sheneese to contemplate their new life and the challenges of the task ahead.

CHAPTER 9
SHACKLETON CRAT

P ompodur Rossen Adarok, President of the Xilinex
Corporation's Lunar Mining Division, stepped out of his
private shuttle in the primary spaceport in Shackleton Crater.
Fortunately, this action did not require him to suffer the
indignity of wearing an EVA suit, as the disembarkation was
facilitated by an umbilical docking port allowing the shuttle's
occupants to enter the city enclave in the comfort of a full one-
atmosphere environment. A process very agreeable to
Pompodur, as his primary purpose here was to project an image
of power and control for the citizens of Shackleton Crater—one
best served by pomp and ceremony.

He strode through the short access route and out into a
wide concourse with several high-ranking Xilinex operatives
following in his wake. His brightly colored flowing robes added
a touch of majestic dignity to the otherwise drab colonist attire
of the reception committee. This was, after all, a surrender

ceremony, and it was fitting for him to look the part of the all-conquering leader, savior of the stranded masses.

The ceremony would be simple: the transfer of control of all FISA sectors in Shackleton Crater to the Xilinex Corporation Lunar Division. Not that the locals had much choice, and many were unhappy about it. Some groups even resisted Xilinex's offer, preferring to go their own way and, unfortunately, willing to put up a fight. They flatly refused to allow access to their sectors, which housed most of the water and food production facilities in Shackleton. A resolution was needed, as achieving food security was the primary reason why the Xilinex Board deferred the attack on the Mass Accelerator facility in favor of securing Shackleton's resources.

General Wagner dispatched a squad to deal with these hold-outs, despite the protests of Ossian Corbell, another Xilinex Director who, in Pompodur's mind, was beginning to display a lack of backbone. He was becoming a festering boil on the corporate board, one that Pompodur needed to lance sooner rather than later to prevent the rot from spreading and his authority being challenged.

The squad eliminated the threat with their usual efficiency, clearing the sector of obstructionists, and managing to capture two of the ringleaders. The General wanted to parade these troublemakers in front of the crowd and execute them publicly as a warning to others. However, Pompodur overruled him, arguing that it was better for the Xilinex Corporation to be seen as liberators and saviors of the people, focused on making things right again. Winning over the people was the goal. He argued that the time for ruling by fear had not yet arrived; it would be necessary in the future, but not right now. So, the General took the two ringleaders to an exterior airlock in a quiet sector and forced them to take a short walk without an EVA suit.

Pompodur and his entourage were ushered into a transport pod and began making their way to what passed for a town square in Shackleton Crater, a wide circular area approximately a hundred meters across with a translucent domed roof. One of the few places in the enclave that had natural sunlight as most of it existed underground or in surface mounds covered in a thick layer of lunar regolith for radiation protection. The large dome only existed because it had an artificially generated magnetic field that protected it from charged cosmic radiation, something only made possible by a copious energy supply from a dedicated fusion reactor.

The core of the current metropolis had its roots in a collection of distinct lunar bases that were established way back in the early days of lunar colonization, mostly during the previous century. Each of these individual bases was operated as a separate entity by whatever agency had established them. But over time, as these islands of human activity began to expand, they eventually coalesced into larger interconnected enclaves—resulting in a labyrinthine infrastructure, with a myriad of architectural styles, all accessed via a bizarre network of tunnels.

Yet, not all the facilities that existed around the rim of Shackleton Crater had been integrated into this new lunar metropolis. Some formed their own micro-enclaves, primarily those controlled by SINO, JAXA-KARI, and CASA over to the west. These were outside the scope of the current Xilinex Corporation takeover—for the time being.

The transport pod sped through a narrow tunnel network and spat them out at a wide concourse, right next to the central dome. Immediately, Pompodur and his entourage were surrounded by Xilinex security, forming a cordon between them and the small crowd that had gathered to witness the handover. Some on the Xilinex Lunar Board had been reticent about this public display, notably Anton Levrosky and the increasingly problematic Ossian Corbell—preferring to do everything on the quiet, behind closed doors. But Pompodur insisted that the best way to bring the citizens of Shackleton on board was to show them the face of the new regime, to show them that Xilinex was here to ensure their collective survival by bringing a level of order and clarity in these uncertain times. Also, Pomodur wasn't going to miss a chance to present himself to the people. This way, they would get to know him. This way, they would learn to love him.

Of course, the formal handover was largely symbolic. In reality, Xilinex now controlled all the old FISA sectors in Shackleton as well as all sectors belonging to their affiliate agencies. Pompodur smiled to himself as he thought of Selene Mene, still stranded on the Axial Luxor orbital. She would be distraught at the thought that Shackleton was lost. She had been trying for a long time to offer herself as the de facto leader of the FISA enclaves. But in the end, she had nothing to offer, only words. Soon he would be making a claim on the luxury orbital, offering them the same deal as the citizens here in Shackleton, surrender to Xilinex rule, or be forced to submit. He couldn't wait to wipe the smug, condescending attitude from Selene Mene's face. He would make it a condition that she offer the surrender face-to-face, maybe even have her bow down before him. But he was getting ahead of himself, going off on a daydream. There was much work to do before that future vision would manifest itself. Still, it sent a shiver of excitement through his body at the thought of a vanquished Selene Mene.

It being over one hundred hours into the long three-hundred and fifty-four-hour-long lunar night, the entire dome area was artificially illuminated, the focus of which was mostly on a raised area to one side, which was mainly used to host shows and concerts back when the enclave had a functioning population of several thousands. Now it accommodated a row of somber-looking seated representatives, a ragtag group of reluctant elders scraped together from the remnants of the decimated population.

Pompodur was escorted up onto the podium by a cohort of Xilinex security personnel, who then took up observation positions on all four sides. Most of the people who had come to witness this handover had been kept well back, and Pompodur was relieved to see that Xilinex security represented at least a third of those present. He strode up to the discreet microphone, faced the crowd, and raised his hands in an expansive gesture.

"Citizens of Shackleton," he began. "We find ourselves in unprecedented times where our very survival is uncertain."

There were some nods and murmurs from the crowd, perhaps some thought he was stating the blindingly obvious but, if Pompodur knew one thing, it was that the best way to connect with the rabble was to speak to their base fear, and that fear wasn't just about survival, it was also about the feeling of being abandoned.

"Most of those that once populated this great metropolis have fled for Earth, those that had the connections, the FISA elite. They simply ran when things got tough, leaving you all behind, abandoned. Why?" He let this question sink in for a moment. "Because they don't care about you. You mean nothing to them. You are the bottom rung of this society, here simply to serve them and their so-called great city." He noticed a few heads nodding in the crowd. There were certainly many here that held a grievance. He would build on that.

"But not so the Xilinex Corporation. No. We stayed." Strictly speaking, over half of the Xilinex employees had been evacuated, but Pompodur had a story to tell; why ruin it with facts? "We stayed because we look after our people, all of our people, regardless of their position in our corporate family." More positive murmurings hummed around the dome. He sensed this crowd might be easier to sway than he had first imagined.

"But the FISA propaganda machine is still hard at work." He pointed up in the air, referring to the regular broadcasts that had been coming from the Axial Luxor. "They tell you that there is no hope of ever returning to Earth—but that is simply not true." This got the desired reaction from the crowd. Now he had their full attention. "The Xilinex Aerospace Division has informed me that it will be no more than eighteen months." The previous murmurings from the crowd had now grown into almost a clamor. He had to raise a hand to quieten them down. "Even as we speak, they are working on new ship designs that can safely pass through the debris cloud." It was all lies, of course, and he could see Ossian Corbell glaring at him from the corner of his eye. But these were very useful lies, ones that could be strung out indefinitely. He could simply say, just a few more months, for as long as needed. But today, he was getting the crowd on his side, and that was all that mattered.

He gestured upward again. "And what are FISA doing? Sitting up in their luxury orbital while you all struggle with food security down here. Well, you'll be very pleased to hear that the food production facilities are no longer being held hostage by a small group of FISA troublemakers." He reached up to rub his chin, a signal to the Xilinex plants in the crowd to get to work. Scattered cheers went up from the crowd, along with muted applause.

"They have been secured and will soon be brought back into full production." More cheers. "And so to conclude, I, Pompodur Rossen Adarok, as president of the Xilinex Corporation Lunar Division, can wholeheartedly assure you all of a safe and productive future here in Shackleton Crater." Even more cheers, this time coupled with enthusiastic applause. He had them where he wanted them. Now it was time to move on to the next phase—removing Selene Mene from the Axial Luxor.

CHAPTER 10

BREAKING BREAD

The microwave dinged in the common room galley, signaling the completion of its cycle. Renton pulled open the door and was instantly assaulted by a steaming ambrosial aroma that seeped into every crevice of his hunger. He extracted the hot plate, stacked high with Turkish flatbread, with all the reverence of a priest raising a celebratory offering, and bent his nose to the heart of the fragrant doughy mass, performing a long, slow sniff as his head approached the aromatic mother lode. It was perhaps the most pleasurable smell he had ever experienced in his entire life, and it made him consider that the previous several weeks of starvation might have been worth it, just to experience the physical bliss of this singular moment.

"Hurry up with that bread, Renton," Alice shouted over from the large table where a feast was being prepared in the common room on the Operations level of Moon Base Delta.

For the last hour or so, a select number of the choicest rations had been liberated from the bags of supplies that he and Yuna had scavenged from the seismic monitoring outpost, and subsequently subjected to various preparation processes including industrial levels of rehydration, or bathed in super-heated steam, or, in the case of the flatbread, blasted with high-energy microwaves, all this in service of creating probably one of the most memorable feasts that the crew would ever have in their entire lifetimes.

It would also give them an opportunity to get to know the newcomers. Having had no functioning comms in the janky rover, the first that Alice and Matteo knew of their success was when the rover entered the maintenance hangar in Moon Base Delta and Renton swung open the airlock hatch, stepping out carrying a bag of supplies under each arm. Both Alice and Matteo pounced on the bags, tossing them to the floor and ripping into them with all the frenzy of a pair of zombies extracting the entrails of a fresh victim.

"Jeez, you guys must really be starving," observed Saito as he clambered out of the rover behind Renton and set eyes on the two ravenous occupants of Moon Base Delta.

Neither Matteo nor Alice paid him much attention other than a cursory glance. They only had one thing on their minds —food. Everything else could wait.

Now, though, as Renton brought the hot bread over to the table, they would all have a chance to get to know one another around that most ancient of human rituals, a shared meal.

"When we originally took shelter here, we thought we'd be

self-sufficient. How wrong we were," Matteo was recounting, in between mouthfuls of hot chicken satay. "But there was almost nothing left in storage that was still edible." He gave a sweeping gesture, a chicken skewer still in his hand. "As for the so-called bioreactor, it barely functions. Almost all the cryogenically stored biomass was dead, and the only samples that were still active have performed poorly."

"That's because they're way past their use-by date," said the old guy, Tanaka. "That stuff's bio-engineered to die after one batch. I'm surprised you got anything out of it."

This was news to Renton and the crew; they all stopped eating and focused their attention on Tanaka.

"What do you mean, bio-engineered to die?" asked Renton.

Tanaka glanced around the table, clearly noticing the reaction he was getting from his statement. "All seed-stock and biomass is batch limited," he said matter-of-factly. "After one production run, it dies. The fact you got anything at all must have been just an anomaly, or possibly a really old GM version."

Matteo stared at him intently. "Are you saying that even standard hydroponic crops don't reproduce?"

Tanaka looked at Matteo, then at Renton with a look of incredulity. "Did you guys not know this? I thought you were all scientists."

"We're mostly engineers, not scientists," Alice corrected. "And none of us have spent any time on the surface before this. Mostly we worked out of the Central FISA Orbital."

"But all life-forms reproduce; that's just nature." Yuna said this more as a question, like she was beginning to question her own understanding of food production.

"Not up here on Luna," said Kimura, shaking her head emphatically. "All bio-stock is genetically modified for growing conditions in our low gravity environment."

"And it's all supplied by one corporation—Santomon," Tanaka added. "They modify everything so that it doesn't reproduce, meaning you have to keep buying new stock from them every growing season." His voice did not hide his obvious contempt for this policy.

Renton sat back in his seat as his brain worked through the ramifications of this bombshell. Even if they could get the hydroponics, the bioreactors, and the other food production facilities up and running, it would all run out of steam eventually unless new supplies came up from Earth. And that wasn't going to happen any time soon. "Shit," he said, mostly to himself.

"DOA," Matteo called out to the AI. "How come you didn't tell us all this?"

"My apologies, Matteo. But my knowledge base only extends to events prior to fifteen years ago when I was deactivated. This genetically modified food policy must have changed during that period."

Tanaka nodded. "Yes, it's true. They started changing over around a decade ago."

"How do you know all this?" Alice asked.

"I used to work in aquaponics, back when the Hamamatsu Corporation had food production facilities. They closed them down around a decade ago, just as the new GM crops were coming in. I moved over to general maintenance after that."

"But this is a major problem," Renton stated the obvious. "Has no one else seen this coming?"

"Of course they have. Why do you think SINO moved on Secchi? We just took possession of a huge delivery of supplies, and the first thing SINO did when they entered the facility was put up a security ring around the stores. They know what's coming."

"So, we're all ultimately doomed," said Yuna, pushing her plate away. She seemed to have lost her appetite. "When all the supplies are consumed and we can't produce any more, then that's it. Game over."

"Not necessarily," Saito said. "There are labs in Shackleton that could probably reverse engineer bio-stock. They're probably working on it right now."

"You don't know that for sure," Kimura countered. "It's just wishful thinking."

"DOA, can this... bio-stock be reverse engineered?" Renton decided to enlist the AI's help.

"It's theoretically possible," came the reply. "But since I have no data on the precise changes made to the bio-stock, I can only speculate. Also, I have no knowledge of a genetics laboratory capable of such engineering existing on Luna, nor if there are any scientists with the required skill set. But, bear in mind that my data set is limited."

"Well, that's just great," Matteo sat back and fired a napkin down onto the table. "There could be no way out of this."

"There might be," Renton raised a finger in the air. "What if we simply asked Santomon how we go about reverse engineering these... franken-beans."

"Worth a shot," said Alice. "They would have to help, considering the fate of everyone up here depends on it."

"Then it looks like fixing the Earth–Moon comms system just moved up to top priority on our to-do list," said Matteo.

"That and securing more supplies. Because this batch will be gone in less than a month." Yuna jerked a thumb over at a stack of crates piled against one wall of the galley.

"The other outpost. We should hit that up next," Saito added. "Bound to be supplies there. Maybe even fuel cells for our rover."

"What?" Kimura glanced at her comrade. "You want to go back for it? You still want to get to Shackleton?"

"Yeah, for sure," Saito replied, then gestured across the table. "Thanks for the hospitality and all, but I can't see you guys surviving here for very long."

"If I may," DOA's voice echoed around the common room. "Now would seem an appropriate time to inform you that the Xilinex Corporation has taken control of all FISA sectors in Shackleton Crater."

"It was bound to happen," Tanaka sighed, "and it won't be the last takeover either."

"Where did you get that information?" Saito glanced at the ceiling, directing his question to the AI.

"A report just released from the Axial. It speculates that the takeover was instigated to secure the food production facilities," said DOA.

Saito sat back and let out a sigh. "Nevertheless, I still think

Shackleton holds the best chance for our long-term survival. You should come with us."

Renton thought about this for a moment, then glanced at the rest of the crew trying to gauge their thoughts. All were looking at the newcomers, clearly considering the option.

"I think that's an offer we'd all need to sleep on," he said finally.

CHAPTER 11

UPDATES FROM THE AXIAL

Renton couldn't sleep. He tossed and turned, trying to get comfortable, thumping his pillow every so often, attempting to beat it into a shape more conducive to nodding off. His insomnia was probably due in part to all the food he had consumed earlier, which was more than he had eaten in the entire previous week.

But he was also feeling a little unsettled by the presence of the new people they had picked up at the seismic testing station: Saito, Kimura, and the old guy, Tanaka—who turned out to be Kimura's father. They had seen what Moon Base Delta had to offer and decided that their prospects of survival would be best served by leaving.

This did not fill Renton with confidence. Yet, maybe they were right. Maybe heading south was the best option. After all, Shackleton was the largest population center, even now after mass evacuation. It had food, water, power, and to some extent, stability, even with the Xilinex takeover. And if any new developments were to be made in resolving the food production issue, it would probably happen in Shackleton first. So on a purely rational assessment, it made a certain amount of sense.

Eventually, Renton gave up trying to get any sleep. Instead, he got up and padded down the corridor toward the operations area. He had a vague plan to check out any new reports that might have come in from the Axial Luxor. He should really contact Selene again soon. They hadn't talked since he and Yuna had left to investigate the outpost.

He stopped off at the common room to make himself a mug of tea—maybe that would help him sleep. There was a light on when he entered and he saw Matteo sitting on one of the sofas, reading from a slate. He looked up when he heard him coming in. "Can't sleep?"

"No, too much food, I think." Renton wandered over to the galley area.

"Me neither. I'm too depressed to sleep."

"Want some tea? Might help," Renton asked as he began rummaging around in the lockers.

"Sure, can't do any harm, I suppose."

A few moments later, Renton came over with two steaming mugs of some herbal tea. He handed one to Matteo.

"I'm heading into the op-room, to see if there are any updates from Selene."

Matteo rose from the sofa while trying not to spill the tea. "I'll join you."

· · ·

Lights flickered on as they entered the operations area. "DOA, any updates from the Axial?"

"Yes, there have been three new broadcasts since you last engaged."

"Play them."

The main monitor blinked to life and a head on shoulders of Nicci Anderson, Selene's old assistant, read out news from the various enclaves that still communicated with the Axial. Most of the items were of little interest to either Renton or Matteo, except for the last broadcast. This was an update on the recent takeover of Shackleton by the Xilinex Corporation. Apparently, several people involved in the opposition to Xilinex control had disappeared, rumors inferred that they were dead, executed by the new regime. Any and all dissent was being crushed, without prejudice.

"Well, I think that might put the kibosh on the newcomers' travel plans," Matteo quipped.

"I dunno. They seemed pretty intent on going."

"If they still want to leave after hearing this, then that's not much of an endorsement for our little club here."

"My thoughts exactly. To be honest, part of me is tempted to head down to Shackleton."

Matteo nearly spilled his tea. "Seriously?"

Renton smiled and shook his head, "No, not really. I'm just considering the options."

"They'll never make it if they're planning to use that rover they left back at the outpost. We've got some of those fuel packs here they could use, but that will only get them so far. Those rovers are only designed for short hops. What they need is one of the big industrial transports with cryogenic hydrogen storage."

"Or solar-electric, and fourteen days of daylight."

"True. But even that would be an arduous trip. Stopping off every few hundred kilometers just to charge up."

Renton studied his friend for a beat. "It's good to have you back, Matteo. I thought I'd lost you to the bioreactor."

"Thanks." Matteo grinned. "There's no real point, now that I know there's a shortened lifespan baked into the biomass. And genetic engineering really isn't my thing." He gestured at the ceiling, "I might have saved myself a lot of time over nothing if we weren't dealing with a geriatric AI who has no knowledge of the last fifteen years of human existence."

"I apologize for my subpar performance in this regard," came the response from DOA. "If I can get access to LunaSat, then I would be able to update my knowledge base."

"Speaking of which, Matteo," said Renton, "Any luck with the X-band transmitter?"

"Actually, yes, Alice and I got it up and running while you were away on your scavenger hunt. Sorry, forgot to mention it. I think I was too focused on the food you brought back." He patted his stomach. "Anyway, it's been transmitting a message on repeat for a day or so."

"What sort of message?"

"Voice. 'Hello, we're here, please respond.' That sort of thing."

"And nothing back? That's a bit disconcerting."

"Not necessarily. You have to remember that we're utilizing the old deep-space network, and there are less than a half-dozen facilities dotted around the globe with a dish antenna capable of picking up our signal. How many of those are still functioning and have someone actively listening while we pass overhead? Here, let me show you." Matteo put down his mug of tea and sat up. "DOA, bring up a map of the old X-band antenna Deep Space network on Earth—just the ones that were operated by FISA and its predecessors."

The holo-table in the center of the operations area came to life with a holographic image of a slowly spinning Earth. "Fortunately, this is old tech, so DOA has all the information."

Several illuminated dots began popping up, showing the locations of the installations. "Right now, we are passing across Western Europe. There's an old site near Madrid in Spain. After that, we pass a few sites across North America, Strawstack Mountain in the east, then Goldstone in the Mojave Desert. After that, we're on to Canberra, Australia. But how many of those are still operational is anyone's guess. Nobody's used this network since all communication began being relayed through the constellations. That's over forty years ago. That said, DOA is of the opinion that the Strawstack Mountain installation might still be operational as it's a military facility."

"So that's our best bet?" Renton didn't sound very hopeful.

"According to DOA." Matteo gave Renton a conspiratorial wink.

"Assuming Space Division and FISA are trying to reestablish communication with the colonies on the Moon, Mars, and beyond, then this site would be logical," said DOA, "But again, I must reiterate, my data is incomplete."

Renton considered this for a moment. The herbal tea

seemed to be making him more alert, not less so. "Surely, the Xilinex Corporation, SINO, and whoever else is still active up here must also be trying to reestablish communications? If they haven't already?"

"I suppose so." Matteo shrugged.

"DOA, what other old comms facilities are still in existence on Luna?"

"The primary facility in use, before my deactivation, was the large array situated on the Malapert Massif, north of Shoemaker Crater. It was privately owned and provided communications services to a wide range of agencies and corporations."

"That's near Shackleton, isn't it?"

"Approximately one-hundred kilometers due North."

Matteo scratched his chin. "If Xilinex are now in control of Shackleton, then I assume they'll take over that facility as well."

Renton finished his tea and felt a wave of tiredness wash over him. Perhaps it just took time for the soporific effects of the beverage to take effect. "Well, my brain has had enough for today. I'm heading back to bed." He stood up and was about to leave when an alarm sounded.

"What the..." He looked up at the main monitor. It showed several exterior camera feeds with a proximity alert flashing in big red letters. At the same time, the hologram of Earth was replaced with a 3D schematic of the Moon Base Delta facility.

"Shit." Matteo jumped up from his seat. "We've got company."

"An unidentified small rover is moving in the direction of

the Southern Gate," said DOA as it enlarged one of the camera feeds on the monitor.

Renton and Matteo stood and watched as a battered-looking machine slowly made its way toward the base, bouncing across the lunar surface.

"Doesn't look like SINO," Renton observed. "Or Xilinex, for that matter."

"Yeah, if anything, that rover looks like a death trap, if you ask me," said Matteo.

"Wait a minute." Renton jerked a finger at the screen. "I think I recognize that machine, or one very like it."

Matteo gave him a quizzical glance. "You do?"

"Yep, I've seen it before. At the seismic testing station. DOA, alert Saito, Kimura, and Tanaka. And get them in here, right now!"

CHAPTER 12
DEEP SPACE NETWORK

After spending a considerable amount of time over the last few days in meetings and discussions with the people who worked at the fortified military facility on Strawstack Mountain, Dr. Han Sundar was genuinely shocked to learn just how dire the situation was in the wider world.

The good news, if you could call it that, was that some order had been restored in the big cities. However, this was only brought about by the imposition of martial law, and all but a fortunate few were now dependent on centralized food distribution. Essentially, everything related to the production, processing, and distribution of food had been taken over by the state. This drastic action had been deemed necessary for two reasons. The first was to ensure food security—now all facilities were physically protected by the military. The second reason was to facilitate equitable distribution, since people had no way to pay for goods now that the digital networks on which a cashless society relied were completely trashed. With no functional monetary system, there was no way to buy anything. To prevent a complete collapse of society, the state intervened, took control of food and energy, and doled it out in sufficient quantities to prevent people from either starving or freezing to death.

While people in the cities had some level of security, it was a different story in the hinterlands. Larger towns had adopted similar systems, but these were managed and policed by locals, leading to the rise of powerful fiefdoms run by unscrupulous militia groups. Beyond the state-controlled cities and militia-run towns lay the badlands. Out there, you were on your own, at the mercy of roaming gangs who pillaged, plundered, raped, and killed with impunity.

It was a story repeated, to varying degrees, all across the planet. However, with the global communications network gone, information from the outside world was scarce and inconsistent. Old ground-based telecom networks and undersea cables still existed, but they had very limited bandwidth in comparison, nowhere near the capacity required for the smooth operation of a hyper-digital society. These precious communication networks were now the preserve of any remaining functional governments, and they were ruthlessly guarded.

Han felt like he was living in the early twentieth century, back when up-to-date news was a scarce commodity, filtered through periodic newspapers and sporadic newsreels shown in cinemas. For the people working in Strawstack, their equivalent of the newsreel was a daily meeting where progress was discussed, followed by snippets of news information from the outside world that the powers-that-be chose to disseminate.

As for the fate of the colonies on the Moon, Mars, and the exploration crews out in the asteroid belt and the moons of Jupiter, very little was known. The large satellites used for the deep space network had also been completely destroyed in the chaotic aftermath of the solar storm. Now there was a scramble to reestablish communication using the old network of ground-based dish antennas, most of which no longer existed, and anything that did had fallen into a desperate state of disrepair. Except for here at Strawstack. This was what they had Sheneese working on; her side passion for old-school radio communications technology was coming in handy in this new post-digital age.

As for Han, they had him doing pretty much what he used to do: tracking orbital debris and developing models to make sense of the chaos that now shrouded Earth. It was a task made even more complex due to the fact that the debris cloud was still a work in progress. Collisions were happening all the time, essentially turning larger pieces into ever-smaller pieces. This process would continue for a very long time. Eventually, it would find an equilibrium, but that might take decades, or even centuries. Yet, impossible as it may seem, the ultimate objective was to establish a real-time understanding of the debris cloud so that they could develop a capsule capable of passing through it intact.

However, both he and Sheneese never lost sight of the fact that they were the lucky ones—securely tucked away in a military base, working for the greater good, so to speak. It meant they had a future. This fact was brought home to them when Han learned from Alan E. Dyson, former head of FISA, that his old colleague, Professor Henriksen, had never made it back to Earth; he had been left stranded at the Axial Luxor Hotel.

It was one afternoon, over lunch in a quiet spot in the large communal canteen, that Sheneese shared the news that had the Radio Astronomy Department abuzz. This was where she worked, and she was breaking protocol by telling him, but he would probably be informed later that day at his own department briefing. They had just received an encrypted signal, on repeat, from Luna.

"Encrypted?" Han asked, after she had given him a breakdown of the transmission.

"Yeah, bizarre. Whoever is sending this is obviously picky about who might be listening."

Han shook his head in disbelief. "You would think they would be desperate for any contact."

"All we know so far is that it's coming from the old transmitter on Malapert Massif, close to Shackleton Crater, the main population center," she whispered.

"That's mainly a FISA base, isn't it?" Han asked as he poured himself and Sheneese more coffee.

"It is, or was. Who knows now? There's speculation that it might be coming from one of the two main blocks that stayed behind. That means either SINO or the Xilinex Corporation."

Han sipped his coffee. "Can you decrypt it?"

"We're working on it, but most of the computing resources are ring-fenced for your department." She made a sad face.

Han gave a sigh. "It's still not enough, nowhere near enough to process the amount of data we're getting in from the S-band array they've managed to get up and running, and we'll soon be getting even more data from the old Space Surveillance Network."

"Surely more data is good, better to identify what's up there?"

"Yeah, I suppose. But we need more computing resources, more processing power if we're going to develop a model... sometime this century."

They were silent for a moment, each concentrating on finishing up their meal as they were both due back soon.

Sheneese cleared her plate with a flourish. "At least Space Division is making sure we're well fed."

Han smiled, "Yeah, no more sauerkraut."

She sat back and sipped her coffee. "What do you think of our chances of getting something through before..." Her sentence trailed off.

"Before the world runs out of Helium-3, all the fusion reactors cease to function, and the world reverts to the Dark Ages?"

"Yeah."

Han shrugged. "Well, the debris cloud isn't a homogeneous mass. It's clumpy, with some areas more chaotic than others. So, since we are strapped for computing power, we're not trying to map every object, not even close. We're working on mapping general density. Then we can focus on the lower-density areas and try to work out what it would take to get something through. The aerospace guys are working on the problem from the bottom up, designing a capsule that can withstand small debris hits. The more robust they can design it, the fewer objects we need to try and track, which is good because a lot of the stuff up there is millimeter-scale. If they can get it up above the ten-centimeter scale, then we might have a chance. In the end, I think it will come down to a roll of the dice. We'll pick a time and a place, throw as many capsules as we can up there, and hope something makes it through. But these will be small packages. It will be a very, very long time before we can contemplate sending a crew. Possibly not in our lifetimes."

Sheneese looked away and across the communal dining area. "Uh oh, here comes Ethan," she said with a hint of trepidation in her voice.

Ethan's most noticeable attribute was that he was young, barely twenty, and there weren't too many of those here in the bunker, unless they happened to be children of staff. But he was a total electronics nerd, with a passion for restoring antique tech. They wanted him because they knew his skill set would be useful. Yet, as far as Han could discern, he was mostly employed as a message runner.

"Professor Richmond? Your presence is required in the radio control room." He spoke very formally.

Sheneese raised an eyebrow. "Oh, why?"

Ethan flicked a glance at Han, not sure how much he could reveal to non-radio astronomy staff.

Sheneese, sensing his unease, gestured across the table.

"This is my husband, Dr. Han Sundar. He has a very high security clearance."

This seemed enough to satisfy Ethan, and he relaxed a little. "We've picked up another signal."

"Encrypted?" Sheneese asked as she tidied up her plate and downed the last sip of coffee.

"No, this one is different. It's a voice message, on repeat, coming from the Sea of Tranquility. From an old facility called Moon Base Delta."

CHAPTER 13

RENEWED PURPOSE

Saito and Kimura shuffled into the operations area, clearly having been woken from a deep sleep. Renton noticed that both were now wearing the standard-issue Moon Base Delta comms units he had given them earlier—probably using the unit's augmented reality function to find their way here.

"The AI woke us up and told us to come here," Saito looked around the area. "Wherever here is."

"So, what's the problem?" Kimura asked, a hint of tired grumpiness in her voice.

Renton jerked a thumb at the camera feed on the main monitor. "Recognize that?"

Saito moved closer, squinting his eyes. "That's... Haruki's rover." He turned to Kimura. "Oh my god, he's still alive."

"How do you know it's... this Haruki guy?" Renton was skeptical.

"It's the same rover."

"Doesn't mean it's still him driving it," said Matteo.

"DOA, can you make radio contact with it?" Renton asked.

"I can attempt a broadcast on the open channels."

"Okay, do it and see if we get a response."

A hissing, crackling sound echoed around the operations area.

"This is Kobayashi Haruki, I'm very low on fuel. Urgently need assistance."

"It's him," said Saito, his voice bright with excitement. "I told you he'd make it."

"DOA, open a voice channel to reply," Renton commanded.

"Confirmed."

"This is Renton Hicks, Moon Base Delta. Bring your rover over to the Southern gate. You can enter the airlock there. Follow the tunnel to the next airlock, where your rover will be decontaminated. We'll meet you at the rover dock on the inside. Oh, and by the way, some of your friends are already here."

"Who? Saito, Kimura? They're okay?"

"Yep, we're still vertical. Me, Kimura, and Tanaka," Saito shouted out.

"I thought you guys were all dead."

"Bring your rover in. We can talk more when you get here. Out." The comms connection closed, and Renton turned around to the others. "We'd better get down there."

"I'll let Alice and Yuna know what's going on," said Matteo. "Never a dull moment, eh?"

"Yeah," Renton replied. "Let's hope he brought his own provisions."

. . .

A few moments later, they were all standing in the rover dock, beside the maintenance yard. Renton, Saito, and Kimura were waiting for the airlock to cycle through its routine when Matteo arrived with a tired and bemused Alice, Oryx trotting beside her, and Yuna, who looked disheveled, clearly not enjoying this new drama.

The airlock door finally opened, and the rover trundled out, coming to a halt with a chorus of hissing and creaking as it continued adjusting to the pressurized environment. The side hatch opened, and Kobayashi Haruki stepped out to be welcomed with open arms by Saito. Haruki seemed a little more reserved, simply giving him a pat on the shoulder.

Saito stepped back to get a good look at his comrade. "Tell me, what happened to the others, Yamada and Kato?"

Haruki seemed hesitant. "Uh... they never made it to the rendezvous. I had to leave without them."

"They never made it?" Kimura sounded deeply skeptical.

"Uh, things got very messy. SINO was all over the place."

Renton noted Kimura's look and realized she didn't trust this guy. Maybe there was a history there. Not so for Saito, who seemed delighted that his buddy was alive and standing in front of him.

Alice began to check out the rover, giving it the once-over. "Did you bring any provisions?"

Haruki's face brightened. "Yeah. I grabbed as much as I could at the outpost. Enough food to last for the journey to Shackleton. No fuel though." He shook his head.

"Same at the other outpost." Saito nodded. "No fuel. That's where we met these guys." He swept an arm around.

"A SINO patrol showed up," said Kimura, "While we were stuck there waiting for you." There was an edge to her voice. "Fortunately, these people were already there and saved our asses."

"How did you know to come to Moon Base Delta?" Renton asked.

"I headed over to the other outpost and saw the abandoned rover. The place was empty, and I thought you guys might have been captured by a SINO patrol. I didn't have much fuel, and I had heard about this place from those broadcasts from the Axial Luxor. Decided to head here." His eyes flicked from Renton to Saito to Kimura. Then he looked around the rover dock and over to the massive maintenance yard. "This place is way bigger than I imagined." He shifted his focus back to Renton and the crew. "I wasn't sure there would actually be people here. It was just... my only option."

Yuna yawned.

"Well, you're here now," said Renton. "Let's get you inside the base and settled in. We can talk tomorrow. We all need to get some sleep."

Saito and Kimura took charge of Haruki, giving him a rundown on how they got here, what little they knew about the place, and then brought him to where he could sleep. Renton and the crew left them to it. They were tired and needed rest. But before retiring, they had a quick confab.

"I don't trust that guy," said Alice when the others were out of earshot.

"I don't really trust any of them," said Matteo.

"We should have DOA keep an eye on them, alert us if they start wandering around," suggested Yuna.

"Agreed," said Renton. "Although, maybe we should take turns on watch. No point in all of us being awake."

"If I may make a suggestion," DOA's voice resonated in Renton's ear through his comms unit. He looked at the others and noticed they all had their units switched on.

"Fire away."

"If any of the newly arrived people should awaken and start to wander around the facility, I could use the robot, Oryx, to follow them."

This seemed like an inspired idea to Renton until he thought about it for a second or two. "But you can see where they go. Why do you need control of the robot?"

"Not all the camera feeds are working. Unless each of them is wearing a comms unit, then I could lose track of them."

"It's fine by me," said Alice. "I'll set up a quick patch-through for you. Then I'm going back to sleep."

Matteo just shrugged.

"Whatever," said Yuna.

"Okay, I suppose so," said Renton. He was dead on his feet by now anyway and didn't have the energy to argue.

They all drifted off back to their bunks, leaving DOA and Oryx on guard duty.

Renton awoke several hours later to the smell of freshly brewed coffee. He opened his eyes to see Alice entering his module. She had a mug in each hand. "Morning, I brought you a coffee."

He sat up and ran his hand through his hair to get it under control—he really needed a haircut. Alice bringing him morning coffee was the last thing he expected. They had drifted apart during the grim weeks of forced malnutrition, each retreating into their own personal safe spaces, just like Matteo and Yuna. Now, though, it seemed Alice was reaching out again. So he extended a hand and took the mug.

Alice sat down on the edge of his bunk. "Guess what?"

Renton took a sip and almost immediately he felt his brain gaining a degree of clarity. "Uh... Oryx murdered all the new people in their sleep."

Alice locked eyes with him, an expression of feigned shock on her face. "Yes, how did you know?"

"Just a wild guess." He grinned.

"No, nothing so dramatic. The news is we got a reply back from Earth."

Renton's coffee mug halted halfway to his mouth. "Seriously?"

"Yep. We received a message on repeat from someplace called Straw-stack, or was it Shaw-shank?" She stared at the ceiling for a moment, trying to remember. "Anyway, they have acknowledged our transmission and are ready for two-way comms."

"Shit, I'd better get to the op-room." He leaned over to put the coffee mug down on a locker.

. . .

Alice raised a hand. "Hold up, there's no panic. We won't be in line-of-sight with that region of Earth for another two hours."

Renton relaxed, retrieved his coffee, and took another sip. He lifted the coffee mug in salute. "Thanks. This is good. The last time you brought me a coffee, it was in a pouch, and cold."

Alice pinched her forehead in a question mark, trying to remember this.

"On the Aurora," Renton prompted. "After I told Mackenzie to go stick it, remember?"

"Ah, yes," she smiled. "That seems like several lifetimes ago."

"Who would have thought we'd end up stuck here?" Renton waved the mug around. "Clinging on by our fingernails."

Alice's face darkened. "It's not looking great, is it?"

"It's better than it was a few days ago." He gestured with the mug. "Now we have coffee. And we're not starving. We've also got new people, and Earth has finally made contact." He smiled at her.

"Yeah, I suppose. But what about next month, next year, the year after that? We're never getting back, are we?"

Renton's tone was soft and somber. "No, we have to put those dreams out of our heads. All we can do is focus on the here and now, try to build ourselves a future, hard as that may seem."

Alice sighed. "I don't think I can bear being so hungry again, Renton. Or that feeling of being so... isolated, drifting apart from reality."

He reached out and clutched her hand. "Hey, we're all in

this together and we can get through it together. We'll find a way."

She leaned in, embraced, and buried her head in his shoulder. Renton could feel her shake, so he reflexively rubbed her back with his free hand. She lifted her head again, looked at him for a beat, then they kissed. And in that moment, Renton felt a surge of renewed purpose course through his being.

CHAPTER 14
TRANSMISSION

By the time Renton and Alice arrived in the operations area of Moon Base Delta, Matteo and Yuna were already there, preparing for the two-way comms with the Strawstack Mountain Astronomical Facility back on Earth. They were also working to tie communications in with the Axial Luxor. Kimura and her father, Tanaka, were also there, both sitting quietly in a corner.

"Where's Saito and that new guy?" Renton whispered into Matteo's ear.

"Down in the maintenance hangar, checking over the rover and doing a stock take of the supplies Haruki grabbed from the outpost." He glanced over at the two others in the corner. "Kimura got pretty excited when I told her we might be making contact with Earth. I said it would be okay if they wanted to hang out here. Hope you don't mind."

"Not at all. I'm beginning to warm to those two. Not that keen on the new guy, though. He could be trouble."

"I think he's pretty determined to get to Shackleton. So hopefully he'll be gone soon."

"Incoming transmission from the Axial Luxor," DOA's voice echoed around the room as a video feed began to crystallize on the big wall monitor.

Selene, as usual, sat in the center of a row of people all gathered around one edge of a circular table in one of the many executive boardrooms available on the orbital hotel. Renton could see they were treating the imminent connection with Earth as a big deal, as he had never seen so many of them gathered together for a call with Moon Base Delta.

"Hello?" said Selene, tentatively testing the connection.

Several of the crew waved back, including Renton, along with a few vocal affirmations that Selene was coming in loud and clear.

"So what's new?" Yuna kicked things off, as she tended to do since she nearly always managed the technicalities of these sessions.

"We're getting reports out of Shackleton on the progress of the Xilinex Corporation's takeover, and it's not good. At least, not if you are someone who values freedom."

This elicited an immediate reaction from Kimura. "Why? What's going on?"

There was a momentary pause in the conversation, and Renton could see that Selene and her associates were confused by this addition to the population of Moon Base Delta.

"Oh, this is Kimura Aoi," said Renton. "And her father, Tanaka Aoi. We ran into them while we were looking for supplies over at the seismic testing station, along with two others. They're just passing through, planning to journey on to Shackleton."

"Xilinex has taken control of all the food production facilities and stores. They've introduced strict rationing and are cracking down hard on anyone that gets in their way. We've got reports of several people having been executed, mainly former leaders."

"I think you're being overly dramatic, Selene." A squat, bald-headed man spoke up from the periphery of the group that had gathered together on the Axial. And judging by the body language around the table, Renton could sense that this guy was not well-liked. "Someone needs to bring order to the chaos, and I, for one, would prefer Xilinex to SINO. We all know what they're like."

"We've just come from the Secchi Mining facility, northeast of Tranquility," Tanaka interjected, his voice raised so that he could be heard. "SINO came in and did exactly the same thing. They took over our food supplies and eliminated anyone they didn't like."

"They're both consolidating," Selene replied. "Growing their respective footprints and stocking up on resources before they go head-to-head. Make no mistake, war is coming."

"That's why we need to pick a side, sooner rather than later," said the bald-headed guy.

"I beg to disagree. Survival shouldn't be dependent on surrendering to either of those two groups," said Selene, her tone emphatic.

Renton could see that there was tension beginning to grow up on the Axial. Different factions were emerging with different ideas and very different agendas.

"Connection established with the Strawstack Mountain Radio Astronomy facility," DOA's voice interrupted the ongoing arguments coming from the Axial leadership. "I will attempt to initiate two-way communication. Please be aware of the anticipated three-second delay in response time."

A hissing, crackling sound filled the room. Then a new voice could be heard breaking through the static. "This is Strawstack. Are you receiving us?"

It sounded to Renton like something from a bygone age, which in truth it was. Back when the first human stepped on the lunar surface, they communicated in fuzzy, stilted signals drenched in atmospheric interference.

Yuna leaned into a retro-looking microphone that she and Matteo had rigged up to give them better control over analog signal amplification.

"This is Moon Base Delta. We are receiving you." She paused for a beat, then continued. "It's good to hear your voice. Over."

They waited for a tense few seconds before the comms crackled again. "Yes, we're receiving you." There was clear excitement in the speaker's voice. "It's great to hear you too. Please stand by while we attempt to focus in on your signal."

"What are they doing?" asked Alice, who had been pretty quiet up until this point.

"As the Moon crosses that region of Earth," answered DOA, "our signal will get stronger, and more bandwidth will be available. They are attempting to accommodate a video link."

With that, a fuzzy picture emerged in one corner of the main monitor. "Connection established," said DOA, "putting it on screen now."

It was definitely low-bandwidth and hence very pixelated, but they could still clearly make out several people all gathered around a camera feed. Three were sitting close together, others stood huddled about behind—all of them had name tags, although they were too hard to read with the current resolution.

The central figure waved. "My name is Sheneese Richmond." She then gestured to her left. "This is Alan Dyson, Head of FISA." Then to her right. "And this is General Philip Grant, Space Division." They all nodded in turn. "Firstly, we would like to establish protocols for data transfer, as this is the first contact with the Moon since the last of the comms satellites were destroyed—as far as we are aware of. We need to ensure efficient transfer of information, just in case we lose contact."

"Protocols received," DOA announced. "Establishing a new encrypted data channel."

There was a pause as the message crossed the vast expanse of space, back to Earth. Their faces animated when confirmation was received their end. "Can you update us on the situation up there now?" Dyson asked.

"We can send you all the broadcasts from the Axial," said Renton. "DOA, do we have them?"

"Yes, Renton. They have all been archived. I will send in batches, as bandwidth allows."

"The Axial?" asked Dyson. "Is Selene Mene still there?"

"Yes, I am," came the reply, which invoked some confusion with the people at Strawstack.

"Is that you, Selene?" Dyson looked perplexed. "I can't see you. Are you in Moon Base Delta?"

"We're on a side call with the Axial Luxor. You can hear them, but there's not enough bandwidth for full video yet," Yuna gestured at the monitor.

"And Professor Henriksen?" The question came from one of the other people standing behind the three central figures.

"Is that you, Han?" The professor sounded genuinely delighted. "Yes, yes, I'm still here. Missed the evacuation flight. Damn dock exploded. Lucky to be alive. Got your early simulations. Excellent work. Although, I rather wish they had been wrong."

"Me too," said Han, nodding his head. "I'm currently working on new simulations. Trying to figure out how bad things really are in Earth orbit."

Renton reckoned it was time to get what they really wanted out of this conversation, otherwise they would spend all day just catching up.

"We need the access codes for the FISA LunaSat constellation. DOA, the AI that runs the base here, is about fifteen years out of date. If it can connect to LunaSat then it can update its knowledge-base. This is critically important for us." He added in the last qualifier to inject some urgency into this request, not have it swill around in committees and board meetings.

"I can send you those, no problem," said Dyson. "And you can thank your aunt, Selene, for persuading me to part with the codes to activate Moon Base Delta."

"Thanks," Renton replied. "One other thing. You're probably aware that the biomass used in food production is provided by the Santomon Corporation and is genetically modified to require constant resupply—nothing up here is self-sustaining. If we don't get a new stock, then we will all ultimately die. This is the reality that none of us can escape. So we need to find a way to reverse engineer it back to its original, natural form, so that plants can self-seed, and so on. This is literally a life and death situation."

It took a few seconds for the message to be sent and for the assembled group down in Strawstack to digest it. As Renton watched their reactions, he could see that this was news to most of them—except maybe, for General Philip Grant, who immediately leaned in to the mic, being first to answer.

"It's a situation we are acutely aware of and are currently in discussions with the Santomon Corporation to come up with a solution." His tone was formal, like he was reading a prepared statement.

"How long will that take? Time is of the essence." Matteo pushed him.

"We can't say for sure. You have to understand that things are pretty chaotic down here on Earth. We're still dealing with the fallout from the loss of the constellations. Communications are extremely problematic and we're not certain what institutions and industries are still functioning," he added.

"How bad is it down there, really?" asked Alice.

There was much side-eye going on when they heard this question—who was going to be the one to answer that? In the end, it turned out to be Dyson. "With no data transmission infrastructure, we have no distribution networks and no financial system to pay for anything. To be blunt, it's catastrophic. The entire society is effectively on state aid. And the security situation is volatile."

"My god," Matteo exclaimed, "that bad?"

"Yes, it's that bad," said Dyson. "And it could get much worse. We're a fusion society relying on Helium-3 fuel that comes almost exclusively from the Moon—at least, it used to come from there. Nothing can get through now, so that's what we're working on down here, finding a way."

"There won't be anything heading to Earth if we're all dead from starvation," Alice added.

"That's why we are working hard to find a solution, for all our sakes," said Grant.

"And what's the possibility of that happening? Xilinex and SINO are both spreading it around that it will be two or three years before this debris cloud clears enough to get craft traveling through it again."

The reaction to this question seemed to elicit a wave of general discomfort, with much shuffling and head scratching.

"Eh, it's a complex situation, and we won't know with any certainty until we've collected enough real-time data to create a model of the cloud." Again, it was the General that answered.

"So is it a year, two, ten, a century?"

"Look, the situation is this. The debris cloud will never clear without our direct intervention. Therefore we are working to understand its dynamics and build craft that can engage with it, and yes, even pass through." The General's tone was becoming a little patronizing for Renton's taste. "These will not be crewed, but robotic, and extremely robust. We're under no illusion here as to the difficulty of the task ahead of us. But just bear in mind the global stockpile of Helium-3 will be exhausted in a few months. So we're throwing everything we can at it. And that means helping you to survive up there."

"If you want to do that, then food security is top priority. We need to find a way to reverse engineer current GM stocks," Renton replied, with a hint of exasperation.

"Of course. As I said, we're already deep in discussions on how best to proceed."

At that point Renton lost interest in the conversation. He had heard everything he needed to hear. He sensed that the military in charge of this operation were hedging their bets. Maybe they had already made contact with SINO or Xilinex, or some other group, and weren't saying—not even to their own people. All this just reinforced Renton's view that if they were going to survive up here, then they would have to find their own way.

CHAPTER 15

POWER AND CONTROL

E ventually, the transmission began to fragment as Earth's inexorable rotation progressed, finally dying when Strawstack was no longer in the direct line-of-sight of Moon Base Delta. It would be another sixteen or more hours before comms could be restored. By this time, everyone was talked out, so the connection with the Axial was also terminated, and they all began to drift back to the common room.

Renton, having skipped breakfast, was hungry. All he was running on was the coffee that Alice had brought him earlier. "I'm starving; I need to eat something," he informed her as they made their way toward the rear of the common room where the galley was located.

"Me too," she replied. "All that talking has drained my energy levels."

"All that talking about nothing," said Renton, almost to himself.

"What do you mean?"

"Oh, it's just I have a feeling we're not getting any help from Earth anytime soon. Maybe we'll get the LunaSat access codes, but not much else."

"What about help with solving the GM food issue?" said Matteo.

Renton looked around to see both him and Yuna also coming into the galley.

"I wouldn't hold my breath. It sounded to me like that General Grant guy was just bullshitting us."

"Yeah," agreed Yuna. "I got the very same vibe, like he was hiding something."

"Like what?" Matteo had a puzzled look on his face.

Yuna shrugged. "I dunno, just something."

Renton began rummaging around in a food locker. "We'll need to get back to a rationing regime, or we'll go through these supplies in no time."

"We might be able to help with that."

They all turned around to see Haruki entering the common room along with the rest of the people they picked up at the outpost.

"Oh, how so?" asked Matteo, adopting a confrontational stance.

"We can trade for hydrogen."

"So you're heading for Shackleton?" asked Alice.

"Too right. Not staying in this... graveyard." Haruki looked around him as if surveying the sad and sorry state of Moon Base Delta.

"We're not going with you," Tanaka announced, his arms

folded, his stance solid. Beside him stood Saito and Kimura, looking resolute.

"We've discussed it between ourselves," his tone soft and resigned. "We'd like to stay here, if you'll have us."

Renton looked at his comrades, trying to judge their reaction. He had known them long enough now to get a good idea of what they were thinking just from their faces and body language. None of them seemed to be objecting.

"Sure." He opened his arms in an expansive gesture. "You're more than welcome to stay. It would be nice to have some more people around."

"No way, Saito. You bailing out on me? After what we've been through? You just going to hole up here like a frightened rat and slowly die of starvation?" Haruki was clearly surprised by this announcement.

"Screw you, Haruki." Kimura took a step forward. "You were never planning to meet up with us after we got out. You would have left us there."

"That's bullshit. You know it is." Haruki appealed.

"You think Shackleton will be better?" Kimura continued. "There's already rationing going on, and who's to say, with Xilinex now in control, they will even let you in?"

Haruki was silent for a beat. "Fine, have it your way. Stay here and die for all I care. But I'm heading for someplace with a future." He turned to face Renton and the crew. "So, do we have a deal on the hydrogen? You guys have got plenty of it here."

"Sure, but you split whatever supplies you have four ways. You keep one for yourself; that should keep you going for a while." Renton offered.

"Uh... I don't really have that much. And it's a long journey down south."

Alice pointed at the ceiling. "DOA has done its own audit of your supplies, back while you guys were checking over your rover. So don't bullshit us. We know more about what you have than even you do."

Haruki looked shocked. "You're all brainwashed by that AI," he tapped the side of his head, referring to the comms units they all wore. "It's turning you all into slaves."

"That's the deal." Renton gestured at the door. "Unless you want to try to get to Shackleton on fumes?"

Haruki just scowled back. He knew he had no choice.

Renton then turned his attention to Saito, Kimura, and Tanaka. "If you want to stay, then the provisions you get from Haruki all go into the central supply." He gestured at the food lockers behind him. "At some point, we might have to start rationing again. I wish we didn't, but if it comes to it, then DOA will allocate food based on body mass, activity, and so on. Are you all okay with that?"

Kimura and Tanaka were quick to nod that they were. Saito followed, clearly not so enthused by the idea of going hungry.

"Fine, all settled," said Renton. "We'll refuel your rover... just as soon as I eat something first."

Later that day, after Haruki had finally departed for Shackleton, they all gathered again in the common room for an evening meal, but this time the vibe was different. There was a celebratory atmosphere. They were welcoming new people,

people who had chosen to join their little tribe, and with it came a feeling of hope within Renton. These people had chosen them over a Xilinex-controlled Shackleton. It was an endorsement of sorts. The mood was relaxed as they all chatted, sharing stories, and trading information.

Kimura turned out to be the most open about what they had come from. She worked for the JAXA-KARI agency in Secchi in Human Resources and knew quite a bit about the inner workings of the Hamamatsu Corporation. But during the evacuation, a whole group of them were left stranded, just like in many other places. In the beginning, it was the broadcasts from the Axial that kept them informed—and kept them from falling into despair. But very soon, two factions began to form: one wanted to go it alone, while another faction wanted to reach out to other groups. The latter faction got the upper hand and began to see SINO as a possible partner. They made the mistake of opening the doors and allowing them in, and once in, SINO wasted no time in taking control.

Saito worked as a maintenance engineer for Hamamatsu and, like Kimura, could see the way things were going with SINO. So they hatched a plan with his friend, Haruki, along with a few others, to commandeer two rovers and head for Shackleton Crater. But things went wrong from the very beginning. What exactly happened? Neither Saito nor Kimura would say. But it was clear that Kimura blamed most of it on Haruki.

Tanaka didn't say much during this, preferring to let his daughter do most of the talking. But when he did speak, it was to drop a bombshell.

"This is probably going to surprise you all, but I used to work here, at Moon Base Delta, back in the day. Must be twenty years ago now."

"What?" Matteo almost choked on the morsel of food he was in the process of chewing. "You were actually here? Why didn't you tell us?"

"Why didn't DOA tell us?" said Yuna.

"I asked it not to. Not until I was ready to reveal it. It kindly obliged. Now that we have decided to stay, it's only right that I should inform you."

Renton wasn't sure what to make of this admission by Tanaka. "So what did you do back then? What was it like?" he asked.

Tanaka took a sip of his drink and collected his thoughts. "Oh, I was young, around your age." He nodded at Renton. "It was my first time on the Moon, I came up with JAXA-KARI, working as a data analyst. This base," he waved a hand around, "was supposed to be a model for a new way of organizing a society, very experimental, and the AI was central to that; it ran everything, including the day-to-day work schedules. And, much to the surprise of a great many skeptics, it all seemed to work out just fine."

"So what happened? Where did it all go wrong?" Alice asked as she relaxed back into her seat.

"Yeah, we heard some strange stories of the AI becoming neurotic, or something," Matteo added.

Tanaka laughed and shook his head. "Ha, nothing like that. It was simply down to certain groups feeling that the way things operated here was a threat to their power base. I think, ultimately, humans aren't wired to function for very long in what was, in effect, an egalitarian utopia. Some see it as an emasculation of the baser desires for power and control. Most assumed the project would be a failure, but when it turned out to be a success, then certain groups felt threatened. How could they have power and control in a society that was operated by an AI? You can see the problems. So they set about restricting this tech, too powerful, a danger to society. In the end, they got their way, and the AI was taken offline, and things returned to a more traditional organizational structure based on power-mongering between factions." Tanaka paused for a moment, taking a sip of his drink.

"Have you ever considered just how powerful that AI is?" Tanaka continued, gesturing with a thumb in the general direction of the operations room.

"It's rather extraordinary, for sure," said Yuna. "I've never come across anything like it before."

"None of us have," said Matteo.

"There's a reason for that. It's because it's restricted tech," he explained. "Only state security agencies and the military have access to such powerful AI. Back on Earth, anyone found operating an advanced general intelligence is committing a serious crime, one punishable by a very long stay in prison."

There was a long silence as this revelation from Tanaka was digested by the others, along with the meal.

"That's quite a story," said Renton eventually. "I wonder why FISA or Space Division never told us any of this."

"Why would they? They were just as instrumental in the

collapse of the project as everyone else. Power and Control." He tapped the side of his nose in a conspiratorial gesture.

"Like what's happening right now?" said Alice. "Everyone is fighting for power and control when most people just want to survive."

"It's just human nature," said Tanaka. "You can't stop it. You can only ever hope to contain the fallout."

"So, if what you're saying is true, then surely that would put Moon Base Delta at the top of the list of facilities to take over," Renton ventured. "You know, use DOA to gain that extra edge in the battle for ultimate control of the Moon."

"It would. But at the same time, there's an irrational fear of the place in the older population," said Tanaka. "People prone to the propaganda of those times."

"Seriously?" Matteo's eyebrows reached peak levels.

"People had to be persuaded of the dangers of advanced AI, so that it could be restricted, only allowed to be used by those in power."

"So that's where all those mad stories came from," said Alice. "I always thought there was more to it than what FISA was saying... or not saying. They were very tight-lipped when asked anything about this place."

"When Selena Mene and the other remnants of FISA, up on the Axial Luxor, were broadcasting about here being a safe place, a lot of people still harbored those old fears. That's why few would consider coming."

"But you did," said Renton.

Tanaka sucked in a long breath. "I knew the place, knew

what it was really like. So I tried to persuade my daughter to head to Moon Base Delta."

"I'll admit, I wasn't keen on the idea." Saito raised a hand. "Haruki had me focused on Shackleton, so, in the end, that's where we decided to aim for." He looked around the common room. "But I have to say, Tanaka, you were right. This place is... something else."

Their conversation was interrupted by a message from DOA. Since acquiring the access codes for LunaSat during the transmission with Strawstack, it had been busy harvesting all the data it could from the multitude of connected FISA facilities still operating on Luna, filling in the gaps in its knowledge base. "If I may," it announced. "Just to let you all know, I have completed my initial data scan of several distributed FISA data-stacks, from which I've compiled an up-to-date geographic and political map of Luna. It is available for you to study as a 3D rendering in the operations room, if you so wish."

"I suppose we should go take a look," said Renton as he rose from his seat. The others did likewise.

As they all walked out of the common room, Renton felt a warm glow emanating from deep within him. It was a long time since he'd felt this content—long before the crash landing of the Aurora. Maybe it was the food in his stomach, maybe it was the relaxed conversation with new friends, or maybe it was his growing relationship with Alice, who had just slipped her arm through his as they made their way to the operations room.

CHAPTER 16
A NEW NARRATIVE

Three robotic rovers cautiously advanced toward the southwestern edge of Scott Crater, a one-hundred-and-eight-kilometer-wide impact site and home to one of the primary SINO-controlled food production facilities on Luna. Behind these slowly moving machines, three more armored rovers equipped with plasma cannons followed, and behind these were a plethora of support vehicles transporting approximately forty well-armed Xilinex mercenaries—all feeding real-time information back to the Xilinex Corporation lunar orbital.

What had once been a spartan corporate boardroom on board the orbital had now been transformed into a frenetic, cluttered war room. Rows of technicians sat at consoles along each wall, attending to a multitude of data feeds for communications, satellite imagery, and robotic vehicles operating down on the surface. The central boardroom holo-table displayed a 3D topographical map of the Scott Crater region, an area of the Moon that had been firmly established as SINO's home turf, but was soon to be under assault from Xilinex forces.

Pompodur Rossen Adarok sat at the head of the holo-table. To his right sat General Wagner, flanked by a number of subordinates. To his left sat Director Anton Levrosky, along with a number of lesser administrative mortals from the Xilinex Corporation. Director Ossian Corbell was not present as he had taken ill the previous day. It seemed that there was something in his tea that didn't agree with him. Something that Pompodur had put in there—an exotic, genetically engineered neurotoxin that he had commissioned many years ago, and had reason to use on at least two prior occasions.

Ossian Corbell would, of course, die, probably within the next day, and that would be one less insufferable fool that Pompodur would have to put up with. Poison was such an elegant solution to a great many problems, Pompodur considered. No surprise that it was often seen as a diplomat's weapon. Why resort to the brutality of the blade when a rival can simply be seduced into consuming a tainted morsel? Then they would drift off to die in a quiet corner—that is, if it was done right.

Corbell complained of feeling unwell and was hauled off to the med-bay, where the doctors were at a loss as to the nature of the ailment. They prescribed fluids and rest—pending blood sample analysis, which returned inconclusive, as Pompodur knew it would. He also knew that Director Corbell would no longer be a thorn in his side by midday tomorrow. The other subtle benefit of using poison was that he could visit his colleague on his sickbed and offer kind words for his quick recovery. It was always a nice touch.

Tensions ratcheted up noticeably in the war room as a camera feed from one of the robotic scouts materialized on the huge wall monitor. A cracked and broken monochrome landscape stretched across the screen. As the scout advanced over the crest of a low rocky ridge, the broad sweep of the SINO base came into view. It consisted of a large central domed structure covered in a dense layer of lunar regolith, with several smaller structures of similar construction nestled around it. Many of these bristled with antennae and gun-pods. The scout's purpose was to draw fire so that the exact location of any plasma weapon systems could be identified. The second and third rover scouts advanced from either side, all three slowly closing the gap to the SINO facility. Everyone in the war room was on high alert. No one spoke as they waited for the first shots to be fired in the first off-planet war ever to be conducted by human civilization.

A flicker of light flashed from the peak of a mound and a blue ball of incandescent plasma seared across the lunar sky at 10,000 kilometers per second—three percent of the speed of light—and slammed into the lead scout rover. Its camera feed fizzed and crackled and then went dead.

"Scout one down," announced a technician in the war room.

Pompodur sat up, mesmerized. He'd never seen a plasma cannon in action and had only heard of their destructive power from the General. They could deliver a highly destructive physical and thermal punch equivalent to around three kilograms of TNT, but they also produced significant electromagnetic radiation, scrambling any unprotected electronic circuitry. Their downside was that they needed an enormous amount of power, supplied by a substantial capacitor array. This meant there was a relatively long period before they could be used again while the capacitor bank charged. Tactically, this was what the General wanted—to force SINO to execute its first volley and then rush forward.

The satellite feed zoomed into the site of the lead scout rover. All that remained was a shattered, blackened hulk squatting in a broad oval patch of scorched and sintered regolith.

"Request order to return fire," a square on the vast wall monitor now showed the head and shoulders of Lieutenant Ben Wilson, the Xilinex commander on the ground, currently hunkered down in one of the rear transport vehicles.

"Hold fire," the General commanded. "Keep advancing. There's probably another plasma weapon. We need to locate it."

"Confirmed," answered Lieutenant Wilson.

A second dome flicked as another ball of high-intensity energy raced across the sky and slammed into another of the robotic scouts. This seemed to be the trigger for the General as he jumped up from his seat shouting "Go, go," swiping the air with an agitated index finger.

From the satellite feed, Pompodur could now see scores of mercenaries pour out from the transports, taking up positions using the machines for cover. The advance began to pick up speed. Two of the armored machines crested the ridge and loosed a salvo of missiles that streaked across the intervening space, great clouds of dust and debris blossoming out from the impact sites.

The main thrust of the assault force now crested the ridge and straight into a hail of small weapons fire from positions located all around the perimeter of the SINO facility. The noise volume in the war room escalated into a cacophonous maelstrom as the multiple audio feeds filled the room with shouts of men impacted by projectiles of one form or another. Rising above this chorus of death and destruction, the General gave the command to return fire.

Another hail of small weapons fire, this time in the opposite direction, smashed into the sides of the domes, coupled with even more missile salvos. Soon, the entire area was one massive cloud of dust, obscuring the satellite feed, with only the flash of weapons blossoming in the maelstrom giving any clue as to the progress of the Xilinex forces.

"Get me some visuals," Wagner shouted out to the techs.

The main monitor tessellated into a myriad of individual bodycam feeds. Each one a jerking, blurry vision of what looked to Pompodur, to be utter chaos. A short moment later, the main airlock entrance of the SINO facility came into view from Lieutenant Wilson's bodycam feed.

"On me! ON ME!" The Lieutenant's voice barked out. "Breaching team on me at the main entrance. Keep those shooters busy, keep them pinned down."

Judging from the video feed, he was taking cover in the recess of a massive airlock door. Several others rushed over, sliding to a halt at the door's edge. One got hit before reaching cover. He collapsed on the ground, clutching his neck, clawing at his visor. A comrade reached out and dragged him in. The Lieutenant came in closer to get a better view, and those in the war room witnessed the life drain away from this fighter as the oxygen in his suit evacuated into the vacuum of space.

"Leave him. Let's get this door opened," the Lieutenant commanded.

A rugged case was opened, explosives extracted, and hastily placed at various points around the door.

"Okay, take cover." The team moved clear, the charges detonated, and the door, or what was left of it, shot out across the surface. The Xilinex mercenaries poured in.

It was hard for Pompodur to follow the progress of the battle from the bodycam feeds, as it was an incomprehensible dance of movement, flashes of weapons fire, and the screams of the fallen. But even with only these chaotic images to work with, it was clear that Xilinex had the upper hand. They had breached the entrance, more were piling in, and they were making short work of any resistance the SINO had managed to put up. The mood in the war room became electric as everyone sensed victory. Bodycam feeds stabilized, and Lieutenant Wilson reported in, talking directly via another camera. "Main resistance has been overcome. Situation is under our control. I'm sending a team to mop up any other holdouts."

A cheer went up in the war room, with much fist-bumping and air punching.

Suddenly, there was a huge explosion at the facility. The Lieutenant dropped to the floor, as did everyone else.

"What the hell was that?" he asked, alarmed.

"Major explosion, sir?"

"I fucking know that. Where?"

"Silos, I think."

"Shit. Anyone in there?"

"Complete depressurization, sir. Anyone in there will be in orbit by now, sir."

"Goddamnit."

"Satellite feed, get back the satellite feed," Wagner roared out to the techs.

The feed reemerged on the main monitor.

"Holy shit," someone voiced out loud what everyone else was thinking.

The entire northern section of the facility was gone, blasted into nothing. The storage silos, the vertical farms, the bioreactors. All gone, all destroyed. Rather than lose it to Xilinex, SINO had just vaporized enough food to feed the entire lunar population for half a year.

"Those crazy bastards," shouted the General. "Eliminate everybody in there. Take no prisoners. They're only more mouths to feed."

But SINO wasn't finished just yet. Out from the edges of the mayhem, they came rushing at the Xilinex mercenaries in one last glorious charge. They piled out, overcoming the unsuspecting, shooting and hacking with everything they had. In response, the mercenaries unloaded into the writhing mass of crazed attackers.

It was all over within a few minutes. The bodycam feeds now showed scenes of utter devastation. Bodies piled on top of bodies covered every inch of the floor. Mercenaries walked through the fallen, popping off shots when someone didn't look quite dead yet.

"Lieutenant Wilson?" Wagner called out. "Status?"

"Eh, the base is... secured, sir."

"Good job, well done."

"We lost a lot of men, sir. Food silos gone, production facility destroyed," Wilson added.

"No matter, we'll make them pay at the Mass Accelerator. The fewer SINO people that exist, the fewer mouths there are to feed."

Pompodur looked around the war room, sensing the shock and trauma experienced by the tech team at the carnage—they needed a pep talk, needed a new narrative to make sense of this bloodlust.

He stood up and raised his voice above the chatter. "This is why we must be victorious." Everyone turned to look in his direction. "The insanity of SINO will destroy us all unless we eliminate them. Remember, we fight for our very survival, we fight for our very future. Today is a great day. Today is the day we start to secure that future."

He caught the General's eye. The old general gave a wry smile and an imperceptible nod in return. He knew the score. A new script was needed to focus the minds of those putting their lives on the line. They needed to know what it was they were fighting for. What it was that would win them victory. And Pompodur's job was to provide that reason.

CHAPTER 17
LUNASAT

"I have been interrogating a multitude of data assets thanks to my recent access to the LunaSat constellation," DOA began, "enough for me to create a reasonably accurate map of the lunar surface, including infrastructure, population densities, and the degree of control currently being exerted by the various factions now operating on the Moon and its environs."

A highly detailed topographical map of the Sea of Tranquility radiated out across the holo-table in the operation room of Moon Base Delta. "These areas of control are highlighted in color," it continued. "The intensity of which indicates the level of control."

"Is this red area SINO territory?" Renton asked, pointing to the very eastern edge of Tranquility. They had all migrated into the operations room after their celebratory meal.

"Yes, as you can see, a large area east of Couchy Rille is all controlled by SINO," said DOA as the 3D map panned to reveal more of this region. "However, these areas in a lighter red color represent outposts and facilities that they have recently taken over."

"That's Secchi, our old mining facility there." Saito pointed to a big industrial outpost, now highlighted in light red.

"I can zoom in on that facility and display real-time images from LunaSat, if you wish," offered DOA.

"Sure," said Saito. "It would be interesting to see what's going on there now."

The map zoomed in to give a 3D rendering of a sprawling complex of buildings interspersed with a multitude of heavy mining machinery. On the periphery was a compact shuttle port, one ship sitting on the pad.

Renton leaned in to get a better look and then tapped on the identification marker hovering above the lone ship parked in the shuttle port. *Light Cargo Vessel XV-345. Schedule: provision transport. Destination: to be determined.*

"They're moving all the supplies," observed Kimura. "Shipping them somewhere else."

"Stealing, you mean," said Saito.

"They're not going to clear everything out in one ship." Tanaka noted. "They would need several trips for that."

"My estimates put it at thirteen if they were using this size of ship," DOA informed them.

Renton did a double-take when he heard this from the AI; it seemed a very precise answer. "Is that just a guess or do you somehow know exactly what's stored in Secchi?" he asked.

"Utilizing LunaSat, I have been able to interrogate their

stock systems and have obtained a detailed inventory of what is currently in storage," DOA replied.

"Wow, that's incredible," said Alice. "What else can you do?"

"LunaSat has given me a new level of awareness. Not only have I been able to update my knowledge base, but I now have access to real-time data from a vast array of sources—excluding certain heavily encrypted core assets."

"Powerful AI," said Tanaka, with a wink. "You can see why they wanted to outlaw it."

Renton was intrigued by this step change in DOA's abilities. "Do you have any information on the number of people currently in Secchi?"

"Approximate population is fifty-seven. Consisting of forty-three people formerly employed by the Hamamatsu Corporation, and fourteen affiliated with SINO."

This seemed a relatively low number of SINO operatives to Renton. How did they manage to take over this place with such a small group? Maybe they had superior weaponry, or maybe someone just let them in. Still, if the current remnants of the Hamamatsu Corporation really wanted SINO out of Secchi, then it could be done. An idea was beginning to form in his head, one that might solve a lot of their problems.

"This may seem crazy," he said, forewarning the others, and scratching his chin at the same time. "But what would it take to wait until that ship was fully loaded with provisions, and then... steal it?"

"You're not seriously considering that, Renton." Matteo looked at his buddy as if he had somehow lost his mind.

"It would keep us supplied for quite a long time, and we would also have a shuttle—it could be very useful."

"That's just bonkers," said Yuna. "How would we even get there? We have a beat-up old solar-electric rover with limited range?"

"SINO would see us coming, and we would just end up back in that same place they kept us after the crash," said Matteo, waving a hand in the air dismissively. "Except this time, we'd have no Spider to get us out."

"Assuming they didn't just kill us all," added Alice.

"If I may make a suggestion," DOA interrupted.

"Of course, fire away," said Renton.

The map panned westward, back in the direction of Moon Base Delta.

"The seismic testing station has power to recharge the rover. You could use it as a pit-stop on the way."

"Sure, but SINO almost caught up with us at that outpost," said Saito. "They probably have patrols all around that place."

"I observe no patrols currently in that area. If you choose to travel, I can monitor all SINO movements and alert you to their exact positions in real-time."

There was a momentary pause as each of them began to contemplate this crazy plan, some thinking that it might have merit.

"We would need weapons," said Alice.

"No, no way, Alice. It's too... crazy," said Matteo, shaking his head and slicing the air with the side of his hand.

"Crazy can be good sometimes," she replied. "Crazy fought

off both SINO and Xilinex in the AI room when Renton was trying to reactivate the base."

"Could you remotely operate our robots that far out?" asked Renton.

Matteo threw his hands in the air. "I don't believe what I'm hearing. Have you all lost your minds?"

"Consider it a mental exercise, Matteo," said Yuna, who was clearly beginning to warm to this idea of Renton's.

"It is possible," confirmed DOA. "A satellite from the LunaSat constellation directly overhead would have more than adequate bandwidth to remotely operate several of the industrial maintenance robots."

Again, they all went quiet, each studying the topographical map hovering above the holo-table, each lost in thought.

"We know people still in there that might help us," said Kimura, finally seeing merit in the plan.

"You're talking about Yamamoto and that crew?" Saito turned to her, a fearful look on his face.

"No way, I wouldn't trust them not to double-cross us. Anyway, they're too close to Haruki, and look how that turned out. No, I'm talking about Kato Tsubasa, from the maintenance sector. He's reliable, and he's got an axe to grind." She looked over at Renton. "SINO killed his brother."

"Yes, he would be very good," Tanaka confirmed, nodding his head. "I had asked him to come with us when we were making our escape, but he didn't want to leave. Still, he'll be looking for an opportunity for vengeance."

"We're not planning a coup," said Renton. "We're just

stealing a supply ship. As quietly as possible. Get in, get out, without anyone raising the alarm until we're long gone."

"Yeah, the last thing we need is a hothead, out to create chaos and take everybody down with him," added Matteo, who, while not yet fully endorsing Renton's idea, was at least beginning to consider it.

"My apologies for interrupting your deliberations," said DOA, "but there has been a new development of some significance."

"What? Don't tell me it's another goddamn solar storm," said Matteo.

"No, this is not a cosmic event. I'm receiving data about an attack by the Xilinex Corporation on a SINO agri-facility in Scott Crater. Early indications show massive destruction to the base. All supplies and production facilities have been exposed to the vacuum of space."

"My god, that's a significant loss," said Alice. "Don't they realize we're all going to these facilities to survive?"

"My understanding is that SINO destroyed it rather than letting Xilinex take control," DOA added.

Renton shook his head in disbelief. He knew there would be a moment when the two powers faced off against one another; it was inevitable. But this was on another level. If this war between SINO and Xilinex became an ideological battle, where both sides refused to concede defeat, then they would take everyone down with them. "Can you show us where that is?" he asked DOA.

The map panned south, all the way down to Scott Crater,

and zoomed in on what remained of a cluster of domed structures. "Any real-time visual?" prompted Yuna.

"This image was taken around thirty-seven minutes ago," said DOA as a high-resolution image of the area rendered over the topographical map. They could all now see the scars of battle, the shattered domes, the wrecked machines, the dead bodies.

"This will be our undoing," said Tanaka, rather cryptically.

"What do you mean by that?" asked Yuna.

"What I mean is, in a war where nothing is gained, then there can be no winners."

"That still doesn't make any sense to me," she said, shaking her head.

"I think what my father is trying to say is that if both sides are willing to destroy their assets rather than have them taken by the other side, then this war will only succeed in destroying everything," Kimura clarified.

But there must be people, ordinary people, within SINO and Xilinex that see this as completely crazy?" said Matteo.

"They're usually the first to be silenced," said Tanaka.

"Jeez, aren't you the cheery one," said Matteo.

"Look, we need to focus on solving our own problems, here, in Moon Base Delta," Alice's tone was emphatic. "Those being, how to find the supplies we need to survive. Otherwise, it's hand over control of the base to one of these two warring factions and hope for the best."

"No way we're doing that," said Matteo. "No way."

"We might have to in the end. Or even abandon this place and try to make it to Shackleton," Yuna added.

"This friend of yours," Renton directed his question at Kimura. "Could he get us inside?"

Kimura pursed her lips and nodded. "Yeah, it's possible. He used to oversee the entire maintenance sector, for all the big mining machines. So he might be able to get us in that way."

"Assuming he hasn't gone and done something stupid and got himself killed," Saito cautioned.

Kimura gave a reluctant nod. "Yes, that's also a possibility. But if he still has his head down, then I'm certain he's our best bet on the inside. We just need to find a way to contact him."

"That should not be a problem," said DOA. "I can now facilitate secure comms outside of the SINO network."

"Don't tell me," said Matteo, "LunaSat. The gift that keeps on giving." He grinned.

"Indeed, but we still have to get there without being spotted," Renton cautioned, as he leaned in to study the topographical map. "Yuna, what do you reckon is the best route to minimize being seen?"

The map panned back toward The Sea of Tranquility. "We could keep this side to the Couchy Rille," said Yuna, waving a finger along the eastern edge of Tranquility. "That would bring us out here. But after that, it's very exposed for around twenty kilometers, no place to hide."

"What if we were expected?" everyone turned to Alice. "I mean, is there a way of masking our identity, pretending we're SINO, a scheduled delivery, something that they wouldn't look too closely at?

"It's possible. Kato would probably know what's coming and going," said Kimura.

"Matteo?" Renton looked at his friend, trying to gauge whether he was in or out of this fast-developing plan. "You game?"

Matteo sighed. "I much preferred you as a rookie engineer than as a heist mastermind." He studied the map for a moment. "Let's say we do all this. Get inside, take the shuttle, and bring it back. Won't we have a trail of angry, gun-toting SINO operatives hot on our asses? How are we going to deal with that?"

"Currently, that's the only shuttle at Secchi." Renton pointed at the image. "So it would depend on the nearest SINO shuttle port. DOA, can you show us where these are?"

The map panned further east, to a small SINO base where several shuttles could be seen parked up around the pad.

"That's around a half-hour away," said Yuna. "So that's all the time we would have, after we land back here, to unload and retreat inside the base. Unless..."

"Unless what?" prompted Renton, as all eyes turned to Yuna.

"When I was exploring the base, back when we first arrived here, I came across a large shuttle maintenance hangar, enclosed, with complete atmospheric integrity. It's located in the old JAXA-KARI sector. DOA, can you show it to us?"

The 3D topographic map of the lunar surface was replaced by a schematic of Moon Base Delta, with the shuttle hangar highlighted in blocky illumination.

"It hasn't been reactivated yet, but it could be an option. There's a pretty big landing pad that will allow us to taxi all the way into the hangar. It would be quicker if we have the doors open beforehand. We'd be inside within ten minutes of touchdown."

There was a much longer moment of silence now, as they all thought through the intricacies of this bold heist.

"It would be prudent to keep a close eye on the fallout from the Scott Crater disaster," cautioned Tanaka. "Security around food supplies will become a priority for SINO, now that they have significantly reduced their capacity to produce more."

"Okay," Renton finally said, stepping back from the holo-table. "Let's not make any decisions on this just yet. Kimura, see if you can contact your guy on the inside, and see if he's in a position to help us. In the meantime, we'll find out what it will take to get that hangar operational."

There was a muted acknowledgment from the others, communicated via nods and grunts. They were all in, Renton could feel it. If Kimura came through, then a lot of their problems might be over—at least, for a little while longer.

CHAPTER 18

A WORLD ON FIRE

D r. Han Sundar stood on the circular observation platform that ran all the way around the dome of what was once an ancient optical telescope, long since decommissioned. It now capped the roof of the Strawstack Mountain canteen, affording those who chose to venture up here a glorious view of the valley, from the Chippapeake mountain range that demarcated the horizon to the west, all the way around to the more populated plains to the east.

The air was fresh and clear this morning. A light breeze blew in from the northeast, and with it came a slightly acrid smell. Han turned his head toward the source and could see three separate smoke trails billowing up into the atmosphere. Something was on fire way over in the town of Petersville.

He sensed movement in his peripheral vision and glanced over to see Zachary Garcia, one of the lead engineers at the base. He stepped out onto the observation deck, and seeing Han, came over.

"Any idea what's going on over at Petersville?" Han asked, pointing in the general direction.

Zachary stood silent for a beat, simply observing the rising smoke. "Turf war, they say. Two rival gangs fighting for control of the town. It kicked off last night."

"Can't anything be done to stop this mindless violence?" Han said this more to himself rather than expecting an answer to what was a seemingly intractable problem.

Zachary gave a long sigh. "The state's security apparatus has its hands full just keeping the sanctuary cities stable. They've effectively abandoned the hinterlands to the locals."

"You think we're safe here? Any chance these guys might see us as a big fat prize to be won?" Han was thinking back to his own naivety at the security arrangements he and Sheneese had set up back in the observatory. At that time, he considered they might be overkill. How wrong he was.

"I think we'll be fine here," the engineer replied with a sweep of his hand. "Just look at all that military hardware."

Han cast his eye around the compound. It certainly looked well-secured, with tall electrified fencing, guard towers, gun emplacements, and a conspicuous contingent of heavily armed military. Yet Han couldn't quite shake the uneasy feeling he got while observing the columns of thick smoke billowing up from the town.

He took another sip from his morning coffee. "So what's happening over at Engineering? Any new thoughts on capsule design?"

"Funny you should mention it, but we just got some design parameters from up on high." Zachary jabbed an index finger in the air.

Han gave him a curious look. "Seriously? How's that possible? We don't even know what we're dealing with yet."

"This is something different, something else entirely."

"Oh?"

Zachary glanced around, checking that they were not in earshot of the other people who were up here grabbing some early morning fresh air. "The specs are for a small capsule, about a meter in diameter, and three meters long." Zachary measured off the approximate dimensions with his hands.

Han thought about this for a moment, as it made no sense to him. Why limit a potential design to something so small when they could loft hundreds of tons into space, not a problem, and they would probably need that mass just to design something robust enough to survive a journey through the debris cloud? Then it struck him. It wasn't for an Earth launch; it was for lifting off from the Moon, specifically for a Mass Accelerator. The only issue with that was that neither FISA nor Space Division, nor any of its affiliates, possessed such a machine.

"You know that's for a Mass Accelerator setup," said Han.

"Yeah, we figured that out as soon as we saw the specs. The design parameters were obviously for a return capsule, no mistake. But hey," he raised his hands in the air in mock surrender, "who are we to question our master's bidding?"

"Indeed. But it's very... odd."

Zachary just shrugged. "My turn to ask you a question. How

are those models going? When are we going to have numbers to work with?"

"Soon. Very soon. Just checking over a few things." Han resisted the urge to say more.

Zachary slapped his hands together, rubbing them for heat. "Well, I think that's enough fresh air for today. Time to descend back down into the bunkers." He gave a mock salute and wandered off, leaving Han to wonder about this revelation that the engineer had let slip—because he was pretty sure that the information on the capsule design was highly classified. If this was indeed what Han assumed it to be, then it was designed to get Helium-3 back through the debris field. But the only facility of that type was owned and operated by SINO. So, was Space Division now in cahoots with their archenemy? It seemed impossible to Han that they could be working together, but as he looked out at the faraway smoke trails, he realized that the world he knew was long gone. This was a new reality, and such was the desperation by the state to secure a future, that it was not inconceivable that they were willing to bury the hatchet and join forces with the opposition.

But then, surely SINO was already working on such a design? Why would they need Space Division to help them? Was it that they didn't have workable models of the debris cloud? Again, this seemed unlikely. He eventually gave up trying to think it out, took another sip of his now cold coffee, and tried to enjoy the fresh air, and find a view of the landscape that wasn't interrupted by military hardware or the smoke of battle.

"I smell something burning."

He turned around to see Sheneese sniffing the air as she came over.

He pointed at the distant smoke columns. "Big turf war over in Petersville, apparently."

Sheneese looked over and shook her head. She had just come off a night shift, so she was trying to catch some air before heading to bed. It had been like that for a while. They would meet each other like passing ships, a quick exchange of information before moving on. Fortunately, the shifts would change around again in a few days to something resembling normality.

"Long night?" he asked, more as a statement.

"For sure, boring mostly, although we did make contact with the Moon again. I was talking to your old friend, Professor Henriksen."

"How are they holding up?"

"As well as can be expected. Now that a war has kicked off up there."

Han raised an eyebrow. "War?"

"The Xilinex corporation attacked a SINO food production facility in Scott Crater. Complete destruction."

"My god." He looked over at the smoke trails. "It seems they're faring no better than we are down here."

"Yeah, and they keep asking about the GM food issue."

"And?"

"Same thing back from General Grant, 'we're working on it.'"

He was going to tell her about the capsule design

parameters but decided that should be a conversation for another time, when Sheneese wasn't so tired.

"You best get to bed. You look like you need it. All this will be in the daily brief, I assume. I can catch up on it then."

She nodded and cast her eye over the landscape. "Most of it will be. But some stuff they deem too... sensitive. There's talk of restricting future communications to military personnel."

Han's eyebrows joined forces with his hairline. "You're joking?"

"This new war that's started between Xilinex and SINO has them all spooked. Even the people on the Axial have been given an ultimatum to surrender control to the Xilinex Corporation. That sent Dyson into a flap."

Han shook his head. "Something weird is going on."

"You can say that again."

"When are they thinking of implementing this... communications lockdown?"

"Oh, I don't know. It's just talk for the moment."

"Would it be possible for me to talk to Professor Henriksen on the Axial, during the next time slot?"

"I don't see why not. Assuming it's advancing your work, then they're hardly likely to refuse."

"Good, as I get the sense that the last remnants of FISA are going to be sacrificed on the altar of resource control."

Sheneese looked at him quizzically. "What do you mean?"

"Oh, nothing, don't mind me. I'm just rambling. We'll talk later, after you've got some sleep." He gave her a hug and a kiss.

She nodded, stifled a yawn as she took one last look around her, and headed back down to the accommodation sector.

Han finished the last of his cold coffee and sniffed the air. There was a change in the wind, and with it came the smell of a world on fire.

CHAPTER 19
SHATTERED DREAMS

Selene Mene sat slumped on a sofa in one of the many deserted lounges of the Axial Luxor Hotel. In one hand, she held a glass containing the last drops of her stash of Kentucky bourbon. In the other, she held the shattered remains of all her dreams.

It was not so much that the solar storm destroyed her vision of a vibrant, enlightened lunar civilization—although it certainly did that. It was more what followed after that eroded all her carefully contrived certainties. Her firmly held belief that a new and progressive society could be fashioned from the remnants of the stranded colonists—where everyone pulled together—was fractured beyond anything she had ever thought possible.

True, she could be accused of just a little hubris in seeing herself at the helm of this new community of can-do colonists, but she could never have conceived of how it all would descend into chaos so quickly. She had been unbelievably naive, like a child with little or no understanding of the world, only to be cast out of the warm comfort of her home into the dark and dirty streets of reality.

She gazed out through the panoramic windows of the lounge at a brilliant Moon far below. Somewhere on that tortured surface, two powers were locking horns, pulverizing the ground beneath them, destroying the very things that were needed for their own survival—and everyone else's, for that matter. What madness, she thought. She no longer had a dream or a vision for the future. Because, truth be told, she had no future.

The Xilinex Corporation would probably take control of the Axial Luxor, assuming they prevailed in this war. It was only a matter of time. Then she would be at the mercy of that pompous popinjay Pompodur Rossen Adarok, who she suspected would make sure to humiliate her as much as he possibly could, assuming he didn't simply have her killed.

Xilinex was already making entreaties for them to come in and take control, offering to save them from isolation, save them from starvation. And already two camps had formed within the Axial. One with Selene as its de facto leader, urging restraint, advocating independence. They were still well supplied and could hold out here for many more months. The other camp was headed by Gabriel Grando, formerly the lead negotiator for the Non-Spacefaring Nations, who advocated for a quick and speedy takeover of the Axial—and every day, the voices in that camp were growing louder and louder. Selene knew deep down that it was only a matter of time.

Any hope she had of forging a broader alliance with stranded remnants that were not affiliated with either Xilinex or SINO, and forming a counterweight to these two powers, was long gone. There was no hope of that now. Even her nephew, Renton, and his colleagues in Moon Base Delta were barely able to feed themselves. It wouldn't be long before they were also taken over. She sighed and downed the last of the bourbon.

"Selene, there you are. I've been looking all over for you."

She turned around to see Professor Henriksen walking into the empty lounge. *Oh God, what does he want?* she thought, as she gave him a feeble wave.

"You weren't there for the call with Strawstack. I wondered if something might be wrong?" He sat down opposite and gave her a concerned look.

She gave a vague gesture with her empty glass. "Why? Did I miss something?"

"Well, it's just, uh… it's not like you to miss a conference with Earth. So we, uh… I thought, you know, something might be up with you."

She didn't answer. Instead, she glanced at her glass in the vain hope that it might have magically refilled itself while she was holding it. "I have come to a stark realization, Lars."

"Oh, what's that?" He shifted in his seat, leaning in, interested in hearing Selene's insights.

"We're all screwed. That's the profound conclusion I've come to."

"Well, that's a bit... nihilistic. I wouldn't quite say it's that bad."

"Oh, really?" She cocked her head at him. "That's because you still have faith, Lars. Because you still believe in the fundamental goodness of humanity." She could sense his increasing discomfort at the way this conversation was going. He had not seen this side of Selene Mene. To be fair, not many people ever had.

"We're in a death spiral, a doom loop," she continued, almost enjoying the articulation of the brutal reality that she saw before them. In a way, it was cathartic, a release. Of sorts. "We've got two powers duking it out for dominance, destroying what we all need to survive. Did you hear about what happened at Scott Crater?"

The Professor nodded. "Yes, it was a disaster."

"If they keep that up, then there will be nothing left. And I haven't even got to the Damoclean sword that's hanging over all our heads. Don't get me started on that."

"You mean the GM food issue?"

"Doesn't anybody see this? Unless we start putting our heads together and solving that issue soon, then we will all starve to death. This is an inevitability. And what horrors will befall us as that end nears? Do we all turn to cannibalism?"

"Uh, I don't really think it will come to that. I'm sure a solution will be found. Earth will not let that happen to us."

"I admire your optimism, Lars. I really do. The reason I wasn't present during the call with Strawstack is because all I hear is talk, nothing more. Even Renton and the crew down at Moon Base Delta don't join in anymore. They too have grown tired of the endless talk, with no sign of action being taken. Where's the progress on the GM food issue? Have they sent any scientific data that's going to help us reverse engineer the seed stock up here so we can have a future? No. Nothing. It's as if they want us all to die."

The Professor screwed his mouth up and scratched his chin, thinking. "Uh, I came to tell you that there has been a development from the team at Strawstack."

Selene did a double-take. "Oh? Some movement on the food issue?"

He shook his head. "Not as such. But I've been talking to Dr. Han Sundar."

"Who's he?"

"He was the analyst at MASTERM that first brought the solar storm impact assessment to our attention. Space Division recruited him to do some analysis work on the debris cloud. His wife, Sheneese, is the one who has been coordinating the comms link."

"Don't tell me... there's another solar event on the way. Good. Maybe it will finish us all off quickly."

"No, nothing like that." The Professor's face revealed mild exasperation at Selene's black mood before turning serious. He leaned in a little. "Dr. Sundar, uh... thinks he's found a way."

This finally got her attention. She put her empty glass down on a side table and tried to push the worst of her depression aside. "A way to do what?"

"He's sent me some data, some analysis he's been conducting on the cloud. He had managed to identify and map the complex wave patterns that resonate within the mass of debris. Long story short, he's identified a period of low intensity, low enough for a sufficiently well-engineered capsule to possibly get through. He's sent it to me to review his theory."

Selene took a long, slow intake of breath. "I see. Well, I don't, actually. But I get that it's at least some progress in the right direction."

"This is not a crewed capsule." The Professor waved a hand. "We're a long, long way from that. This is a small, robust cargo vessel with very limited capacity." He lowered his voice. "He's also sent me some encrypted data, for my eyes only, so to speak. In it, he says that the preliminary designs being contemplated by the engineering team back at Strawstack are for a return capsule. And, there's talk that further communications with us up here at the Axial and over at Moon Base Delta are to be restricted to high-ranking Space Division personnel only."

Selene's black mood was being pushed further away as her natural curiosity took over. That, and her innate ability to smell a political plot at play. She thought about this new information for a moment, almost regretting the numbing effects the bourbon was having on the analytical section of her brain.

"This is good news, I suppose. If they can get something through, then that means they can send us new seed stock and biomass for food production." She sat up a little. "Maybe they really are trying to solve the food supply issue."

"It's a positive development. But, bear in mind, it's currently theoretical. Nothing has been built or tested yet."

"And this... return capsule, I presume this is for Helium-3."

"Correct. H3 is an existential issue for Earth."

"Yes, I know. It's the one thing where we have some hold

over Earth. Without it, they will be heading for the industrial dark ages."

"Unfortunately, this is so."

Selene's mind began to shake off a little more of its stupor as auxiliary brain cells were now being called into action. "So then, possession and control of this... cargo capsule technology would convey enormous power to anyone who controlled it?"

The Professor looked a little perplexed, as if he had never considered this. "Yes, now that you say it, I suppose it would."

"Then the fundamental question is, who gets to control it?"

"Well, I don't know. But the design that Dr. Sundar revealed seemed to suggest that it would be for a Mass Accelerator."

Selene's eyes widened. "That's a SINO facility. That doesn't make any sense. I can't see Space Division working in partnership with those guys unless things have become desperate. Surely it would be possible to loft this capsule toward Earth just with a standard rocket?"

"One would think so, or something of a similar design. But alas, I am not an aerospace engineer, so I have no idea of the limitations of such a design. But I do know that the Mass Accelerator is probably an order of magnitude more efficient than a rocket launch."

"Then there are the rumors of a possible Xilinex assault on that facility," Selene ventured.

"Yes, I've heard them too."

She sat up straight and gave Professor Henriksen a considered look. "Well, Lars, you've succeeded in sobering me up. Not only that, you have done the seemingly impossible and given me hope. So, thank you for that."

He smiled. "Happy to be of service. And glad to hear you're back to your old self."

"I wouldn't go that far, Lars. This orbital will be taken over by Xilinex Corporation, that's for sure. It's only a matter of time. The war will escalate, causing death and destruction, as all wars do. And there's still very little hope of developing a counterweight to the Xilinex-SINO axis of evil. But this information from your friend Sundar has added an interesting new element to the political formula. Plans are being concocted down on Earth, plans to get them what they want, which are the necessary resources from the Moon to keep humanity from completely falling apart. And I suspect they don't care who gives it to them as long as they get it. But if I were Space Division and developed a technology to get these critical resources back to Earth, I would want some way to keep control of it, some way to exert pressure on the lunar partner."

Again, the Professor looked perplexed. Being an academic, he could never conceive of such political machinations. "You really think so?"

"Oh, I know so. Remember, Lars. This is what I do, try to second guess the opponent. Figure out what it is that they're really up to. So let me ask you a question. How would you go about keeping whomever you partnered with up on Luna on a short leash?"

The Professor stroked his chin and furrowed his brow as he brought a seldom-utilized sector of his brain into operation. "Eh, food supply, possibly?"

"Very good, Lars. My guess is that's exactly what they'll use. So all this stalling on the GM food issue starts to make sense, but they don't want to solve that problem. They want to find a way to keep supplying us with time-limited seed stock. That keeps us needing more. We send the Helium-3, they send us food."

"My god, that's..."

"Blackmail? You have a lot to learn about the real world, Lars. Trust me when I tell you that this is exactly what their plan is." She stood up and walked over to the viewing window and looked down at the lunar surface. "My guess is that Space Division has sided with the Xilinex Corporation." She turned back to the Professor. "They're the ones they reckon can deliver for them. The last remnants of FISA will be sacrificed for that end. That's why they will soon restrict communications."

Professor Henriksen looked visibly shocked.

"But they didn't reckon on one thing," Selene continued.

"Oh, what's that?"

"Your friend Dr. Han Sundar, who has inadvertently revealed to us the ultimate plan. We now know what that is."

"Yes, I doubt even he has worked that out yet."

"I trust you have not told this to anyone else?"

Professor Henriksen shook his head. "No, well... the usual suspects know I've been talking to Dr. Sundar on data analysis. But nothing about the capsule design."

"Good. Keep it that way. Our only advantage here is that they don't know we've figured it out."

He nodded but looked like he really didn't understand how any of this was of use to them in their current situation.

"We need to get off this orbital, Lars. As soon as humanly

possible, and get to Moon Base Delta. If we can do that, then we may have a chance of using this to secure a better future."

"That's impossible unless we hitch a ride with the Xilinex vanguard."

"Nothing is impossible. It can be done if we really want it. All we have to do is play dirty. It's time to stop trying to bring these lunatics together. Instead, we need to start trying to bring them down."

CHAPTER 20

SURFACE TENSION

R enton stared out the cockpit window of the old rover at the cracked and broken monochromatic landscape beyond. *Home,* he joked to himself. *And it's anything but sweet.*

Beside him, Yuna gripped the controls of the ancient vehicle like her life depended on it. Her eyes flicked from the path ahead to scrutinizing the various readouts on the dashboard.

"How's it holding up?" Renton asked, more by way of making conversation than any desire to gain insight into the performance of the machine. He knew it intimately; after all, it was he who had taken it apart and rebuilt it.

"It'll get us there... eventually." She glanced down at some readout. "We should have more than enough juice to get the job done."

Renton gave a satisfied nod and settled into his seat.

"So, what do you think of that last message from your aunt?" Yuna asked. Renton wondered if, like him, she was just making conversation, or if she genuinely wanted to know his thoughts. He sucked in a breath. "Hard to say what's going on."

He reflected on the encrypted video message that Selene had sent them, just a few hours before they had set off on this mission to steal a shuttle full of provisions from the Secchi mining facility. Like the rest of the crew at Moon Base Delta, he was happy to technically facilitate two-way communication with the Strawstack facility on Earth, happy to act as a relay station and not much else. He had not bothered joining any of the recent conversations they had had with the Axial. So perhaps this encrypted message from Selene was a way for her to get his attention.

The recorded visual comprised Selene, Henriksen, and two others that Renton vaguely recognized, talking in hushed tones, casting conspiratorial glances at each other. The gist of the message was that some bright spark down in the Strawstack facility had figured out a possible path through the debris cloud. However, this was for tiny capsules only—there would be no crewed mission, no rescue ships. And they also seemed to infer that it had been designed for the Mass Accelerator, which, as far as Renton understood, belonged to SINO. After that, the message descended into a paranoid rant about betrayal and plots within plots. *Typical Selene*, he thought.

He wondered why anyone would bother with politics. It seemed like such a nebulous endeavor, constantly trying to divine the machinations of various power blocs, and then trying to outplay them at their own game. It was like trying to catch shadows. None of it was real; it was all just a delusion. It was no wonder a great many politicians went mad in the end. How could you not?

That's why he was an engineer. There was an immutable certainty to it. One plus one equals two—and it always would, no matter how you try to spin it or manipulate the information. It was absolute certainty. And it was that scientific certainty that enabled humanity to build a spacefaring society. You can't do that by simply talking about it.

However, what was also certain, a scientific fact, if you will, was that they would all eventually starve to death unless a solution to the genetically modified food supply issue was found. And even more certain was that Renton and the crew in Moon Base Delta would be long dead even before that, if this mission they were now embarking on failed.

"I guess it's good that they might have a way to get something through the debris cloud," he said finally. "But we're a very, very long way from sending a crew, not to mention sending a big Starliner. They're just very small capsules, at best."

"Better than nothing, I suppose."

"Yeah, but it doesn't help us much. A capsule that size will hold very little, certainly not enough to resupply the stranded population up here. And I suspect there will be a very high attrition rate. Maybe one in twenty might make it through."

"What about the so-called plan to abandon all FISA assets to Xilinex?"

"What about it?" said Renton. "It's not up to them. We're on our own up here. What happens, happens—there's nothing the assholes back on Earth can do about it. All they really care

GERALD M. KILBY

about is getting supplies of Helium-3. That's why the capsule design is for the Mass Accelerator. They only care about themselves."

She glanced over at him. "You've become very cynical in your old age, Renton."

"Yeah, well, starving to death and being shot at—both at the same time—will do that to a person."

Saito's head appeared through the companionway door into the cockpit. "Where are we now?"

Yuna pointed to a navigation map. "Around halfway."

Saito nodded. Then continued to study the landscape through the cockpit window. He was nervous and agitated. This plan, for the most part, rested on their guy, Kato Tsubasa, coming through for them. So far, he had proven his worth. His job was project manager for the maintenance of heavy mining equipment, and so knew a considerable amount about the facility. The mining operation came to an abrupt halt when the evacuation began, but SINO had pressed a portion of it back into service. Kato was also persuaded to go back to work with offers of food and security. Although, Kimura reckoned he only agreed so that he could find a way to screw them over. He was now about to get his chance.

Having an asset like Kato on the inside finally persuaded Renton that they should try and steal the supply ship. After that, it was simply a matter of figuring out who should go to Secchi and actually do it.

Yuna insisted that she was best placed to fly the shuttle, so she was in. Saito wanted to come as he knew this guy, Kato. He was the contact. As for Renton, he was not going to conceive such a risky plan and then stay at home watching it all unfold on a monitor, so he too was very much in. Then, Alice also insisted she go, arguing that they would probably need her to control the robot, Oryx.

Matteo, on the other hand, decided not to go, as he would be needed to operate the recently reactivated hangar systems. He also helped them weaponize two maintenance drones. One was a unit, typically used for work in space on ship's hulls and orbital infrastructure, but could also be used for aerial surveillance in a low gravity environment such as the Moon. The second was a micro-drone for use only in a pressurized environment. All these robotic assets were fitted with scavenged rail-gun parts, enabling them to spit out metal slugs with enough momentum to cause considerable damage to a soft target. They weren't very accurate but would probably scare the hell out of anyone on the receiving end of a hail of flying metal. The final member of the team was the AI, DOA. It could communicate with them via the LunaSat constellation and keep tabs on surface activity. Kimura and Tanaka would stay behind with Matteo, and wait it out.

The radio speaker in the rover cockpit cracked and hissed. "Maintenance vehicle, Beebop, this is Central Control, come in."

Renton sat up, as did Yuna. Saito almost jumped out of his EVA suit. "That's Kato calling. He said he'd use the name 'Beebop' if there was a problem."

Renton hit the comms button. "Uh... this is Beebop, go ahead Control, over."

"We have a maintenance issue with a surface machine over

at sector five. Please make your way there and await instructions, out." The comms went dead.

"What the hell?" said Saito. "Something's up. This wasn't the plan."

"Just stay cool. It's probably just a minor reset." Renton turned to Yuna. "Where is that sector?"

She pointed to a spot on the navigation map around two kilometers from the main Secchi facility, just as Alice popped her head in. "Trouble?"

"Yeah, I think so." Saito was moving toward peak panic.

"No," said Renton emphatically. "No trouble, just a change of plan. Instead of meeting at the previously agreed location, Kato has diverted us to one of the mining sites."

"Any explanation?" Alice asked, a twinge of concern on her face.

"Sadly lacking in detail," said Yuna as she plotted the new course.

"DOA," Renton opened a comms channel again.

"Yes, Renton."

"Is there any new activity around the sector five mining site?"

"I have tracked a maintenance rover departing from the main Secchi base and heading in that direction."

"Is it a SINO rover?" asked Saito.

"No. It's a standard maintenance machine of the Hamamatsu Corporation."

"Then, that's probably Kato. He's coming to meet us outside." Renton pursed his lips as he wondered what this change might mean.

"Thanks." He closed the channel.

"This is not good," said Saito. "Maybe we should think about it a bit more."

"Just calm down." Yuna sounded exasperated with Saito. "We'll never pull this off if we stall at the first hurdle. We'll find out when we get there," she added, with a stern look at Saito.

CHAPTER 21
NONNEGOTIABLE

Approximately one kilometer from the rendezvous point, Renton carefully unpacked the maintenance drone, placed it in the rover's airlock, and once the outer door opened, sent it soaring overhead in order to scout the surrounding area. Despite DOA's ability to provide them with detailed visuals via LunaSat, the drone had the distinct advantage of having an integrated weapons system, offering them some much-needed cover should the situation get tricky.

Back inside the tight confines of the cockpit, the four members of the team huddled around a compact monitor, displaying the live camera feed from the drone hovering above, scanning the terrain for any signs of movement.

Yuna's eyes narrowed as she caught sight of something. "There," she said, pointing a finger at a rover gradually coming into view on screen. "That must be him."

They continued to monitor the movement of the solitary rover, tracking its steady advancement as it gradually approached their position.

"He seems to be alone," said Renton eventually. "I don't see any other movement out here. I'd say let's just get on with it and meet up."

Alice nodded. "Agreed. No point hanging around."

Yuna powered up the rover again, and they cautiously made their way across the lunar surface using a low ridge of mine tailings as cover. When they finally came out from behind it, they could see the other rover parked up, flashing its lights at them.

Yuna brought their own rover to a halt.

"Someone's getting out," said Alice. "And waving. I think he wants us to come closer."

Yuna started the rover again and rolled up beside the lone figure standing on the surface. He was signaling that he wanted to enter their airlock.

Renton leaned over the dashboard and entered the command to allow him access. They waited as the airlock cycled through its pressurization routine. Eventually, Kato Tsubasa stepped into the cabin and unclipped his helmet.

"Sorry about all this," he sounded flustered.

Saito grabbed him by the shoulders in a gesture of friendship. "It's good to see you again, Kato." Then he stood back a little, looking into his friend's face. "What's going on? Why the change of plan?"

Kato drew in a long breath. "There's been a marked increase

in SINO activity at the base. New people coming in, they seem anxious to get the supplies moved." He turned and gave them all a hard look. "More security around the shuttle port. I think they're preparing to lift off very soon, possibly within the next few hours."

"Shit, that soon?" Saito asked with a concerned look on his face.

"That would make sense," said Renton. "If the reports from Scott Crater are true and the food facilities there were completely destroyed, SINO is under pressure to get more supplies distributed."

"Is there still a way in?" asked Alice.

"Yes, absolutely." Kato nodded. "I will take you all inside the base in my rover. It won't be checked. You'll need to leave yours here and transfer. Once inside, we will be able to make our way to the port as before."

"And the guards?" asked Alice.

"Uh... with the increased security, there are extra guards posted around the supply store and the shuttle."

"How many are we talking about?" Renton was not comfortable with this new development.

"I counted six, but there could be more."

There was a brief silence as they all contemplated this change in circumstance and how it affected their carefully constructed plan.

"The diversion is still our best chance," said Alice, her face resolute. "Even if there are more guards, it doesn't matter. They should all go running."

"Agreed. It doesn't change the plan. I say we continue." Renton looked to Yuna.

She nodded. "We've come this far, no point in turning back now. And even if we did, we're still left with the same problem."

"Okay, let's get going." Renton went to grab his helmet.

"There's, uh... just one other thing?" Kato seemed hesitant to come out with this new wrinkle in the plan.

"What?" urged Saito. "Out with it."

"I want to come with you. I want out." He searched their eyes for signs of confirmation. "The situation on the base is getting more... brutal. So, I want out."

"I'm guessing this is nonnegotiable?" Renton asked, with a sigh.

Kato nodded, his face stern. "Also," he continued. "My wife and son."

"That might be a problem with weight," said Yuna. "We could be overloading the shuttle. It's only designed for two crew, now we'll have, what?" She did a quick mental calculation. "Seven, plus all the supplies, which are heavy."

Kato straightened up. "I'm not doing this without your word that my family and I can all get out."

"You had your chance with me and Kimura, and you bailed on us." Saito's tone was one of anger. Clearly, these two had history.

"If it were just me, I would have joined you." Kato offered a placating gesture with his hands. "But I had to think of the boy. He's very young, and I just couldn't take the risk."

"How old is he?" asked Alice.

"Twelve."

"Twelve? What the heck is someone that young doing up here?" Alice's incredulity was shared by all the others. The under-eighteens demographic was not well-represented in lunar colonies, primarily because the low-gravity environment was seen as a health risk to physical development. Any woman who found herself expecting would be on the next flight back to Earth. It was a law common to all agencies that operated up here. No one argued with it because the realities of bringing a baby to full term, even in the one-gee environment of an orbital, were very risky. No expectant mother wanted to take that chance.

"My wife and son were on vacation, up on the Axial Luxor." Kato explained. "I was to join them there for a time. But I pulled a few strings and got a pass for them to come down here for a few days. I wanted to show my son where I worked, what it was like. He was very excited about it. He'd be the envy of all his school friends back on Earth if he could say he was on the Moon. Anyway, the storm hit and..." he trailed off.

"I assume this is also nonnegotiable?" said Renton.

Kato simply nodded.

"Okay, then we'll ditch some of the supplies if we need to. We'll get you out." He looked from Alice to Yuna for backup.

"Yeah, we'll find a way," said Alice.

"Yuna, Alice, and I will go with you," said Renton, now moving up a gear. "Saito, you take the rover back to Moon Base Delta."

"What, you're leaving me here?"

"We need to save weight. I'm sure the four of us can handle it," Renton replied.

"Along with Oryx." Alice gestured at the robot that was sitting quietly in a corner of the rover.

"It'll be fine, Saito. I'll see you back in Moon Base Delta." Kato grabbed Saito's arm by way of assurance. Then he turned to the others. "We'd better get going. Time's running out. Hopefully, the supply ship is still on the pad when we get there."

CHAPTER 22

THE SECCHI HEIST

Kato Tsubasa's rover was cavernous by comparison to the dainty vehicle that Renton and the crew had used to get here—it could probably fit comfortably inside this one and then some if it were not for the chaotic collection of spare parts, tools, and maintenance droids that occupied its interior.

All of them had assembled in the wide, spacious cockpit for the initial part of the journey to Secchi. This would take them directly through the primary mining area.

Across the vast flat landscape, great autonomous machines scraped up huge volumes of lunar regolith and transported it to a central processing facility, itself another giant structure—fully automated. This seemingly impossible scale was made possible by the low-gravity environment that existed on the Moon. On Earth, these machines and structures would simply collapse under their own weight. But up here, the fantastic could be made real.

Renton had never spent much time on the surface before the storm. Neither had Alice nor Yuna. Therefore, this vast scale was something new to them. Hearing about this lunar gigantism was one thing, but it could not really prepare you for seeing it up close.

"Would you look at the size of that thing?" Alice said as she stared wide-eyed at one of these leviathans as it churned up the landscape, great fountains of dust gushing from its base.

"It takes the regolith over to the electrolyzer, where the oxygen is stripped out, leaving the metallic ore," Kato pointed at a massive squat cylindrical structure. "The oxygen is stored in tanks, but the ore is transported back to the main processing plant. We're going to join in with the trail of autonomous ore carriers. That will bring us into the main plant without being bothered, and we can make our way to the supply hangar from there."

As Renton gazed out on this tortured landscape, he could see only a few of these great machines were in operation. Most stood still and silent like abandoned hulks from some long-forgotten war among a nation of giants.

It didn't take long for them to see the silhouette of the Secchi mining facility outlining the horizon. They were now following a clearly defined road with long rows of beacons on either side identifying its boundaries.

"Best get down below," said Kato. "We'll soon be entering the facility. Wouldn't be good to have you all up here in plain sight."

The rest of the trip was spent trying to discern the outside world through the sounds and movement of the maintenance rover. At one point, Kato talked on the radio, but it was too muffled and indistinct for Renton to make out what was being said. Yet the tone seemed calm. A short while later, the machine finally came to a wheezing halt and Kato shouted down to them. "We're here. You can come out now."

They clambered back into the cockpit. Renton could see they were inside a vast maintenance hangar. Rows of machines with indeterminate functions stretched out in all directions. It was so cavernous that a thin haze hung high up along the gantries, obscuring the ceiling from view.

Kato gestured at a control surface on the rover dashboard, and a 3D schematic of the facility flickered into existence above a small holo-slate.

"We are here, the main maintenance hangar. That's the shuttle port over there, accessed through this tunnel. At least that's how we'll be getting there."

"And where are the ore silos?" Renton asked as he studied the map.

"There's a lot of them, but the one you want is here. I'll bring you to the airlock. Then you're on your own. Hopefully, we'll see you back at the landing pad."

Alice gripped his arm. "Be careful, won't you?"

Renton grinned. "No, I'm planning to be reckless and blow up a silo full of powdered aluminum. What could go wrong?" His grin expanded.

"Just get back to the pad in one piece. Don't screw around, okay?"

"You got it." He hefted a bag containing a homemade explosive device fashioned from an old, and volatile, energy pack along with a rudimentary mechanism for shorting it. This should hopefully cause a runaway reaction, burning at an intense two thousand degrees Celsius without the need for an additional supply of atmospheric oxygen. He estimated the burn time to be around two minutes, just enough to melt a hole in the silo and touch off the highly flammable contents. Renton's only concern was that while it seemed like the perfect plan to create a distraction, he didn't want to burn down the entire facility, which this had the potential to do. However, Kato convinced him that the fire protection systems would immediately kick in, suck out all the oxygen in the sector, along with a number of other extreme fire-suppressing measures. The bottom line was that it should be enough for the SINO guards to drop what they were doing and start adopting firefighting measures. That would allow Alice and Yuna to sneak onboard the shuttle, deal with any stragglers—how that was going to happen wasn't quite clear, but it seemed that Oryx would play a major role in this—and wait for Renton, along with Kato and his family, to catch up. The entire plan was predicated on the assumption that SINO would not be expecting anyone to try to steal their supply ship; they would be taken completely by surprise.

When he exited the rover into the vast maintenance yard, he checked his EVA suit once again to ensure it functioned correctly. He would be needing this later when making his way across the landing pad. For the moment, they were still inside a pressurized environment, so he left the helmet visor open.

He put his bag on the ground, reached in, and pulled out the small weaponized micro-drone, lofted it in the air, and checked that he had control of it through his comms unit. "Comm check," he voiced. This resulted in a chorus of acknowledgments from the others as they confirmed their units were working.

In one corner of his visual field, he could see an aerial view from the drone. Hopefully, it would help them avoid being spotted as Kato led them through a labyrinth of back passages and deserted areas.

As they trod their way through these passages, Renton was reminded of a saying attributed to some late twentieth-century boxer: *Everyone has a plan until they get punched in the face.*

That punch came when they exited a short passage into the storage yard housing the silos. Renton had sent the drone ahead and did a quick sweep of the area. All looked clear. But what he, nor Kato, had reckoned on was a pair of SINO guards who had decided to slack off and find a quiet place where they could chat and drink. They had concealed themselves in an alcove that the drone did not see.

"Hey, what are you two doing here?" one of the guards shouted as he sat up.

"Uh... maintenance crew. Here to check on one of the silos," Kato replied with authority that impressed Renton.

The guard scrutinized them for a beat, then waved a hand. "Well, get on with it then."

Renton was about to breathe a sigh of relief when the other guard decided to pull rank. "Wait a minute. Hold up." He stood up, picked up his weapon, and came over. His eyes fixed on Renton.

"So what's a FISA tech doing here?" He hefted the weapon

and pointed it at Renton. He seemed particularly interested in his EVA suit.

It was then that Renton realized that it was always the little things that trip you up. He had been so focused on the big picture aspects of the plan, he forgot that the EVA suit, which he had refurbished from Moon Base Delta stock, had the FISA insignia emblazoned on his shoulder. How had he not seen it? How had none of the others not seen it? Perhaps they had been working on the assumption that they would not be spotted. It was a stupid mistake, and now it would be their undoing.

"Ah, it's an old suit we had lying around, so what?" Again, Kato sounded like this was just an irritation stopping important work from being done.

By now, the other guard had come over. "What's in the bag?" He pointed with the muzzle of his weapon.

"Why don't you boys go back to your drinking and let us get on with our work?" Kato began to move but was rewarded with a firm push backward. "You just stay right where you are."

"Should we call it in?" asked the other guard.

The first raised a hand. "In a minute. But first, slide that bag over here. Let's see what these guys are really up to."

Renton sensed they were now past the point of no return. Any attempt at talking their way out of it was going to fail, and taking these two guys on was also not an option. So he did the only thing he could think of.

"Sure." He smiled breezily. Then slowly unshouldered the bag. At the same time, he used the movement to disguise a quick instruction to the drone, which was now overhead, to open fire.

Two short bursts emanated from the underbelly of the drone, spraying the two hapless guards with a hail of sharp metal slugs. It was so fast that all Renton witnessed was the jerking movements of the guards as their bodies were perforated with a hail of barbs.

They dropped to the floor, a thick pool of blood oozing out from where they lay.

"Goddamnit." Kato jumped back in shock, his eyes wide.

"What the hell else could we do?" said Renton, shaking his head at the carnage.

"Yeah, I know, I know. Us or them. It's the way it is now." Kato seemed to have regained his composure remarkably quickly.

Renton was still transfixed by the sight of the dead bodies. He had just killed two people, shot them dead, simply because he and his friends needed to steal food to survive. It all came down to that in the end. It shocked him to his core.

"Come on," Kato pulled at his elbow. "We need to keep going. Let's get this done. And don't feel too sorry for these guys. They would have killed us just for the contents of our pockets."

Renton pictured Alice and Yuna anxiously waiting for the diversion to happen. He couldn't let them down. "Yes, let's go."

They hurried through the storage silos until Kato finally halted. "This is it. It's about half full of powdered aluminum." He swept a hand upward. "This should create one hell of an emergency when it goes up."

Renton nodded and unshouldered the bag.

"The airlock exit out onto the landing pad is just there." He pointed to a doorway festooned with signage, alerting people to its function. "Once you're outside, the ship will be sitting around three hundred meters to your right. We'll be further down in the maintenance hangar waiting for the, uh... show to start. I'll make my way back now. Give me five minutes before you kick it off."

"Got it. Good luck." He patted Kato on the upper arm.

It didn't take Renton long to identify the weakest section of the silo, attach the homemade incendiary device, and activate the remote. Since this micro-drone couldn't fly without an atmosphere, he called it back and packed it away in his bag. He did one last check, then headed for the airlock.

Outside, the bright lunar day bathed the shuttle port in harsh monochrome light. He could see the shuttle, just as Kato had said, off to his right, about a hundred meters out from the edge of the main facility. Supplies would have been stored in sealed, pressurized containers, designed to keep perishables at a reasonable temperature. Rather than the extreme degrees Celsius, it currently was during the long Lunar day. He could see the cargo bay ramp still open, with four guards milling about.

He worked his way along the edge of the facility using a combination of stacked containers and maintenance equipment as cover. When he had reached what he considered a reasonably safe distance, he checked his time. The allotted five minutes had passed.

"Ready?" he called into his helmet comms.

"We're in position," came the response from Alice.

He took a deep breath and activated the incendiary device.

For a moment, nothing happened. He anxiously looked over at the airlock where he had just exited the storage depot a few moments ago, then looked back at the guards over at the base of the shuttle. They didn't seem fazed.

Maybe his cobbled-together device malfunctioned, or wasn't powerful enough to melt through the metal wall of the silo? He contemplated going back and checking when the side wall of the storage depot blew out in a ground-trembling explosion of energy.

"Shit." He did not expect that. A cascade of debris was ejected from the depot as the atmosphere inside was expelled. This got everyone's attention.

He poked his head up from behind a stack of storage crates and saw a figure bounding across the landing pad to the shuttle. The figure was beckoning to the guards to abandon security duties and follow him back inside the main facility. Renton could have been mistaken, but that figure looked very much like Kato. He watched them leave their posts and disappear back inside to deal with whatever mammoth explosion he had caused.

Immediately, he saw Alice and Yuna break cover and run across the landing pad toward the open cargo bay ramp. Fast on their heels were two more figures, one of which was wearing the smallest EVA suit Renton had ever seen. Oryx was first to the ramp and now stood guard at its base.

Renton bolted. He ran as fast as possible in low gravity. He was around halfway to the ramp when he saw Kato running out of the base, except he was being chased by the four SINO guards.

"Kato's in trouble," he shouted into his comms.

"Goddamnit, what just happened?" Alice's panicked voice echoed in his helmet.

Renton pulled out the small rail-gun he had stowed in the breast pouch of his EVA suit and turned to shoot, just as one or two of the guards opened fire. Kato stumbled and fell.

Renton returned fire. Not a bright idea, as he was the next target. The ground around him spat dust as a burst of fire just missed him by inches. He kept running toward the fallen man, firing as he went. It was probably the stupidest thing he could do, but it was just his instinct to try and help Kato, who had now managed to right himself and was hobbling toward the ramp.

Both he and Renton were nearly knocked over by Oryx, bounding out from the shuttle. In a few hops, the robot had planted itself between Renton and the oncoming guards, then opened fire. Two guards fell, and the others scattered, racing for cover.

Renton grabbed Kato and shoved him onto the ramp where Alice helped pull both him and Renton inside.

Yuna was already up in the cockpit, powering up the engines. "Everyone on board yet?" she called out through the comms.

"Yeah, go, go."

The ramp began rising, but Oryx bounded back inside before it closed fully. The craft rose fast. Yuna wasn't hanging around. A moment later, the craft leveled out. By then, the ramp had closed, and the cargo bay had pressurized. Renton unclipped his helmet and moved over to where Kato was being tended to by his wife, Rina. The kid, Ryou, looked on anxiously.

A blot of bright red blood bloomed across Kato's left hip. "I'm okay, I'm okay," he kept saying, even though he clearly wasn't.

Rina was remarkably calm. Maybe that was for the kid's sake. "Just stay still, don't move, keep pressure on the wound."

Renton was no expert on combat wounds, but he reckoned the old guy would probably be okay. He might not be able to walk without pain for a while, but he should pull through.

He leaned his back against the inner hull of the ship and slumped down on the floor. Alice came up beside him and did the same.

"That was intense." He looked over at her and grinned.

She grinned back, then looked at the mountains of supply crates crammed into the cargo bay, and gave a satisfied sigh. "But worth it."

CHAPTER 23

MIND THE GAP

Renton's giddy joy at pulling off the high-risk theft of a SINO supply ship was short-lived. When he and Alice entered the cockpit, they found Yuna listening to an alert from DOA.

"We've got two shuttles on our tail." She glanced up at them as they entered. "One from Taruntis and another from DaVinci. Both are about twenty-five minutes away."

Renton strapped himself into one of the co-pilot seats. "DOA, is Matteo there?"

"I'm here," came an excited response. "I can't believe you guys pulled it off, you crazy bastards."

"We're not back yet. Is the hangar ready?"

"Yeah. The doors are wide open. You just gotta land and taxi in. It's a five-minute operation, tops."

"Slight problem."

"Oh?"

"This machine has no wheels, no way to taxi. It's just got fixed landing struts for basic up/down operation."

"Damn, what sort of a supply shuttle is that?"

"It's just a repurposed transport shuttle, I think, not designed as a cargo hauler."

"Then we'll just have to drag it in. Can't leave it out there if you've got trouble on your tail."

"How? The rover's not going to be powerful enough—I presume Saito got back okay?"

"Yeah, just now. And you're right, no way the rover will drag a fully laden shuttle. What about dropping the loading ramp and using the rover to just drag in the supplies?"

"That's possible, except it's all separate crates and containers. It would take several trips. And I don't think we have that time."

"How high are those doors, how much clearance have we got?" shouted Yuna.

"You're not seriously thinking... what I think you're thinking?" Matteo replied.

She tilted her head this way and that. "If you mean that I'm thinking of flying it in, then yeah. I know it sounds crazy, but it's not impossible," she looked over at Renton and Alice with a steely expression on her face.

Renton stabbed at the comms again. "DOA, what height is the hangar entrance?"

"Ten point five meters."

Renton looked over at Yuna, who nodded. "Tight, but doable."

"Did you hear that, Matteo? Yuna's going to... fly it in."

"That's very risky. If she hits the entrance doors and damages them, they might not close properly, or the ship could just... I don't know... explode!"

"I suppose we're going to find out. You just be ready to close those doors as soon as we're in—hopefully in one piece."

Yuna flew low over the undulating lunar terrain, keeping the ship close to the surface. Renton presumed she was doing this to make them harder to spot. Although their vector on take-off from the Secchi mining base would make it relatively easy for SINO to work out where they were heading, no doubt the supply ship was a blip on a SINO radar somewhere.

Soon he could see the squat central structure of Moon Base Delta. A formidable-looking circular concrete domed column that capped off a lava pit into which it had been constructed. It reminded Renton of ancient war fortifications, with its thick concrete walls and recessed windows. But this only represented a small part of the base, as most of it existed underground. And even the sectors that did exist on the surface were covered in a thick layer of lunar regolith to protect its occupants from cosmic radiation and micrometeorite strikes. So it was hard to tell where the base began and the lunar surface ended.

Yuna banked the shuttle to starboard of the central structure, toward a bright patch of yellow light that reflected off a flat, smooth landing pad. As the ship came around, Renton could see the light was emanating from the wide-open doors of a maintenance hangar built into what looked like the entrance to some high-tech burrow. It also looked like a very tight gap.

"Here we go. Probably best you all strap in." Yuna looked over at Renton and Alice. "Just in case."

"I'll go tell the others and sit with them." Alice rose and made her way back to the cargo bay.

The cockpit comms crackled into life. "I don't wish to add any more pressure on you, but just to let you know the first of those SINO ships is a little under ten minutes away," DOA advised.

"Okay, got it," Renton snapped back.

The shuttle's engines shifted in tone as Yuna brought the craft into a hover over the pad. They changed again as she almost touched down, its rigid landing struts thumping off the ground. The ship rose again and moved forward slightly, skirting the ground as it did. Yuna's face was a study in concentration as she fought to maintain fine control of the ship.

She had it centered on the open doors, but her focus was on keeping it low enough to fit under the roof of the hangar, yet high enough so that it didn't drag on the surface. She inched it forward accompanied by a lot of thumping and engine whine.

The nose of the ship nudged its way in through the gap, the light from the hangar interior illuminating the shuttle cockpit. Something caught on the port side, and the shuttle began to rotate. Yuna compensated by raising the right-hand side but overdid it, and there was a thump from the roof.

"Crap," she shouted in frustration, lowering the craft again. "Time to stop messing around." She applied more power to the engines, and the machine suddenly lurched forward, hitting the back wall of the hangar before Yuna could apply enough reverse thrust. Renton felt the seat's restraining straps cut into his shoulders, preventing him from bouncing off the cockpit window.

Yuna shouted into the comms. "We're in! Shut the doors, shut the doors!"

She slumped back in her seat. "Don't ever let me do that again."

"Hey, you got us in." Renton gave her a thumbs-up, accompanied by a huge grin.

It took a full five minutes for the doors to completely close and the hangar to pressurize. Only then did they exit the craft to the sound of cheering from the others, their joy tempered by the sight of Kato. He was conscious but looked pale. They rushed him to the med-bay, where Matteo and Tanaka set about tending to his injuries. When they had removed his EVA suit and stemmed the blood flow, Tanaka indicated that he would take over. He seemed to have much more medical training than Matteo, who was more than happy to have someone who really knew what they were doing take the lead.

He nodded and turned to Renton. "Let's go check out what these SINO guys are doing out there."

They made their way to the operations room, where Alice and Yuna were already sitting, watching camera feeds from the maintenance hangar landing pad. Two SINO shuttles had come down, and a number of their operatives were milling about, weapons in hand.

"What are they doing?" Renton asked as he entered and sat down.

"Nothing, just standing around," said Yuna. "I'm not sure

they know what to do. They don't look like they're trying to enter."

"I've got several of the industrial robots unloading as we speak," said Alice, flicking to an interior feed showing the unloading process inside the hangar. "If SINO tries to get in that way, then we can set the dogs on them. And DOA has taken control of a few more and placed them around the other entry points."

Renton began to relax a little. They had pulled it off, secured enough supplies to last a very long time. But he couldn't fully decompress with SINO lurking outside like a pack of hungry wolves waiting for any sign of weakness, any chink in the armor. Still, it didn't seem like they had any heavy weapons with them, and the ships were not military, just standard transports. So, hopefully, they would grow tired and leave soon. In the meantime, all they could do was wait.

CHAPTER 24

UNO ISLAND

Uno Island is a one-hundred-square-kilometer patch of tropical paradise, some eighty kilometers off the west coast of a small African nation once known as Guinea-Bissau. It was acquired by the Xilinex Corporation about half a century ago as a part of reparation agreements for the enormous debt the then-government ended up owing, on loans from the corporation, for its failed national development plan.

Xilinex promptly evicted the three thousand inhabitants of the island and set about building an uber-futuristic corporate facility for its chief executives to enjoy their wealth and privilege in peace and quiet, far from the noise and attention of the masses.

Over time, other islands in the Bissagos grouping were acquired and, being conveniently located close to the Equator, soon became the primary Xilinex Corporation spaceport, dealing with all of its lunar exploration activities.

Shortly after the Carrington Event that pulverized Earth's network constellations, these islands rapidly became a primary administration center for the Xilinex global corporation. This came about for many reasons. Firstly, there was already considerable technical and scientific infrastructure there due to its importance as a space hub. Secondly, its borders could be completely controlled, providing an unparalleled level of security during the current period of societal collapse. Furthermore, the mainland was extremely underdeveloped, with the primary activity being small-scale farming. With little exposure to advanced technology, this activity continued almost unaffected by the collapse of the so-called meta-modernist world. Other than a return to early twentieth-century forms of communication, life went on as before, growing food and raising animals, as it had for centuries. This meant that the Xilinex corporation workers on these islands would not go hungry any time soon.

For the past few weeks, flights had been arriving on the main island, bringing people in from less well-secured corporation facilities all over the globe. In tandem with these, a flotilla of cargo ships had also arrived at the island's small port, bringing supplies for the army of Xilinex Corporation employees that now called Uno and its sister islands home.

On one of the smaller islands in the group, construction workers and electrical engineers had been busy, laboring around the clock, to build a twenty-five-meter-diameter X-band radio antenna along with the necessary ancillary buildings to house all the electronic equipment needed for its operation.

Coupled with this new feature on the subtropical landscape were a nest of microwave dishes that pointed to relay stations on each of the other islands and then onto stations along the coast. These, in turn, beamed data, station-to-station, through a new network of corporate communications in a post-constellation world.

The culmination of all the building work arrived today—when the giant antenna would be switched on, and, at a time when the Moon was high in the nighttime sky, a comms channel would be opened with a similar, if somewhat more ancient, antenna on the Malapert Massif, northwest of Shackleton Crater, now under the control of the Xilinex Lunar Corporation. This would be the first time since the Carrington Event that a two-way conversation would take place between these two elements of the Xilinex corporate empire. Tests would be conducted, and very soon, the head office on Uno Island would find out just how things were going up there. And if their man, Pompodur Rossen Adarok, was playing ball.

Pompodur, for his part, was currently experiencing that rare feeling where everything he touched was turning to gold. Even the operations that had not gone quite to plan were turning out to have worked in his favor. The destruction of the food processing facility at Scott Crater had now put SINO under extreme resource pressure. So much so that there were rumors of a rebellion breaking out at DaVinci Crater, a place so rooted in SINO doctrine that few could have anticipated such a turn of events.

Even those annoying little shits in Moon Base Delta were

inadvertently helping the Xilinex corporation turn the tide in this war. By stealing a fully laden supply ship that had been scheduled to deliver to DaVinci, the very place the supposed uprising was happening.

Pompodur was in no doubt this ripple in the otherwise smooth pond of SINO discipline was in no small part due to his propaganda machine spewing doubt and discontent into the SINO ranks. And this message manipulation did not end at the airlocks of SINO enclaves. He was utilizing the very same techniques to galvanize Xilinex people, as well as FISA and others, into seeing SINO as the barbarians at the gates—and that only he, Pompodur Rossen Adarok, could save them all from annihilation at the hands of the SINO madmen.

The only irritation in this carefully concocted narrative was the incessant broadcasts from the Axial Luxor by that self-aggrandizing windbag, Selene Mene. But he had a plan for her, a plan that was already in place. Soon, the Axial would be his, and Selene Mene's oh-so-self-righteous bleatings would be put to an end.

Even the news that the Xilinex techs over at Malapert Massif had made contact with the corporation's new headquarters on Earth could not dampen his spirits. He was about to enter into a video conference in the war room, but unlike his last conversation with the Xilinex board, prior to the Carrington Event, this time he knew he was the one in the seat of power.

Back then, he was expecting admonishment only to be seduced by the prospect of great wealth, and yes, power. In truth, they had bought him. Now, though, after all the successful campaigns by both the mercenaries under Wagner and his own formidable propaganda machine, he had had an epiphany. Once SINO was defeated and the last dregs of FISA and their affiliates were brought into line, Pompodur Rossen Adarok would be the most powerful person on Luna. Not only that, he would have control of all mining resources and, if and when deliveries could resume, he would be the most powerful person on Earth too—as he would control the supply of Helium-3. The prospect made him almost faint with joy.

So, as the wall monitor in the war room flickered to life with the grainy images of the Xilinex board members, he was not going to be taking any crap from them. He would make sure to let them all know who was boss.

After a moment or two of testing the connection, checking that everyone could hear and see, the President of the Xilinex Corporation, Lane Zeebos, seated in an opulent chair with a backdrop that looked to be of a clear blue ocean, began the meeting.

"I, along with the entire board, would like to take this opportunity to congratulate you all on a job well done. It would appear from the preliminary reports we've just received that the mission to acquire all stranded assets and make inroads into the areas controlled by SINO is progressing beyond even our most ambitious targets."

Pompodur gave only a cursory acknowledgment of this pronouncement; instead, he spent his time studying a plate of dainties that his new chef had created, searching for the perfect accompaniment to the cup of herbal tea that one of his new servants was preparing for him.

"Thank you." He waved a hand in the general direction of the screen. "It has been going rather well."

"Indeed," replied Zeebos after an awkward few seconds' delay. "And it also seems that plans to secure the Mass Accelerator at Clavius Crater are well underway?" The Xilinex President inferred that this was a question requiring a proper reply.

"Yes, sir." General Wagner almost snapped to attention. "We have eliminated the reserve contingent at Moretus Crater and have moved our forces into position. It won't be long now until the facility is under our control."

Again, there was another awkward silence as they all waited for the reply.

"Excellent. We on the board cannot stress enough how important this facility is to securing both the future of the lunar population and that of Earth."

Pompodur reflexively glanced up at the screen, a part of him found this statement curious. What exactly did Zeebos mean by securing the lunar population?

"We have been working with scientists and aerospace engineers here on Earth," the President continued, "to analyze the debris cloud and design a capsule that is capable of passing through it safely. Work is well advanced, with real-world tests currently being conducted. The results of these early tests are very encouraging, and we are confident that we will have a workable system for the transport of small quantities of cargo very soon."

"Are we to assume that this... capsule design can be utilized in the Mass Accelerator?" Anton Levrosky asked.

"Correct, Director Levrosky. It has been specifically designed with that return system in mind. This will enable the resumption of Helium-3 supplies to Earth, something that is absolutely critical. Failure to resume these supplies has the potential to plunge the already fractured society here on Earth into a new dark age. As you can imagine, this has now become an existential issue."

Pompodur couldn't help but do a mental air punch. The Xilinex board had just admitted how utterly dependent they were on Helium-3 being supplied from the Moon—and that resource, along with its delivery, would soon be completely under his control. Pompodur fought the temptation to cheer out loud; instead, he rummaged through the plate of cakes to calm himself down, best not give away what he was truly feeling. He gathered himself to make his play. "I imagine, given the existential nature of the issue, that suitable compensation will be forthcoming?" Pompodur reckoned that there would never be a better time to turn the screws on the board and extract the maximum compensation possible, given that the continued functioning of the modern world now depended entirely on him.

It took a moment for this request to be registered by the board, who instantly muted the comms and entered into a brief internal discussion.

Pompodur imagined they were discussing the vast sums of money and assets he would be offered. When they finished their little discussion and Zeebos spoke again, "Compensation will be by way of continued supplies of food, specifically bio-stock."

"What?" Pompodur exclaimed. Had he heard this right? Were they trying to make a fool of him, denigrating his intelligence with this insult? He was so stunned that he didn't get time to speak before Zeebos resumed talking.

"We assumed that you all have realized that your current food supply is finite. Everything that is produced up there is from genetically modified bio-stock that has a limited reproductive capacity. In short, you will ultimately run out of food because the bio-stock will be exhausted."

Pompodur felt the floor beneath him disappear. He turned to Levrosky. "Is this true? Why didn't anyone tell me this?"

"I'm afraid so," His fellow director looked slightly bemused. "We've all known for some time. I assumed you did as well."

"There was a report produced on the situation," said the General, glaring at Pompodur. "I presume you read it?"

"Eh..." said Pompodur.

"It turns out that the bio-stock utilized by the entire population on Luna is produced by just one company, the Santomon Corporation," Zeebos continued, ignoring the tête-à-tête going on in the war room. "This corporation has now been nationalized by the Western Alliance, as it is seen as critical to national security. The issue of supplying the lunar colonies with bio-stock is now the preserve of Space Division, the military wing of FISA."

"I don't bloody believe this!" Pompodur could feel his body go limp, a cold sweat broke out on his forehead, his mouth hung open. FISA, of all people, it seemed impossible to rid himself of these pompous, interfering bastards.

"The Xilinex Corporation is also not immune to this new

paradigm," Zeebos leaned in a little closer to the camera. "So, to stave off a threat of nationalization, we have come to a mutually beneficial agreement. Space Division will supply and deliver bio-stock to lunar orbit. In return, Xilinex will supply Helium-3, and other important raw materials, to Earth, exclusively to the Western Alliance. To assist us in this mission, Space Division/FISA will request that all remnants of their assets on Luna be surrendered to the Xilinex Corporation and to assist us in our fight against SINO. I think you'll all agree that this is an excellent arrangement. You, on Luna, will have all the bio-stock you require, and be one step closer to complete control over all resources. The Western Alliance will have Helium-3 for its reactors, which will stave off a potential social apocalypse, not to mention that exclusive access to these resources will give them enormous global power." He paused for a beat.

"However, this... arrangement is predicated on Xilinex taking control of the Mass Accelerator. Should you fail to do so, Space Division has let it be known that they are not averse to doing a similar deal with SINO, although this would not be their preferred option. So it is incumbent on you to ensure the capture of this vital asset."

Pompodur's general state of mind transitioned from one of shock to one of stunned silence. He had to admit it was genius. Space Division, through their development of the capsule technology and acquisition of the food source, had turned the tables completely. They now held the gift of life over everyone who existed up here, ensuring that Helium-3 delivery kept coming. If they failed, then there would be no bio-stock supply. Without that, unnecessary hardship would endure.

In the space of a few minutes, Pompodur had gone from being the most powerful person in the known universe to a mere slave, begging for food from his master's bowl. He felt sick, very sick. He rose from his seat in the war room, rushed to the sanitary facilities, and promptly threw up all those beautiful dainties that his new chef had so lovingly crafted.

CHAPTER 25

INNERMOST RING

S elene gathered together her closest associates, those she could trust, those who had stuck with her since the beginning. If the FISA analyst Dr. Han Sundar was to be believed, then Space Division was about to sacrifice them all to the Xilinex Corporation. The question now was, what were they going to do about it? And was there even anything that could be done?

They had assembled in one of the upper levels of the Axial —which, by the counter-intuitive physics of centrifugal force, meant that they were on the innermost orbital ring. It was a quiet sector; few people came here as it was mostly used for maintenance and storage.

Professor Henriksen was here along with Nicci Anderson, Selene's former assistant back in the day. Now she mostly did her own thing, which seemed to involve a lot of jogging. Selene would often meet her in passing on one of Nicci's many laps of the outer ring. Jeff Bodega was here as well as Deejay Bale, the two people she had first met on the fateful day when she had tried to evacuate. Then there was Dr. Maria Jensen, a medical doctor who had been seconded to the FISA team during the negotiations, and Theo Girard, a human resources manager and former employee of the Axial Luxor. It was a motley crew, but they all had one thing in common: a deep mistrust of the Xilinex Corporation under the increasingly messianic leadership of Pompodur Rossen Adarok.

They gathered in an abandoned rest area formerly used by some of the hotel's maintenance staff, taking up random seating positions as Henriksen ran through a version of the story he had told Selene some time ago.

"But this is good... isn't it?" said Nicci. "If they get this... capsule thing to work, then we can get food supplies from Earth."

"Yes, that's correct. Except my guess is those supplies, whatever they are, will be under the control of either Xilinex or SINO, depending on which of them prevails in the battle for control of the Mass Accelerator facility," Selene explained.

"But Xilinex and the other mining corporations have been lobbing stuff back to Earth for decades; why do they need this Mass Accelerator thing?" Theo asked the obvious question.

"They used big cargo ships, repurposed Starliners," said Deejay. "They would transport everything up to the orbital spaceports and then load it onto these massive cargo ships. But now those big ships would never survive passage through the debris cloud."

"So why don't they just design smaller ones, based on this

supposed capsule design that Space Division is working on?" Theo continued.

"Lots of reasons why that would be difficult," Henriksen began. "Mainly because almost eighty percent of the Lunar population has been evacuated, so they probably don't have the engineers or maybe the technical people to operate the manufacturing facilities. All manufacturing has ground to a complete halt, everyone is living off stored supplies, and any labor bandwidth is going to either food production and management or the war."

"We've got word that's already started," Jeff Bodega added. "There's been a big buildup of Xilinex forces around the Accelerator site down on Clavius Crater."

"And they've taken over Shackleton, Amundsen, and large swathes of the nonaffiliated sectors have ceded control to them," Selene explained. "On top of all that, they're making steady inroads into SINO enclaves. I think it's fair to say there's no stopping them. The outcome is almost certain." Selene gave a resigned look.

"So, we're next then?" said Dr. Jensen. "And with the blessing of Space Division?"

"It's an inevitability." Selene nodded. "We have to face reality; this orbital will ultimately be handed over to Xilinex— sooner rather than later."

"And there's nothing we can do about it?" asked Theo.

"We could just refuse. You know, just tell Xilinex to go screw themselves," offered Nicci. "If we shut down the dock, then how are they going to get in?"

"They'll just starve us into submission," Selene countered.

"And it wouldn't take long. Already, Gabriel Grando and his followers are just itching to fling the doors wide open and let Xilinex waltz in."

"Maybe it wouldn't be so bad?" said Nicci. "I mean, what's the worst that could happen?"

Selene could see that this took a few of them by surprise. She raised a hand to quell any negative reaction. "In theory, yes. What's the harm? They'll keep us fed and all that. But we can already see what's happening in Shackleton. Leaders being executed, rationing being dependent on fighting for Xilinex under that psychopathic General Wagner. As for everybody else, we'll all, in one way or another, become slaves to the corporate overlords."

"You paint a grim picture of the future, Selene. One that we seem powerless to oppose," observed Dr. Jensen.

"There is one, eh... possibility." Selene threw this out and let it rest for a beat, scanning the faces of the group. They all looked at her expectantly. "We evacuate to Moon Base Delta."

"How?" Jeff Bodega opened his arms, inviting an answer. "We have no ship; we can't leave here. That's been our fundamental problem since the beginning."

"Moon Base Delta now has a shuttle." Selene looked from one to the other to gauge their reaction.

"They have a shuttle? Since when?" Bodega's eyes widened.

"Deejay, tell them what you heard." She turned and nodded to the young tech.

"I was talking to Matteo Cristoforetti, one of the original crew from the service vessel Aurora—just a few hours ago. A casual conversation, just me and him. Anyway, he informed me of a daring raid they carried out on the Secchi mining facility, which was recently taken over by SINO. The upshot is they stole a transport shuttle full of supplies. It's now parked up in one of their maintenance hangars."

"So... uh, they're planning to evacuate us?" asked Theo.

"Well, no, not exactly." Selene paused for a beat just to gather her thoughts. "Nothing has been discussed. What I mean is we haven't asked them if they can do it. The thing is if we do ask them, we would need to be very careful how we do it. Remember, Grando and his gang are itching to invite Xilinex into the Axial. If they were to get wind of an evacuation plan, then they would almost certainly try to scupper it."

"Why would they do that?" asked Nicci. "Surely if people wanted to go, that would be up to them?"

"Because Pompodur would probably go nuclear if more people were to arrive at Moon Base Delta. It's the last thing he wants," said Deejay.

"Look, maybe he would and maybe he wouldn't have a fit," Selene added. "But if we were to seriously consider this, then it would be best for all concerned that we keep it under wraps."

"So, I assume you have a plan?" asked Dr. Jensen.

"Deejay, maybe you should explain it?" Again, Selene turned to the tech.

"First, we need to contact the crew at Moon Base Delta and see if it's technically possible, and if they'll agree to attempt it. If so, then we find out the capacity of the shuttle, gather up as many supplies as we can, and head for one of the functioning shuttle docks. We can lock down that part of the dock—no one gets in or out. If Grando finds out and sends a group after us, they won't be able to gain entry to the shuttle dock."

"Won't we need EVA suits?" Theo asked.

"No, we can embark and disembark in a pressurized environment at both ends," explained Deejay. "But that'll mean waiting for the dock to pressurize before we can get out. Probably the riskiest part because we'll be vulnerable at that point."

"How so?" Dr. Jensen asked.

"We won't be able to fend off any attempts to gain entry to the dock if we're all inside the shuttle."

"So..." Selene raised her voice to get everyone's attention. "That's the plan. The question now is, who's in?"

"Before anyone answers that," Dr. Jensen interjected, "there are a few issues that people need to be aware of. I know some of you will be well versed in the rigors of space, but others may have only experienced it from the comfort of this luxury orbital. By evacuating to the Moon base, we'll be going from a comfortable, Earthlike environment here on the orbital to a very low, point-one-seven-gee, on the surface. Prolonged exposure to that environment can have a detrimental effect on the human body."

This made everyone sit up and think. "How detrimental?" asked Nicci, whose one experience of space was the Axial Luxor.

"Decreased bone density and increased muscle loss over time. However..." She raised a hand before anyone could say anything. "With a rigorous daily exercise regime, and periodic exposure to increased gravity environments, these issues can be mitigated, even eliminated. I'm just putting this out there so that everyone knows what they're getting into."

"Thank you for that, Dr. Jensen," Selene responded. "It's important to understand the challenges of life on the lunar surface. Given that, how do you feel about us all evacuating?"

The doctor thought about this for a moment, and Selene sensed that she might bail on them. "I would still rather live my life under my own control down on the surface rather than be subjected to a very uncertain future up here. In the end, even if we stay here, who's to say that Xilinex will not ship us off to some lunar gulag, given time? So, to answer your initial question, I'm in." She gave an emphatic nod.

"Who else?" Selene asked again, looking from one to the other.

Slowly, one-by-one, they all raised their hands.

CHAPTER 26
ORBITAL INJECTION

Renton felt the strain on his muscles as he pushed for an extra ten lifts. On Earth, he would be lifting the equivalent of two hundred kilos, but here it was only around thirty. He needed to start doing more resistance training—operating in low Lunar gravity was fine for short periods, but as time went on, his body would start to lose muscle mass, his bones would become weaker, and he would struggle if he were ever to find himself back in normal Earth gravity. Not that there was much chance of that happening any time soon—if ever.

Kimura and Saito had taken it upon themselves to try and get one of the many gym areas back into action. Having spent a lot of time working on the lunar surface, they were acutely aware of physical degradation. Every twenty-four hours, they would do at least one hour of a workout carefully calibrated to mitigate the effects of low gravity on the body. Along with that, every few months, they would be shipped off to one of the many orbitals for some rest and recreation, and a full one-gee environment.

Renton and the crew, on the other hand, had spent most of their time in space in the relative comfort of the FISA central maintenance orbital, so developing such a rigorous physical routine was not such an issue for them. But after a long conversation one evening over rehydrated Thai green curry and several cups of Shackleton's Finest Sake, the new people from the Secchi mining facility explained to them, in graphic detail, just how totally screwed up one's body can get if you don't do those physical routines every single day. Not that Renton and the crew were completely green in this department. Renton had been trying to make it a priority—prompted by DOA's incessant reminders—but since most of his time in Moon Base Delta he had been busy starving to death, it didn't seem all that important. Now, though, with enough supplies to feed an army, their bodies started to complain about other things.

This gym area was two levels down in the central core of the base, on one of the main accommodation levels. There were many others on different levels and sectors, but they picked this as it was the closest to the upper operations area where they spent most of their time. He still didn't have a very good mental map of the entire facility; it was just too vast, too labyrinthine, with way too many levels and sectors.

A few rows along from where Renton strained his arms and shoulders against the heavy weights, Alice was running on a treadmill. A tether around her waist pulling her down, mimicking the forces of gravity as she ran. Her body glowed with a thin film of sweat, her face a study in focus. She was pushing for the next level.

Renton forced the last lift out of him, racked the weights, and sat up on the bench. His heart pounded, and he took a moment to catch his breath while wiping the sweat from his face with a towel. When he had recovered somewhat, he glanced down to where he had left his comms unit lying on his shirt; it was blinking an alert. He reached down, picked it up, and slotted it over his right ear. He tapped to connect and got Matteo.

"Yeah, what's up?"

"Weird message in from your nearest and dearest up on the Axial."

"The usual political paranoia?"

"And then some. You best come up here and get it in full 3D surround sound."

"Okay, just finished here, see you up there in a minute." He tapped to close the connection.

"Gotta head up to operations, something in from the Axial Matteo wants me to see."

Alice waved an acknowledgment as she continued pounding the treadmill, clearly not willing to expend any more energy than necessary on trying to talk.

Renton sat for a moment in operations, having listened to the comms from his aunt. "How did she know we have a ship?" he asked Matteo.

"I was talking to Deejay, their tech, about your exploits over at the Secchi mining facility. To be honest, it sounded like he really needed to hear something more exciting than the usual dull reports."

Renton thought for a moment. Selene and her merry band of followers were looking for a way off the orbital before it was taken over by Xilinex. All very well in theory, but there were a lot of unknowns in this request.

"So what do you think?"

Matteo screwed his mouth up, "Well, there's the slight problem of getting that shuttle in and out of the hangar. And, oh... the fact that there's still a bunch of SINO heads milling around outside just dying to find a way in."

"DOA, what are they doing out there?" Renton asked the AI.

"Assessing their options," it replied. "But they will depart in less than an hour."

"What? How can you know that?" Renton exchanged a surprised glance with Matteo.

"While you were spending time improving your physical well-being, and Matteo was helping himself to a protein bar and a glass of Shackleton's Finest Sake, the Xilinex Corporation finally launched their assault on the Mass Accelerator facility in Clavius Crater. In tandem with that, they also launched several other assaults on various SINO facilities. As such, the cohort that is currently outside Moon Base Delta will be called back to help reinforce the base at DaVinci."

Yuna then arrived in the operations room along with Kimura. "Got an alert from DOA saying the SINO guys might be getting lost soon."

Again, Renton was amazed at how DOA could perform

multiple parallel conversations. No doubt Alice was also being informed, and possibly the others. Although Renton had begun to notice that DOA was choosy in who it informed of what, and when—like it was being selective, informing only those who might prove to be productive in some way. If he were prone to paranoia, he might go as far as to say that the AI was manipulating them—just a little.

"Yeah," said Matteo. "And it looks like we might be going on a rescue mission soon."

"What?"

"Here, have a listen," he replied. "DOA, play that comms from the Axial again."

Halfway through the playback, Alice came in. "What's going on?"

Renton gestured at the monitor, where his aunt was pleading in hushed tones for them to come and evacuate her and a small group she had assembled, some fifteen people.

"Is it possible? Can we do it?" Alice asked when the comms terminated.

"Sure," said Yuna with confidence. "The shuttle's empty, so getting it out of the hangar is easy."

"DOA, how far away is the Axial?"

"At its current orbital position and estimating the average speed of a SINO transport shuttle, it would take approximately twenty minutes to rendezvous."

There was silence in the room as everyone, especially Renton, considered what they were about to embark on.

"What about bringing all these new people back to the base? What about supplies?" Kimura was first to voice her primary concern. And Renton began to understand why DOA had brought her into the loop.

"She's my aunt, and we wouldn't even be here if not for her. She got us the access codes to reactivate the base—and it cost her her freedom; she missed the evacuation flight. So we owe her, big time." Renton was inviting no argument. They were doing this, end of discussion.

Renton felt a surge of adrenaline course through his body as he, Alice, Yuna, and Matteo entered the EVA suit locker room to get ready for the flight. At least he assumed it was adrenaline, although it was more subtle, less like how he imagined a great warrior might feel heading out to battle and more like how someone would feel embarking on an adventure. *Was this really him?* he wondered. On the trip to Secchi, he had been terrified; he just didn't show it. Now, after the success of that mission, he felt a sense of invincibility. He looked around at the others and wondered if they felt the same way.

At first, he had considered doing this on his own, wondering why the others should risk their asses if they didn't have to. But they would hear none of it. Yuna insisted she had to pilot because Renton would probably crash the shuttle just getting it out of the hangar. Alice said he couldn't possibly manage without backup in the form of Oryx and several weaponized maintenance drones, which she was best placed at operating. And Matteo was adamant that he wasn't going to be left behind again. No way were they going to leave him out of all the fun— his words.

That left Saito, Kimura, Tanaka, and the three new people they picked up at Secchi. Renton had his reservations about leaving them in charge of the base—did he really trust them that much? But it seemed that DOA had, as usual, been several steps ahead.

Tanaka came to him with Ryou in tow, letting him know that they would all help organize things for their return. A new accommodation area would be got ready with all the basic home comforts, the med-bay would be prepped, should anyone arrive back injured, and food would be prepared, ready and waiting for the new arrivals.

Renton was impressed; why didn't he or any of the others think of all this? It turned out that DOA had been in Tanaka's ear about getting this done, along with Saito, Kimura, and even Rina and Ryou—seemingly by playing on their need to feel useful. Not that Renton cared how it was done. But he couldn't help getting that uneasy feeling that the AI was way ahead of the game. Which led him to consider what might happen when fifteen or so new people came in and all plugged themselves into the AI matrix via the comms units they had all now taken to wearing.

"You okay?" Alice asked. "You look like you've seen a ghost."

"Uh? Oh... No, nothing. Just thinking, you know," he replied, a little unconvincingly. Then wondered if it was just him having these thoughts, or did the others sense it too?

As predicted by DOA, the SINO operatives piled back into their transports, lifted off, and headed back to their base in DaVinci Crater. Matteo and Yuna had already communicated with Deejay, up on the Axial, going over the details of the planned evacuation. So, everything was set. They piled into the shuttle, having given it the once-over to ensure the hull still had integrity after Yuna's bumpy arrival into the hangar.

She was strapped into the pilot seat and running checks. "Okay," she finally announced into the comms to DOA. "All systems nominal. Time to open the doors and let this bird fly."

The hangar took a few minutes to depressurize, the doors opened, and Yuna powered up the shuttle. Being now empty of supplies, it was lighter and easier to maneuver. Yuna gently lifted the craft off the hangar floor a fraction, then rotated it a full 180 degrees, and slowly eased it out through the opening, before powering up and orienting the craft for orbital injection along the path of the Axial Luxor.

Renton felt a surge of energy as the shuttle quickly broke free of the puny Lunar gravity well and he began to float free. He felt like he was home again, out in space, where he belonged.

CHAPTER 27
DEVELOPING SITUATION

P ompodur watched as all the pieces of the Xilinex military machine moved into position and began to let rip. Several groups of mercenaries began to assault SINO facilities all over the lunar map. As these attacks began, satellites tracked the movement of SINO assets, hoping that the cohort garrisoned at the Mass Accelerator facility would panic, thinking that they had been thrown a curveball and the much-flagged attack on the facility was just a feint by Xilinex. It was not entirely mission-critical, but the General's fear was that SINO might be planning to do to the Mass Accelerator what they did to the food production facility in Scott Crater, and that is to destroy it completely rather than let it fall into Xilinex hands. This threat needed to be negated before any full-frontal assault could be put in motion.

Techs in the war room on board the Xilinex orbital filtered incoming data from satellites and ground units, and displayed it on the main monitor as map data. From where Pompodur, Wagner, and the other few remaining members of the board were sitting, they had a full visual image of exactly what was happening on the ground in real time. As the various assaults got underway, it looked like the General's assessment of what would happen was turning out to be correct. Techs in the war room began to detail movements of SINO assets being redirected to the besieged bases.

Three rovers leaving Jansen, transport shuttle en route to Balmer, and so on. But one update caught Pompodur's attention. *Two SINO transports departing from Moon Base Delta for DaVinci Crater.*

"What?" he shouted over at the tech. "What was that last report?"

The tech examined his readouts. "Looks like they were chasing down the shuttle from the supply heist at Secchi."

"I knew those transports wouldn't stay there," the General added. "They would be redeployed as soon as the pot got stirred."

Pompodur didn't think much more on it until, around a half hour into the campaign, the same tech called out again. "Eh, there's a shuttle transport leaving Moon Base Delta. Looks to be civilian."

"A shuttle? Where's it going?" Pompodur sat up, intimidating the tech.

"Eh... best guess is... orbital intersection with... the Axial Luxor Hotel."

"What?" Pompodur stood up so fast he nearly spilled his cup of tea all over his plate of cakes.

"That's probably Hicks and the others, planning something with that witch Mene. We've got to stop them."

The General waved at him to sit down. "Not important, we need everything we have for this fight."

Pompodur became increasingly flustered. He couldn't simply let this go. They were up to something, and he didn't like it when things were happening beyond his control. "General," he spoke in the most persuasive voice he could manage. "There is an anti-Xilinex faction functioning freely on that orbital, broadcasting vile propaganda against us. I have tried to keep a lid on it by employing some of my own, eh... agents to counter this reactionary element until after this campaign is completed —and we can deal with them more robustly, by getting rid of them." He did a cutting motion with his hand across his neck. "But if that shuttle is what I think it is, then those very same people will be relocating to Moon Base Delta. And as you said so yourself, that's a hard nut to crack. So we need to deal with this now, or it will continue to be a large thorn in our side."

The General thought for a moment, giving Pompodur's entreaties careful consideration. In the background, techs continued to give vocal updates on the various ongoing battles.

"All our assets are committed," he said with an earnest expression. "I appreciate what you're saying about the propaganda, but we are truly stretched to the limit. However, depending on how things shake out over the next hour or so, we might be able to get a ship to intercept them before they return to Moon Base Delta."

Pompodur nodded, happy that at least the General was seeing the bigger picture here. If the windbag Selene Mene managed to relocate to Moon Base Delta, then it would be a hard task removing her. It would be done eventually, of course. He knew it was only a matter of time before they launched an assault on the base and captured it. But she could be a real pain in the ass in the meantime. Best to cut her head off now before she could do any more damage.

"Very well. But make sure this is a priority. In the meantime, I might be able to delay them on the Axial, keep them trapped there until we have a unit free." He pushed his seat back, gathered the folds of his robes together at the front with one hand, and headed out of the war room.

He returned to his private quarters, the largest such space on the entire orbital. It was two of the grand suites combined into one unit. Not palatial by any means, but adequate for his needs and his stature as President of the Xilinex Lunar Corporation.

It was a title that didn't sit well with him of late, now that the path to complete dominion of all lunar resources had been set. He needed something more befitting a man of such rank and power. Something regal, something that rose above the mundanities of civic or corporate power. Not King, too old-fashioned. Not emperor, too pretentious. *Chancellor,* he thought. It had an old-world regal quality to it, yet not so much that it would seem like a caricature. *Chancellor Adarok,* he said to himself, trying on the title. *Pompodur Rossen Adarok, Chancellor of Luna.* He liked it.

But that was for another day, when he could officially adopt it at a big, lavish ceremony of some sort. First, he needed to deal with that Selene Mene gasbag. He flopped down in a large comfortable sofa, gestured at the big wall screen, and called his agent on the Axial Luxor, Gabriel Grando.

"President Adarok, how nice to see you." Grando's head and shoulders materialized on screen. He also looked to be in his quarters, which Pompodur noted were considerably more opulent than his own—Grando being on a luxury hotel, and Pompodur having to slum it on a utilitarian, corporate orbital.

"This is indeed a wonderful surprise," Grando continued.

Pompodur waved a hand, signaling that he was in no mood for pleasantries. "There's a situation developing, and you need to deal with it."

Grando's face changed to almost one of horror at the thought that he might actually have to do something. "But of course, please enlighten me."

"A shuttle just took off from Moon Base Delta. We believe Renton Hicks is on board, and he, along with his motley crew of troublemakers, is planning to meet up with his aunt, Selene Mene, either to evacuate her or for some other purpose yet to be determined."

Grando looked aghast.

"Your job is to keep that shuttle there once it arrives. Do not let it leave. We will be sending a squad to deal with them. But you must prevent Hicks from leaving until that team gets there. I don't care how you do it. In fact, I don't even care if you kill them all, but they must not return to Moon Base Delta. Do you understand me?"

"Eh, but... eh, how do I do that?"

"Use your bloody initiative, find a way. Unless, of course, you're not up to the job. If so, tell me now and I will find another person within your entourage who sees the bigger picture here. Someone who really appreciates the prospect of being the ruler of the, soon to be, Xilinex Corporation orbital facility. And, who's not afraid to step up to the plate and get their hands dirty."

"No, uh... I mean, yes, of course, you can count on me. I'll keep them here. I won't let you down."

"You'd better not. Space can be a very uncomfortable place if you're not dressed for the occasion." Pompodur couldn't be sure, but he thought he heard Grando gulp just before ending the connection.

CHAPTER 28

THE SHUTTLE DOCK

They chose only those they could trust, a group of around a dozen or so. However, there would be others that they would have to abandon, since the shuttle coming could only hold so many. This did not sit well with Selene's sense of fair play. Yet, what could she do? Stay and fight the good fight? She knew how that would end.

Once they received confirmation from Moon Base Delta, they quickly collected as many supplies as they could, then all gathered at the concourse area for one of the few shuttle hangars that had survived the disastrous explosion at the primary dock used for the big Starliner spaceships. They did this while keeping their activities under the radar. If any whiff of their plan were to get out and make its way back to Grando or his followers, then it would be game over.

Selene, Deejay, and Jeff Bodega decamped to the control room for the shuttle dock, where there was a series of monitors displaying feeds from several exterior cameras. This way, they would be able to see the shuttle's approach and start the depressurizing sequence for the hangar. No one spoke; there was a palpable air of anxiety resting over the entire group. What would happen in the next few minutes would define their lives from now on.

"There." Deejay pointed at a glistening speck that entered one of the cameras' field of view. He checked a readout on another monitor. "ETA, four minutes."

Selene breathed a sigh of relief; at least this first part of the operation looked to be on track. "Okay, I suppose it's time to open the hangar doors."

The tech gestured at a control interface, and another monitor indicated that the hangar was now undergoing depressurization. In a minute or two, they would be able to open the big outer doors. Hopefully, Renton, or whoever was piloting the shuttle, would see this and know where to come in.

Selene left the control room and let the group outside know what was happening. She, once again, went over the boarding procedure with them, determined to get this done as fast as humanly possible. She felt a slight vibration in the handrail she was holding and floated back around to stick her head into the control room again.

Jeff gave her the thumbs up. "Doors opening."

The camera feed from inside the hangar showed the far wall split open, and the great doors slid back to reveal an ever-widening black rectangle of space. Framed in its center was the shuttle, slowly advancing, growing bigger with each second. They had remained in radio silence, not wanting to risk their communication with the shuttle being overheard, even if it was encrypted.

More people squeezed their heads into the control room to watch this graceful ballet in motion. It would be the first time a ship came into dock at the Axial since before the evacuation, which seemed a lifetime ago.

The shuttle slowly entered, then hung in space for a moment before spinning around to point its nose back out the way it came in. It then drifted down to the floor of the dock, where great magnetic clamps swung into place over its landing struts. Deejay gestured again at the control interface, and the outer hangar doors began to close.

If Selene had been a nail-biting person, her fingers would have been chewed down to nubs by now. A deep emotion began to well up inside her; she could feel herself starting to shake. It was all she could do to hold it together as she watched the monitor indicating the rising pressure in the hangar. When it finally reached the required atmosphere, the inner access doors slid open, and the group rushed in.

The rear cargo ramp of the shuttle began to lower, and out stepped Renton Hicks, along with a young woman that Selene took to be Alice Tyler, and a sinister-looking quadruped robot complete with a top-mounted weapons system. Selene pushed her way through the group and swung her arms around her nephew. "Oh my god, Renton. I thought I'd never see you again."

He grinned. "I'm hard to kill."

She stepped back and examined his face. It had lost all its boyish charm; he looked to have aged a decade. His face was thin and gaunt, with eyes that had a look of someone who had seen and done things that could not be undone.

"Best get everyone inside as quick as possible," he said. "Time enough to catch up when we get back."

Selene nodded. "Yes, of course." She snapped back into administrator mode and began to urge the stragglers to hurry inside the shuttle.

Then something moved in her peripheral vision. She spun around to see the inner hangar doors closing. Odd, she thought. Who's controlling those?

The answer came when several new figures could be seen moving on the other side of the long viewing window beside the inner doors. The others in the group saw them too, and there was a moment where nobody was sure what was going on. That was until Selene saw Gabriel Grando coming up close to the window, with a sinister grin on his face. Someone handed him a remote mic, which he clipped over his right ear, tapped it twice, and began speaking. The public address system squealed into action, and Grando's voice began to echo around the hangar.

"So, Selene Mene, our supposed great leader has chosen to run away, like a thief in the night."

"Goddammit," someone said. "How the hell did they find out?"

"I'm very disappointed in you," Grando continued. "Not only did you hold us all back by constantly blocking any offer from the Xilinex Corporation for our future security, but you now choose to abandon even those idiots who were foolish enough to believe your bullshit. Off to Moon Base Delta, are we? Your Eldorado, your fantasy, the fabled city in the wilderness. Delusional. That's what you are."

How did he know all this? Selene wondered. How could he possibly have deduced that this shuttle was coming, let alone know it was her nephew from Moon Base Delta? Someone much higher up the food chain must have informed him. This went a long way to proving her suspicions that Grando had been acting as an agent for Xilinex all along.

"Well, I think not, Selene Mene. You and your collaborators are going nowhere. We have control of the hangar." He glanced over at someone out of view for confirmation. "Those outer doors are not going to open. You are trapped here, and here you will stay until Xilinex arrives and takes control. Which, in case you're interested, will be very, very soon."

The public address system went dead, and Grando moved out of view.

"Who is that guy?" Selene turned to see Renton standing beside her.

"Gabriel Grando, one of the biggest thorns in my side and now appears to be a Xilinex agent."

"Well, that complicates things a bit," said Alice, not sounding too put out by this unexpected change in events.

"I'm sorry, Renton." Selene shook her head. "I should have known; I should have anticipated this possibility."

"Get everyone inside the shuttle." Renton's tone was firm. "This isn't over yet."

CHAPTER 29

DRONE ATTACK

"Still glad you came along, Matteo?" Renton asked as he floated into the shuttle cockpit.

"Wouldn't have missed it for the world. Beats sitting back at base and listening to DOA drone on about doing more strength training." He grinned.

"I can't raise DOA," said Yuan, glancing over from the pilot seat. "I can't get any comms while we're stuck inside."

"Selene says the control booth for the hangar is on the other side of those inner doors." Renton pointed out across the open space to a set of thick steel access doors.

"The hangar is still pressurized so Oryx should be able to prize them open," offered Alice.

"And then what?" asked Matteo. "We start a firefight?"

"Selene," Renton called back into the cargo hold. Selene extracted herself from the small group of anxious faces and floated over to him.

"How many people does this Grando guy have? And how many know their way around a weapon?" he asked.

Selene thought about this for a moment. "He has at least seven core supporters, but quite a few more followers. There could be fifteen out there. As for weapons, most of the stranded hotel security staff are with him, and they have training," she advised, concern growing on her face.

"Risky," said Matteo. "I know I said I needed some stimulation in my life, but a shootout might be taking it too far."

"Might be our only option," said Renton. "If Xilinex gets here, then we're probably dealing with mercenaries. And that would be a whole different level of stimulation."

"We'd better decide something, and quick, before they get here," demanded Yuna.

"Selene? How were you planning to get out without someone manually operating that control booth?"

Selene drew a blank at this. Then called into the cargo hold for Deejay and asked him the same question.

"There is a procedure I set up, ready to go," explained the tech. "Once it's activated, you've got one minute before the hangar starts to depressurize."

"That's cutting it a bit tight," Renton observed.

Deejay just shrugged. "We weren't planning on hanging around."

"Okay, here's a plan—sort of." Renton turned to the crew. "Yuna, you power up the shuttle, pressurize the cabin, and get ready to take off. Myself and Matteo will suit up, take Oryx, and prize open those inner doors enough to send in the maintenance drone. That will start shooting up the place and hopefully scatter everybody enough so that we can get to the booth and run that procedure. Then we've got sixty seconds to get back inside."

"I see a slight problem with that," said Matteo. "What if they regroup once we're gone and halt the procedure?"

"I could keep Oryx in the corridor, taking potshots at anyone who approaches the booth," offered Alice. "But just so you know, Oryx is difficult to maneuver in zero-gee, and it would mean sacrificing the robot; there'll be no way to retrieve it."

"I'm okay with that," said Renton. "All right then, are we doing this? Or does anyone have a better crazy plan?"

No one did.

A few minutes later, Yuna had the ship powered up. Renton and Matteo exited via the side airlock, along with a maintenance drone that immediately took to the air, and Oryx, who was tethered to Renton. They both wore EVA suits, not that they needed them in the pressurized environment, but more as body armor against anybody who managed to get off a lucky shot.

As they traversed the hangar, the group on the other side of the window began to pay attention, no doubt wondering what they were up to. They reached the inner doors, and Oryx began to prize them open with its powerful grippers. Renton and Matteo took up positions on either side.

A hail of metal barbs bounced off the robot as the doors split apart. The drone then dropped down and let loose a return barrage for a brief second before flying through the gap.

Oryx followed—both machines spitting sharp metal barbs in all directions. Grando and his people ran for cover.

"Alice?" Renton shouted into his helmet comm. "How's it looking out there?"

She was controlling Oryx from inside the shuttle cockpit, seeing what it saw. Yuna controlled the maintenance drone.

"They've all moved back down the corridor," she replied. "They're taking cover where they can. Go, now! Before they get organized."

Renton pushed his way through the gap in the doors, followed by Matteo. A few slugs ricocheted off the side walls, but they were way wide of the mark. The drone darted around, this way and that, returning fire, keeping their opponents pinned.

They worked their way up along the corridor to the control booth, and Matteo floated in. Renton stayed outside, keeping him covered while he activated the procedure that Deejay had set up. A second or two later, he floated back out again. "Done, let's go."

More slugs bounced around; one smacked off Renton's helmet visor but did no damage other than a scratch—but it did make him move quicker. They made it back in through the doors. "Yuna, bring the drone back."

A moment later, it whizzed back into the hangar, leaving Oryx clamped to a handhold in the corridor, keeping Grando's people pinned down.

They clambered in through the shuttle airlock, to a sea of very anxious faces. "That was crazy, Renton," Selene's face full of concern for her nephew.

"We're not out yet," he said as he took off his helmet and headed for the cockpit.

"How are we looking?" he asked.

"Still pinned down," Alice pointed at the central cockpit monitor displaying a feed from Oryx. "But it's taking a beating. It may be tough, but they can still do damage to Oryx with enough firepower."

A red strobe light illuminated the hangar interior as the inner doors shut again and the space began to depressurize.

"Here we go, fingers crossed," said Alice, as she kept the robot oriented on the targets. The screen suddenly went black, and then... nothing. "Crap, they've hit the camera. I'm flying blind."

"Just keep pressing the trigger and spray the place until there's no more ammunition left," Matteo advised.

The outer doors began to slide open. "It's working, look." Yuna pointed at the ever-widening gap. They then felt several thumps as the magnetic grapples disengaged, and the shuttle rose up off the hangar floor. Yuna inched it forward, ready to escape as soon as the gap was wide enough.

"Oryx is out of ammo," Alice shouted, as she waved a frustrated hand at the controls.

"Go, Yuna. What are you waiting for?" shouted Matteo.

"Wait, not enough clearance yet."

The doors halted their sideways motion.

"Uh-oh, I think they're in the control booth," said Renton. "They're closing the doors again."

"Goddamn it," Yuna shouted as she hit the forward thrust and aimed for the gap. "Let's hope it's wide enough."

The shuttle shot out through the gap and into space, with only a slight tremor from the hull. "Damn it, we hit something." Yuna's eyes then danced across the readouts. "We're okay, I think. Hull's still holding pressure."

Matteo clapped her on the back, then high-fived Renton and Alice. "We did it, we absolutely did it."

"Are we out?" Selene's head poked through the cockpit door.

Renton grinned. "You bet we are." He gave her a high five as well, perhaps with a little too much enthusiasm, as she went sailing back through the door and into the cargo hold. A second later, he could hear cheers coming from inside.

The cockpit comms crackled to life. "This is DOA. I am happy to see that you have disembarked from the Axial Luxor Hotel. However, just to let you know, a Xilinex military transport has taken off from Shackleton and is now en route to your location. Intercept in fourteen minutes."

"Goddamn it. Just when I thought we were home free," Renton sighed. "Can we outrun it?"

Yuna shook her head. "Not a hope in hell. This thing's just a delivery truck."

"Also," DOA continued, "I could be wrong, although I never am, but the Xilinex transport has an exterior plasma cannon."

"Jesus, they'll blow us to smithereens," said Matteo.

Renton cast him a sideways glance. "Still glad you came?"

Matteo gave a snort. "Ha, loving it. It's been a blast," he laughed.

"This is serious, Matteo." Yuna did not quite get his morbid sense of humor. "We have no chance against that sort of weapon."

"If I may offer some clarification on the capabilities of the plasma cannon," DOA interrupted.

"By all means," said Renton.

"It's low-powered, so it might not do much physical damage to your ship. However, it is capable of frying all your electronics, similar to a massive solar flare."

"That still means if they hit us, we'll just be floating in space, unable to maneuver," said Renton.

"Or breathe," added Alice.

"We'll probably freeze long before we asphyxiate," said Matteo.

"We could power everything down, like we did on the Aurora?" Alice suggested. "We'll still have momentum; we'll still be heading back to base."

"Theoretically," Yuna said, very slowly, like she was thinking it all out as she spoke. "If we take a direct hit, there's still a possibility we could lose hull integrity, decompression. We'll also be knocked off course."

A proximity alert flashed on the navigation console. "Four minutes, and they'll be on top of us," Alice observed. "We need to do something real quick."

"DOA, what fuel type is that Xilinex shuttle using?"

"Standard hydrogen," came the reply.

"And how long does it take them to recharge their plasma cannon?"

"Based on the limited data I have available on the exact

configuration of this vehicle, my best estimate would be one hundred and twenty-eight seconds."

"Two minutes," said Renton. "We've got two minutes."

"To do what exactly?" asked Matteo.

"Disable that shuttle."

"Sure. But how?" said Alice.

"The laser cutter on the maintenance drone. We use it to disable their plasma cannon, then it can start slicing open their fuel tanks. That will send them running for home."

"Uh, okay, assuming we survive long enough to launch it," said Matteo.

"Yuna, set us on an intercept course. Then we power everything down and launch the drone. If they fire at us, and we survive, we reboot and target the drone on the ship. Then we've got two minutes for it to do its thing."

Everyone looked at Renton, wondering if he was insane or inspired.

"Screw it." Yuna nudged the controls and changed their vector for intercept. "Done," she announced a few seconds later. "Time to power down." Both she and Alice began to flick switches and twist knobs as the lights in the ship went out. "Someone better tell the people in the cargo hold what's happening, or they'll all freak out."

The shuttle went dead, no lights, no heat, not even the ever-present background hum of the life-support system. The only sound was the whimpering of the hapless cargo of evacuees.

"No panic," Matteo called out as he and Renton began moving through the hold to get the maintenance drone ready. "All part of the plan," he smiled.

"But, the ship's dead," a voice called out from the darkness.

"No, it's just, uh... in stealth mode," Matteo assured them.

Renton was sweeping the light from his helmet over the drone to check its systems when there was an almighty jolt to the ship. The cargo hold briefly illuminated with incandescent tendrils of electrical energy arcing all around the interior of the hull. Shrieks of terror erupted from the passengers as Renton and Matteo gave each other a concerned look.

"Damnit, we've been hit," said Renton.

"Powering up," came the shout from Yuna in the cockpit. With that, the cabin lights flickered back on, the life-support system kicked in—the ship had survived.

"Quick," said Renton. "Let's get this drone outside."

They shoved it into the airlock and set it cycling through its routine. "Alice?" Renton called out as he and Matteo made their way back to the cockpit, pushing past the terrified passengers. "It's all yours."

Alice routed the camera feed from the drone to the central cockpit monitor. They could see the Xilinex ship growing bigger and bigger.

"The drone's coming in very fast, going to be difficult to slow it down just with reaction thrusters." Alice's hands danced over the input controls.

Renton felt a shift in momentum as Yuna banked the shuttle away, orienting it back on course for Moon Base Delta.

The drone slowed down considerably but still impacted the Xilinex ship with speed, bouncing off the hull. Alice struggled to get it oriented. On the monitor, they could see the ship slip by as the drone fought to gain some purchase on the hull. It had reached the stern, just over the engine cowling when Alice finally managed to get one of the drone's grippers clamped onto a sensor array.

"Holy cow, that was intense," she said, and she instructed the robot to move back up the hull to the cannon turret.

"Thirty seconds to full recharge," Yuna advised.

"Don't remind me. I'm going as fast as I can."

On the monitor, they could see the base of the cannon turret. "There," said Renton. "Those power cables, cut them."

A bright light bloomed from the monitor as Alice deployed the laser cutter. She stopped for a second to examine the results, before activating the laser again. She did this three more times until the cables were all severed. She looked up at the others. They waited.

"Minus twenty seconds," Yuna said, cautiously. "Minus twenty-five... thirty."

"I think you did it, Alice. I think you absolutely did it." Matteo's voice was almost ecstatic.

"I'm going to be out of control range with the drone in less than a minute," Alice cautioned. "I'll move it back to find the hydrogen storage tanks."

The drone moved back toward the stern of the ship, using its two gripper arms to cling on where it could.

"There should be one on either side of the engine bay, two bulges," Matteo pointed to a section of the ship.

"I'll set it on auto. But the laser is almost out of power. I'll let it run until it's exhausted."

Again, the monitor bloomed with intense light.

"This is DOA." The AI's voice crackled in the cockpit. "Just to inform you, the Xilinex ship has altered course. I calculate it is now heading back to its home base."

"Yes!" Matteo punched the air. "In your face, Xilinex, in your goddamn face." He gave the middle finger salute in the general direction of the damaged craft.

"Also, you'll be pleased to know that Tanaka and his people have done a splendid job of preparing for your arrival. The hangar door is open, and a warm welcome awaits."

Renton's breathing slowed, and his heart rate finally began to calm down.

CHAPTER 30

MASS ACCELERATOR

Lieutenant Ben Wilson, along with five other hand-picked and highly trained members of his mercenary team, busied themselves stripping out of their Xilinex EVA suits and redeploying into standard issue SINO suits. These had just been taken from several captured individuals who had the misfortune of being on the losing side in the recent skirmish for control of the small SINO outpost at Rutherford Crater. This was a relatively insignificant subcrater within the much greater, two-hundred-and-thirty-kilometer-wide Clavius Crater—home to the vast SINO Helium-3 mining facility including their Mass Accelerator. The Lieutenant and his squad had stormed this small SINO enclave for no other reason than as a setup for their main mission.

Their primary objective, the Mass Accelerator, was further to the west, deeper into Clavius, but to assault it with the main force, Xilinex first needed to ensure that any self-destruct system that SINO may have installed was neutralized. This was the Lieutenant's objective.

Several of his squad had been busy scouting what remained of the outpost, to find a still-functioning SINO transport rover, into which he and his team were now in the process of boarding. They had reloaded their light plasma weapons with fresh power cells, stowing a few more into carry bags as well as an assortment of remote-controlled explosives. All of this equipment was loaded into the newly acquired SINO rover along with two large storage crates, the contents of which would determine the outcome of the mission.

They powered up the rover, entered the big industrial airlock, and shot out at top speed when the outer doors finally opened. All of this subterfuge was intended to look like a cohort of SINO operatives had escaped the occupying Xilinex forces and were making a run for the safety of the nearest SINO enclave, the Mass Accelerator facility. The rover skidded on the loose lunar regolith, throwing up dust and debris as it plowed on. It was reckless driving, the type conducted by people fleeing for their lives.

Sergeant Wesley Zhang, whose Mandarin was reputedly flawless, opened a comms channel to the facility and poured forth a loud frantic message: "Rutherford outpost overrun, barely managed to escape being killed, two injured, retreating to the Mass Accelerator facility to help fend off the imminent attack by the capitalists." Or words to that effect. To Lieutenant Wilson's untrained ear, it sounded pretty convincing. And when a return message came, Sergeant Wesley Zhang's face morphed into a broad grin and gave the thumbs up. It seemed they were falling for it.

The road took them through the vast, open-cast, Helium-3 mining fields. Out through the rover windshield, Wilson could see several of the great machines that scraped up the Helium-3 rich surface regolith, all lying idle, like dead mechanical beasts from some long-forgotten industrial era. There was no need for them now, no way to return the precious harvest back to Earth, nor were there any people to operate them—the entire SINO working population had been redeployed to the defense of their facilities and territory.

And, in many respects, this was their fundamental problem, the very reason, in the minds of Xilinex command, why SINO was destined to lose this war. They did not have the foresight to deploy and train military personnel when they had the chance. Now they were relying on internal security, their police, to fight against a well-resourced and well-trained mercenary army. Already, rumors were circulating that the ordinary SINO workers were revolting against this forced conscription. How was a lab tech or an IT guy or a food producer supposed to hold back these killing machines? They didn't stand a chance.

Around a half hour later, the commandeered rover barreled up toward the primary transport airlock of the SINO Mass Accelerator facility. This is it, thought Wilson, time to find out if this deception will work. A challenge broke out from the cockpit comms. It was indecipherable to Wilson, but its tone was unmistakable.

"Who the hell are you guys?"

Sergeant Wesley Zhang came back with an equally animated reply. Then there ensued a back-and-forth dialogue that got more and more animated. Wilson began to fear that their carefully planned ruse was about to fail and end up in a hail of plasma fire. But the comms ended with Zhang pointing ahead—the main airlock doors were opening. It was game on.

The Lieutenant noted the auto-cannon positioned to the right of the main airlock entrance. That would have to go, but the first objective was to disable any self-destruct system that might have been put in place by SINO. Once that was located and rendered nonoperational, then the real battle could begin in earnest. He also noted the body language of the two guards and the medic that approached the rover as it cycled through the airlock and entered the hangar, very casual, very resigned— these were not military people, probably ordinary facility workers who had been press-ganged into guard duty. It took Lieutenant Wilson's team less than thirty seconds to relieve them of their weapons, and another thirty to do the same to the hapless SINO tech operating the hangar control booth.

Wilson then sent a cryptic message back to the main Xilinex force that the "horse was inside the walls," while the rest of his team began unloading an electromagnetic pulse device, an EMP, from its storage crate. Sergeant Zhang activated the device and tossed the remote detonator to Lieutenant Wilson.

A second, empty crate was also hastily unloaded from the rover and opened. Its purpose was to protect its contents from the high-intensity electromagnetic blast. The squad then stripped off their EVA suits and dumped them in this crate along with all their plasma weapons and electronic equipment. It was sealed and carried into the hangar control booth where they all hunkered down. Sergeant Zhang activated the outer airlock doors to ensure they were wide open before giving the signal to Lieutenant Wilson. He nodded his acknowledgment, raised his hand with the remote trigger, and detonated the EMP device.

There was no sound, no shockwave, just an invisible burst of energy that radiated out across the entire facility, overloading electronic and electrical circuits, causing massive systems failures. Immediately the entire area was thrown into darkness as the lights flickered out. The ever-present, pervasive hum of the life support system also ceased. It was deathly quiet, yet somewhere in the background, Lieutenant Wilson thought he heard the sounds of panic rising in the occupants of this far-flung outpost. They wasted no time in getting suited up and armed again. It was the moment to put this mission to bed.

At the same time as the Lieutenant and his squad were preparing for the battle to come, a Xilinex shuttle, with twenty-five highly trained mercenaries, was powering low across the lunar landscape toward the facility, along with two rover transports with a further thirty security personnel cobbled together from Xilinex bases and other enclaves that they had taken over. All these resources were now converging on the main airlock entrance of the Mass Accelerator facility without fear of being spotted by radar or being hit by plasma cannon— all of which were now disabled by the powerful EMP blast.

As the transport shuttle touched down, the mercenaries were already disembarking, making a hurried dash for the entrance. Within minutes, they had blown the interior doors off their supports, creating a massive evacuation of atmosphere from inside the facility. Soon, they were piling in, blowing open internal bulkhead doors as they advanced through the area. What resistance they did meet was quickly crushed. In less than thirty-five minutes, it was all over. The battle for control of the Mass Accelerator was accomplished. The Xilinex corporation was victorious, and SINO was dealt a significant death blow, from which they would struggle to recover.

CHAPTER 31

THE WESTERN ALLIANCE

"What do you think they want?" Sheneese asked her husband with a pronounced tone of concern. "Do you think they found out about that data transmission you sent to Professor Henriksen?"

"No, it's not possible, it was heavily encrypted." Han shook his head, but deep down he wasn't so sure. Maybe they did find out about it, in which case, they would be none too happy.

"We can't afford to get kicked out of here, Han. Did you hear what's going on outside? If we have to leave here, we won't survive for long, I just know it."

"Don't worry, I'm sure it will be fine, they probably just want to do a work review. Hey, maybe they'll give me a bonus." He forced out his best smile.

"I heard rumors that the same gang that took over Petersville last week is planning a raid on this facility."

"Well, that would be suicide on their part. This place is well protected. They would need an army to take it."

"But an army is what they have, apparently. All supplies are coming in by helicopter now. No more trucks. There hasn't been a delivery that way for over two weeks. They say it's just too dangerous, that the gang controls most of the countryside around here now."

"You're worrying too much."

"I can't help it. Maybe you shouldn't have sent that data. And I shouldn't have facilitated. If we're found out and have to leave..." Her sentence trailed off.

"I have to go. The board is waiting for me. Best not delay them." He kissed her on the cheek, straightened up his shirt, and made his way to the council meeting where he was on the agenda.

Sheneese was right, of course, it was a stupid risk he took to send that data to Henriksen. Why had he done it? Risked their privileged position in what was a beacon of security and sanity in a sea of chaos and uncertainty. Yet, he just couldn't leave his old friend in the dark. It was only fair, in his mind, that he should be kept in the loop. Call it academic courtesy, if you will. But, in hindsight, maybe it wasn't such a good idea after all. *Well, time to find out,* he thought as he entered the boardroom.

It wasn't so much a boardroom in the traditional sense; it wasn't some airy, steel and glass cathedral atop a corporate mega-tower. There was no aged oak wood paneling with the walls adorned with oil paintings of past CEOs. No, this was a bunker within a bunker—its predominant feature being concrete. A cold gray windowless space with a circular table fashioned, not from some exotic wood, but roughly polished aluminum, as were the rest of the fixtures in the room. A large monitor took up the entire back wall, on which was displayed an aerial view of a launch site in Vandenberg, where six small rockets had been rolled into position waiting to take off. A big bold countdown timer flashed in one corner. T minus 5:31:48. That would be the moment where his analysis of the debris cloud that surrounded Earth, and the new capsule designs, finally met reality.

"Ah... Dr. Sundar. Great that you could make it. Please, have a seat." General Philip Grant gestured to a chair opposite, facing the arc of authority that sat in a curve around the other half of the circular table, several of whom nodded greetings in Han's direction.

"Big day today," said Grant. His tone was cheerful, expectant, and had the effect of dialing down Han's paranoia levels a notch or two.

Then there was that moment in all gatherings where the substantive news needed to be delivered. It was a kind of unconscious hive-mind dance that all the participants undertook, as they got down to the business at hand—nods, glances, paper shuffling, seat shifting, and pen tapping.

"So, Dr. Sundar," said Grant, with a noticeable air of gravitas.

Here it comes, he thought.

"We wanted to take this opportunity to offer you our collective thanks for the great work you've done for us, and for humanity."

Han wasn't quite sure what he was hearing, so he tried to maintain his best poker face.

"They said you were the best, which is why we went to all the trouble to pluck you out of your castle up there in the mountains, and they were not wrong. I appreciate it's still early days." Grant gestured at the countdown timer on the wall monitor. "It will be a few hours yet before we know for sure. But nevertheless, we wanted to offer our appreciation for your tireless efforts in making this day possible."

There was a pause which stretched out until Han realized Grant was expecting a response from him.

"Oh, eh, well, it's eh… what I do." He shifted in his seat and rubbed his hands on his thighs to dry the sweat.

"We've decided, as a valuable member of the team, to level up your security clearance. You'll now have complete access to everything, and… you'll also be our newest member of this board."

Han was stunned. He had come in here predicting a dark future for himself and Sheneese, and here they were offering a board position.

"I'm… stunned," he replied. Which he truly was.

"However," Grant noted, his tone more serious. "We need to satisfy ourselves that you fully understand the policies we need to adopt if we are to have any chance of saving civilized society from complete collapse."

"Of course," Han replied. "We must do everything we can. Everything humanly possible."

"I'm glad you think that way, Dr. Sundar. Because what I'm about to tell you is known only to a very few select people, and we need your assurance that you understand the implications for human civilization if we fail in this task." Grant leaned in, placing his arms on the table, hands clasped together.

"The Xilinex Corporation has just taken control of the Mass Accelerator facility on Luna. SINO are now in disarray, and it won't be long before all lunar assets are under the control of Xilinex. This leaves us no other option but to work with this corporation in ensuring that supplies of Helium-3 can begin again." He nodded his head at the monitor. "Assuming, of course, all goes well with the test today."

Han simply nodded. Part of him knew this was coming.

"However, everyone still existing up on Luna does so under the Damoclean sword of starvation. Their food supply is genetically modified to only produce a certain volume, after which point the biomass is exhausted, unable to produce any more."

"Then let's hope the tests are successful, that at least one of the capsules makes it through intact," offered Han.

"Indeed, so much depends on it." It was Dyson that now spoke. "Both here and on Luna."

"This Luna-specific bio-stock is only produced by one corporation," Grant resumed, "Santomon, and they have the monopoly on it. However, it has now been taken over by the state as an issue of national security. Their offices and production facilities now have a heavy military presence around them. They are completely under our control."

"Makes perfect sense." Han nodded his approval. "Food security is absolutely critical. Presumably then, they can be directed to produce a self-sustaining bio-stock that reproduces like natural biomass. That would secure the current population on the Moon."

"It would. But that would be a mistake," said Grant, his tone emphatic.

Han did a mental double-take. How could this possibly be a mistake? Giving a soon-to-be starving population the means to feed itself seemed like a moral imperative to him.

"What we need is leverage over Xilinex," Grant explained. "Remember they are a corporation, with a corporate culture that thinks only in terms of profit. Given free rein, they would play us all off against one another, now that they have a complete monopoly on supplies of Helium-3 from Luna. This does no one any good, except them. They would extract an exorbitant price, dangle the risk of a cut in supply over the heads of any country or government that didn't play ball with them."

Han had to admit this was absolutely what a corporation as powerful as Xilinex would do. Yet, it still didn't quite sit right with him, restricting the population's ability to grow its own food."

"So we have brokered a deal between the combined Western Alliance, who now control the food supply, and the Xilinex Corporation who control Helium-3. This goes right to the very top." Grant pointed skyward. "We supply them with enough GM bio-stock to keep them going for a while, they supply us exclusively with Helium-3. Any deviation from this arrangement, such as restricting supply or supplying other countries not within the Western Alliance, will immediately result in the restriction of fresh bio-stock."

"So... you starve them?" Han tried to hide his distaste for this arrangement.

Dyson intervened, his tone avuncular. "Ah, it won't actually come to that. It's just the threat of doing it is enough to keep everybody on the straight and narrow."

"And we, being the Western Alliance, will have the sole supply of Helium-3?" Han asked, looking for clarification.

"Exactly, this is the brilliance of the plan," said Grant, gesturing with both hands. "With control of the food supply, we control the Moon, and with control of the Helium-3 supply, we effectively control Earth."

"Indeed." Han nodded again, as his thoughts went to his friend Professor Henriksen, who had just made a daring escape to Moon Base Delta—if the recent reports were to be trusted. "Will we, I mean FISA and Space Division, be trying to hang on to any assets up there?"

Grant shook his head. "No, these are of no use to us now. Part of the deal is that we hand them all over to Xilinex. It's a peace offering, a way of building trust."

"Including Moon Base Delta?" prompted Han. "That would be quite a prize."

"Including the base, yes." Dyson nodded.

Han shook his head. "I get that we can't go back there any time soon, but sometime in the future it's a possibility. It seems a pity to just, I don't know, hand it over like that."

Grant gave him a long hard look. "You do see the necessity for all this, don't you, Dr. Sundar? You understand what's at stake here. The objective being to secure everyone's future."

Han thought about the earlier conversation with Sheneese,

the concern on her face. He remembered the fear they lived in back at the old observatory, before being magically transported to this base. About the local town that had just come under the control of some new-age warlord, about the reports of chaos and violence outside these walls, about his and his wife's future.

"Of course," he said finally. "I think it's masterful, borderline genius. Everyone's future is secured. And that's all that matters." He provided them with a broad smile.

CHAPTER 32
FAILURE OF DUTY

A Xilinex executive class transport powered its way across the blackness of lunar space en route to the Axial Luxor Orbital Hotel, soon to be the headquarters for the new governing council of the Moon—with a large section carved out as the private residence of Chancellor Pompodur Rossen Adarok.

The old Xilinex orbital, which Pompodur had spent the last few months on, would now be repurposed as a military and security HQ, with General Wagner in command. This would be a better fit for such a utilitarian facility.

After the successful capture of the Mass Accelerator, Pompodur spent the next four days doing what he did best, providing a narrative that the frightened and panicked population could latch onto, one that would give them hope and a sense of security. The Xilinex corporation would ensure that order was maintained and that the day-to-day administration of the newly emerging lunar society would be run efficiently for the benefit of all. Supplies from Earth would soon resume, industries would be brought back online, entertainment spaces would reopen, and above all, food production and management would be given top priority—no one would go hungry, as all provisions would be carefully managed by the Xilinex bean-counters.

A new lunar community would be wrought from the old, more vibrant, more dynamic, and more prosperous. To this end, a new monetary system would be introduced, one that better suited the new and dynamic lunar economy that they were all now building together. Not only would Xilinex bring peace and stability, but they would also catapult the people of the Moon to new, greater heights of wealth that would rival anything Earth had to offer. When flights back to the home planet resumed, as surely they would in time, the lunar population would be looked upon with envy for their wealth and sophistication.

Granted, Pompodur may have gone a bit too far with this last proclamation, but it still had the desired effect of emboldening the naive, inspiring the cautious, and neutralizing the dissenters.

He visited five of the primary population centers in the last four days, giving the same speech each time, meeting with the local leaders, installing those who were loyal to Xilinex in positions of power, and seeking out potential troublemakers. Slowly but surely, he was also building up his network of spies and informants, those who would sell their own mother for an extra supply of rations and the promise of power over their fellow colonists.

The key to control of the people was to ensure that the primary narrative was not polluted by dissenting voices. And the key to doing that was good old-fashioned boots on the ground, loyalists who could sniff out potential troublemakers before they had a chance to gain a foothold in the community. Part of this narrative was exaggerating the threat posed by SINO forces. So long as the general population was kept firmly in a state of fear over the barbarians at the gates, then they would hold firm to the need for support of Xilinex as their protectors.

This was a concept that Pompodur had great difficulty in persuading the General to accept. With SINO forces in complete disarray, they had consolidated all their military resources at two locations. The first was at a sizable base in the Sea of Crises, a fitting moniker for a power in its death throes. The second was at a mining outpost at DaVinci Crater. Yet, rumors abounded that even this latter facility was undergoing its own internal struggles. It seemed that a rebellion of sorts had broken out, so they agreed to let this run its course—no need to send in a Xilinex force if SINO rebels were doing the job for them.

As for the main SINO base, the General wanted to move in fast and crush all resistance there. But Pompodur explained to him the value in keeping the last remaining SINO enclave as a propaganda weapon. They were not much of a threat anymore since Xilinex had established a blockade around it, nothing in, nothing out. But Pompodur could use it as a perceived threat, constantly informing the people that SINO was still active and could swarm over the lunar surface again, destroying all the good work of the Xilinex corporation in bringing peace and stability to the Moon. This would help keep everyone in line, this fear that chaos was only being held at bay by the efforts of the valiant Xilinex mercenaries.

The only thing preventing Pompodur's complete control of the narrative was Moon Base Delta, more specifically Selene Mene and her constant information broadcasts, which had resumed just as soon as she arrived at the base. Something had to be done, and soon. It was a situation that could not be allowed to continue. And that meant sending a Xilinex force and taking over the entire base, once and for all.

The General was in agreement, not specifically because he fully understood the need to control the message, but because he was pissed off that one of his shuttles had been disabled by a bunch of amateurs. His military pride could not let that stand.

But first, they needed to do some mopping-up operations, clearing out enclaves that still had some resistance, stabilizing newly acquired facilities, and consolidating their forces. Once that was done, Moon Base Delta would be brought to heel.

For Pompodur, this mopping-up operation commenced with the Axial Luxor, more specifically, extracting suitable retribution for the failure of Gabriel Grando and his group to prevent Selene Mene and her followers from escaping the orbital. Things would have been much easier for the new Lunar Chancellor if she had not made it down to Moon Base Delta.

As he and the rest of the new administrative council disembarked from the shuttle and made their way to the vast central lobby of the hotel, he began to feel the increase in the simulated gravity produced by the massive rotating hotel torus. It was only around eighty percent of Earth's but much more than that of the Xilinex HQ orbital. He was feeling the additional weight on his body, slowing him down. But he was determined not to let that spoil his fun today.

All current occupants of the Axial had been gathered together into the big central lobby of the hotel, under the watchful eye of Xilinex security which had been sent up in advance to prepare the way for the Chancellor's arrival and the establishment of the new seat of power.

The assembled crowd, of some one-hundred people, would first be treated to a speech from Pompodur—a shortened version he had been giving to everyone else over the last few days. But there would be a very special moment at the end that he was going to enjoy immensely.

Then they would all be individually processed. Those who had worked here in the past, hotel staff, would remain. Others would be reassigned to different areas within the Xilinex Lunar empire and given positions commensurate with their skill set. As for the FISA people, and lackeys of their affiliated agencies that had the misfortune to be stranded here after the evacuation, they would be sent to the harshest mining outpost that existed on the lunar surface. Probably the extremely isolated iron mines in Joliet Crater, reputed to be the absolute worst in terms of conditions and survival rates. There they would be sent, and there they would die.

Seeing how Pompodur was struggling with the extra gravity, Christophe Dubois, his second-favorite servant, reached out to offer him a hand up onto the raised dais that he was using to make his speech. He slapped it away in anger. How dare Christophe make him look weak in front of this crowd of people. He would deal with him later, perhaps another one for Joliot Crater.

He stepped onto the podium and surveyed the assembled group before him. He could sense their fear; this was good, this was exactly where he wanted them to be. He began.

As he talked, he was keen to observe the body language of the group, seeking out those who could be trouble, as well as those that might be eager to serve the new regime. As he came to the end of his speech, he gestured at the wide viewing window that dominated one whole side of the hotel lobby. The group all turned to see that a Xilinex military shuttle had come up alongside the window, its bulk almost obscuring all else.

"Now I want you all to pay close attention to the side airlock of the shuttle."

The assembled group jostled for suitable viewing positions.

"It always pains me to hear of failure, particularly failure of duty. Some failures, of course, are unavoidable, where circumstances conspire to thwart even the most Herculean of efforts. But by the same token, some failures are unforgivable— I'm talking here of failure due to incompetence. This, I regard as a crime." He paused for a moment, just to let that last word sink in.

"It is this very crime that Gabriel Grando and his associates stand accused of in their failure to detain the traitor Selene Mene and her followers. The crime of gross incompetence. And for such a heinous crime there can only be one sentence, and that is death." He gestured at the shuttle poised outside the window again, ensuring that everyone's attention was on it.

The shuttle seemed to drift in a little before the outer airlock door slid open to reveal three figures exposed to the vacuum of space without EVA suits. They jerked and gyrated, clutching at their necks for a brief moment before their frozen inert bodies floated out of the airlock.

Pompodur remained silent so that all assembled in the hotel lobby had time to witness the price to be paid for failure of duty to the Xilinex Corporation.

CHAPTER 33
GOOD WHILE IT LASTED

T he wide central silo that formed the core of Moon Base
Delta was capped by an elegantly domed transparent
roof, manufactured from an amorphous carbon compound that
gave it a hardness above that of diamond, and provided
radiation shielding equivalent to approximately three meters of
lunar regolith. It was coated with a second inner skin that could
regulate its transparency by simply applying an electrical
current to it. This allowed the amount of direct sunlight
illuminating the space beneath it to be dialed down during the
fourteen-day-long lunar daytime but fully open to the heavens
during the equally long lunar night. The area occupied the
entire upper floor of the core and had been designed as a
viewing gallery and communal area, with seating, ornamental
gardens, and a myriad of alcoves where the colonists of the past
could spend some downtime in pleasant surroundings, with
spectacular views of the heavens above.

Now, though, the area had the feel of a long-derelict warehouse. The ornamental gardens were nothing more than a collection of dry, dead twigs. A thin layer of dust covered every centimeter of the area: the floor, the fixtures, the furnishings. But it did have one occupant, Renton Hicks, who was lying flat on his back on a dusty bench, staring up at the cosmos. Beside him, on the floor, lay his jacket and comms unit, which he had taken off so he could get some time to himself, time where he could let his mind rest.

There was a different mood in the base ever since the arrival of his aunt and her group from the Axial a few days ago. Selene had been quite emotional when she arrived. It had been her dream to see the base reactivated. And now, in a strange way, her dream was fulfilled. She also had an encyclopedic knowledge of the place, explaining to the others how it came to be built and much of its history. Even DOA seemed to connect with her in a way that was different from everyone else. Perhaps it had some deeper, historic connection that held more weight in its unfathomable AI mind.

All this gave Renton a sense that the grown-ups were now in control, a childish feeling he knew, but it really did seem that way to him. He felt that he could safely switch off survival mode in his brain and just... kick back for a while. Or maybe it was the several near-death experiences he had been through over the last few months that were finally catching up with him and the rest of the crew.

He had talked about it with Alice, and wasn't surprised that she too was in a similar mood. Recuperation, she called it. Now that they had secured some modicum of a future, it was the body's way of letting you know that it was time to power down and recharge. Because, as she pointed out, there would be more stressful times ahead.

He was beginning to drift off to sleep when he heard the sound of footsteps. "Renton, there you are. We've been trying to contact you. Where's your comms unit?"

He opened his eyes to find Alice standing over him, a concerned look on her face.

"Hello," he said, tilting his head in her direction. "So much for trying to spend some time doing absolutely nothing." He sat up and swung his legs over the side of the bench, feet on the ground.

"Sorry, but there have been some developments."

He gave a long sigh. "Well, it was nice while it lasted." He glanced up at her. "So, what new existential crises are we facing this time?"

"Henriksen has received an encrypted message from his contact in Strawstack. Everyone is down in the operations room and freaking out about it. Sorry, but you need to be in the loop on this one."

Renton sighed again. "Can it wait?" He asked, knowing what the answer would be.

"I wouldn't be here if it could. So, come on." She grabbed his arm to gently coax him up from the bench. "Let's get down there and you'll find out for yourself."

The upshot was that some high-level insider friend of the professor's, a guy called Dr. Han Sundar, had sent him an encrypted message disguised as debris cloud analysis. In it, he laid out the entire deal that the Western Alliance was putting in place with the Xilinex Corporation. It was a bombshell. They were not working on a long-term solution to the GM food issue. Instead, they were feverishly developing a capsule design for a lunar population supplied with the very same GM bio-stock with a limited half-life. In return, Xilinex would keep the Helium-3 flowing. No Helium-3, no food. It was blackmail, pure and simple. Worse, they had officially handed over all lunar assets to Xilinex, even Moon Base Delta.

Over the next few hours, Renton and the crew, along with Selene and some of her people, and even Tanaka and his people all knocked their heads together to work out exactly what all this meant for them.

DOA was set the task of assessing the current situation on the ground and war-gaming various scenarios. It was the AI's assessment that a mopping-up operation was in progress by Xilinex, keeping a lot of their mercenaries busy. But once that finished, and the internal fighting going on at the old SINO mining base at DaVinci had resolved itself, then Xilinex would turn its attention on them. In the end, it all came down to the inevitability that there would be an assault on the base by Xilinex. The only question was when. Best guess, they had no more than seven days to get ready.

CHAPTER 34
ROBOT ARMY

R enton's recuperation period was well and truly over. The day and a half he had spent doing absolutely nothing was a distant memory. Now all his energy was focused on how to repel an imminent Xilinex attack on Moon Base Delta.

Even though the base was built like a fortress—most of it existing underground with a fixed number of access points—it was not invulnerable to a determined assault. If Xilinex managed to gain entry, then it was probably game over, as they had limited weapons and none of the twenty-plus current inhabitants of the base had any skill in fighting, let alone military planning. They did, however, have two things that Xilinex did not possess. The first was a vast array of industrial robots, although most were inoperable. And the second was a very powerful AI that could, in theory, coordinate a defense of the base.

But their initial problem was much more fundamental. Even if they somehow managed to mount a substantive fightback and repel the Xilinex force—a big if—there was nothing to stop the corporation from doing the same thing they were doing to the SINO base over in Mare Crisium, Sea of Crisis: simply blockade them until they starved.

The natural reaction by the bulk of the new arrivals from the Axial to this news was borderline panic. Yet, strangely, as they were all given new comms units and got used to the somewhat disconcerting internal dialogue with DOA, they began to settle down. Renton wondered what sweet nothings the AI was whispering in their collective ears to ease their jitters. It was uncanny. Still, he was not complaining, as it saved him, Selene, and some of the others from having to do this work along with figuring out how they were going to deal with the imminent Xilinex onslaught.

Selene had resumed her broadcasts, in the same format that she and her team had been doing up on the Axial—a quasi-news bulletin-stroke-counter-propaganda narrative, which was only twenty minutes long and repeated every four hours. It had become more sophisticated and detailed, mainly due to DOA's assistance now that it could see most of what was going on across the lunar surface via its connection to the LunaSat constellation. However, Selene refrained from broadcasting details of the new deal between the Western Alliance and Xilinex, on Professor Henriksen's insistence, as this could potentially expose his high-level informant.

Renton, and a few of the others, however, were concerned

that his aunt's "hobby" served no useful purpose other than to anger Xilinex, making a physical assault on the base more likely rather than a blockade. But Selene's argument was to undermine the Xilinex narrative, expose the lies, and stir discontent. It was all politics, something Renton knew next to nothing about nor did he care. All that mattered to him was the same as it had been ever since the solar storm crippled the Aurora—survival, and maybe one day getting back home.

"There are twenty-seven possible entry points into Moon Base Delta," DOA informed the assembled group that had gathered around the big holo-table and were studying a 3D schematic of the entire base.

"There's no way we can cover all of those," said Matteo, shaking his head.

"We don't need to cover them all," countered DOA.

Renton wondered if anyone else noticed DOA's latest quirk of using "we" all the time. Before, it was "I" or "you." Now it regarded itself as one of the team.

"The assault group may be as small as six persons, depending on their confidence," DOA continued. "This was the size of the squad they used to gain access to the Mass Accelerator facility in Clavius Crater. They also utilized an EMP device to disable all electrical systems, thus allowing the main force to storm the base unhindered."

"An EMP, crap, that could do some serious damage," said Renton. "It could even take you offline, DOA."

"It's a possibility, but for that to happen, the epicenter of the blast would need to be very close to my core. But that would require access to the lower levels. That said, one must question whether they regard me as an asset to protect or a threat to eliminate."

"Well, there goes our robot army idea," said Alice. "If they detonate an EMP, then they're all dead in the water."

"Not necessarily," said Matteo. "This is a vast base, covering several kilometers of caverns and tunnels, with thousands of tons of rock and concrete. Even a large EMP blast would be contained within a relatively small area."

"So, we could theoretically stash several groups of robots in different locations, then call on those units that escape the blast and are still operational," offered Renton.

"Standard doctrine would dictate that small groups cover the access points with a larger group held in reserve to rush to the aid of any group that is under attack," said DOA. "I suggest we adopt a similar methodology. Moreover, we will know long before they gain access exactly where they're trying to enter."

"Those industrial robots were fine fighting against opponents with only rail-guns," said Alice. "But these Xilinex mercenaries have plasma weapons, a mini, handheld EMP. They could take out a robot with just a few shots."

"What if..." Renton paused, then leaned in closer to the 3D schematic of the base. "What if we built our own EMP?" He began to sweep his hand over the holo-table. "These guys will be entering fully suited up, making them equally susceptible to an EMP attack, including all their fancy-assed weapons."

There was silence around the holo-table as they began to sense merit in Renton's proposal.

"I like it," said Matteo. "We set up a kill-zone and lure them into it, and bingo, zap them with a high-energy pulse. It would render all their weapons useless."

"Then send in the robots," added Yuna.

"Exactly." Renton nodded. "And we could have them already situated in the zone, protected inside a Faraday cage."

"Can you build an EMP device?" asked Selene.

"Oh, yes. How many would you like?" Matteo grinned.

Over the next hour, a plan began to be formulated. Since Oryx and the big maintenance drone had been sacrificed during the rescue attempt from the Axial, this meant they had lost their two best weapons. So more needed to be refurbished, upgraded, and tested—as many industrial robots as they could manage. It was going to be an army.

They would use a few of these to do a shoot and scoot operation, taking potshots at the assault group and hightailing it, inviting the group to give chase. Assuming that the assault team's objective was to get to the upper levels of the central silo, where the operations room was located, then they could set up an area en route where they could lay their trap. It needed to be a big enough space but not too close to the operations level so that the EMP blast wouldn't damage any of the systems.

Anyone from the Axial that had any technical skills would be roped in to help with the robots under Alice and Renton's supervision. While Matteo would lead a team to build not just one EMP, but two, as a backup.

Yuna, along with some input from DOA, would map out possible routes through the base from each of the possible access points, and work out the optimal area to set up the kill zone. The rest would do whatever they could to help keep the teams working around the clock to prepare the robot army.

CHAPTER 35
DAVINCI

S ix refurbished industrial robots stood in a row, fresh off the production line, so to speak. They were the same model as the two that Alice and Yuna had used to fend off the earlier attack by SINO and Xilinex down in the AI core when they had first arrived. Back then, the attackers were not expecting these machines to suddenly rise up and go on a rampage, but they would be fully aware of their existence for this next assault and no doubt had a plan to deal with them, probably in the form of some heavy weaponry. So if their own plan was going to have any chance of working, they would need a lot more than six robots.

Renton glanced around the maintenance hangar they were using as their workshop, the same one they arrived in when they first entered the base. One group was busy disassembling several of the robots that were in the worst condition, breaking them into usable spare parts. Three other teams, working in pairs, were busy rebuilding and testing the units that had been deemed salvageable. Renton would have liked to be working with Alice, but they had split up so they could support the various teams as needed.

As he looked around, he estimated they had enough machines and spare parts to get ten, maybe eleven, more robots operational. But these were not the only units in the base; there were estimated to be upward of two hundred scattered throughout. Yuna, Saito, and Tanaka had been tasked with finding them, along with any machines that contained the super-capacitors Matteo needed for his EMP devices.

Renton saw that Alice was taking a break over at the ad hoc canteen that the others had set up for them to keep them supplied with food and fuel. He put his tools down on a workbench and went over to her.

"I think we can get ten more out of what we've got here," she said in between mouthfuls of a protein bar. "And Yuna's located another seven. They're bringing a few of them over here now."

He couldn't help noticing that she had a smudge of dirt on the tip of her nose, which he found strangely alluring. "Engineer love," he said, with a nod.

Alice looked at him, perplexed. "Uh?"

"You have the cutest oily nose I've ever seen."

She rolled her eyes and wiped her nose on her sleeve. "Gone?"

"Yes, sadly, I could get used to that look."

She smiled. "Maybe if I don't wash for a week, I could drive you crazy."

He laughed.

There was a commotion at the elevator gates, and they both turned to see Yuna descending with Tanaka and three more robots that looked in pretty good shape from where he was standing.

"More stock arriving," observed Alice.

"I've been thinking," he said, taking a sip of coffee.

"Oh?"

"These machines." He jerked a thumb at one of the robots. "They're not very fast."

"They're industrial robots. What do you expect," Alice snapped back, almost taking this as a personal insult. "They're built to lift and lug, not run around like rabbits."

"I know. But that could be a problem. A human could chase one down very easily."

"Well, we'd better make sure we have a good supply, then." She pointed over at the newly arrived stock. "Come on, let's get back to work."

Selene and her team sat down to begin another broadcast recording. It had become a ritual for them, a thing they did as a routine. Selene found comfort in it, a way to feel like she was doing something, providing a valuable counterpoint to all the clap-trap that was being spewed out by Xilinex and SINO—although they had gone very quiet of late. There was not much official propaganda from them anymore, just snippets of information she could pick up from the LunaSat constellation via DOA, and sporadic communication with those who dared to take the risk of sending information her way. However, she did notice a general uptick in these. Perhaps it was because they were broadcasting from Moon Base Delta now, not some luxury orbital. Possibly this felt more real to people out there in the outposts, and as a consequence, they were more willing to keep providing information on what was happening on the ground.

Today's broadcast focused on the movements of the Xilinex military division, which had all the hallmarks of a mopping-up operation. The primary SINO base in Mare Crisium was being blockaded, and it remained to be seen if SINO would launch a counteroffensive to break it. Then they would list all the other enclaves that were being consolidated into the Xilinex empire —Selene had taken to calling them that more recently, an empire. Then there were reports of the brutal execution of Gabriel Grando and two of his associates up on the Axial, along with a number of other reports of people going missing.

The last item on the agenda was the developing situation at the old mining facility in DaVinci, not too far from where Moon Base Delta was located, and the very same place that SINO had taken Renton and the crew of the Aurora after it crash-landed. What started as a row with some of the workers turned into something more akin to an insurrection with an armed group taking over one sector of the facility. From what they could see from the satellite network, there had been a firefight and a series of explosions in that sector recently, leading them to speculate that SINO security was getting the situation back under control. They also speculated that Xilinex might decide that DaVinci was ripe for the taking, having been destabilized by infighting. This was backed up by DOA detecting several Xilinex shuttles heading in that direction.

. . .

Renton had listened to Selene's recent update over his comms unit while working in the maintenance hangar. It was the first in quite a while that he had bothered to listen to. But since there was now a new mood in the base, a sense that they were all in this together, all making a last stand, he decided he needed to know what was going on outside.

He was intrigued by the developments at the mine; having been incarcerated there, he felt some connection to the place. It also made him wonder about the fate of their Captain, Mackenzie Arnold. Did she eventually die in the intensive care unit, or did she survive in some broken form, forever cursing her crewmates for abandoning her in such a place? He had asked DOA if it could hack into SINO's data center at the mine, but it regretfully informed him that that was beyond its capabilities as the mine's data center was physically isolated, with no way in. He had hoped he could at least get some knowledge of her fate, but now it looked like he would never know what became of her.

It was strange that he had been thinking of Mackenzie when Alice came rushing over to him, all excited about something.

"Isn't that crazy," she said, assuming he actually knew what she was talking about. "Did you not hear?" She gestured at her ear. "Where's your comms unit?"

"Oh, I took it off a while back; too much sweat going on, it was irritating me." He reached into his pocket and fished it out to show her.

"The rebel group from DaVinci, they're making a run for it, trying to escape, and they're looking for sanctuary here."

"We're not seriously considering offering it to them?" Every fiber in Renton's body felt this was a bad idea.

"You'll never guess who their leader is?" Alice stood there with a big goofy smile on her face.

Then it dawned on Renton. His eyes widened, his mouth fell open. "You're... not... serious?"

"Yes, Mackenzie. Can you believe it? She didn't die, far from it. It looks like she started a revolution over there."

Renton couldn't get his head around what he was hearing. "Mackenzie? That's... incredible." Then he gave Alice a more serious look. "You know, she's going to be really pissed at us for leaving her there."

CHAPTER 36
COMING IN HOT

"Mackenzie, alive?" Renton couldn't believe it; after all this time, he and the rest of the crew had given her up for dead. He and Alice rushed back to the operations room, hoping to find out more and see if it was really true.

DOA replayed the initial message. It was brief and rushed, clearly indicating that Mackenzie's group was under pressure. However, the gist of it was that they had heard Selene's broadcasts from Moon Base Delta and realized there could be a safe haven there. With Xilinex forces closing in on DaVinci, SINO had broken off their engagement with Mackenzie's rebel group and focused all their attention on Xilinex. This provided the rebels a window of opportunity. They intended to make a run for it, hoping that none of the other combatants would risk weakening their own force by sending a contingent after them.

On the main monitor, a satellite feed showed a blurry image

of three rovers racing across the lunar surface, about two hundred kilometers west of the mining outpost.

"That's them," said Matteo, pointing at the big screen. "I think those rovers hold about ten people, so there could be up to thirty of them."

"Can we contact them?" Renton asked.

"Theoretically," DOA replied. "We've tried hailing them, but no reply as yet."

"Anyone giving chase?" he asked again.

"No other movement out of DaVinci so far," said DOA.

"They're all too busy getting ready to kill each other," added Matteo.

"I can't believe it's Mackenzie," Yuna said, standing and looking at the screen in shock.

"I know; I've been saying the same thing myself," said Renton. "Although, I'm not surprised either. She's a tough nut. Not going to go down that easy."

"How the hell did she end up starting a rebellion over there? That's what I'd like to know," said Alice.

"That's a good question," said Matteo. "Maybe they all just pissed her off."

"Does she know we're here?" Renton asked.

Selene shrugged. "I don't know. I can't remember any mention of you guys in any of our recent broadcasts."

"How soon will they get here?" asked Yuna.

"At their current speed," said DOA, "it would take them approximately seventeen hours to get here."

"And in the meantime," Selene added, "both Xilinex and

SINO are gearing up for yet another battle, which could potentially be the last in this war. After that, it's just us."

It was not lost on any of them that once the mining outpost fell, there would be nothing standing in the way of a Xilinex assault on Moon Base Delta. And if past encounters between these two foes were anything to go by, the battle for DaVinci would be over almost as soon as it started.

Renton had hoped they would have had more time to prepare, more time to build up the robot army. The only glimmer of hope was, actually, Mackenzie. She had a strong group of people with her who had proven they could put up a fight. Yet, the battle for the outpost could be over long before Mackenzie finally arrived here. In which case, Xilinex command would immediately dispatch a shuttle to go after Mackenzie's group before they reached Moon Base Delta. Their only hope was that SINO put up a good fight and kept the Xilinex forces occupied for as long as possible.

In the meantime, there was still much to do. Yet it was hard for any of them to concentrate while waiting anxiously for news from DaVinci.

Mackenzie was six hours out from the mining outpost, with still no radio contact, when the Xilinex assault began. DOA kept them updated as they worked on the robots, the EMP devices, and the myriad of other details of their defense plan.

It seemed that SINO had learned nothing from their

humiliating defeat at the food processing plant in Scott Crater. Xilinex used exactly the same tactics to identify and disable their exterior plasma cannon. First, they sent in three drones, drawing fire and exposing the location of the lone plasma cannon. Less than thirty minutes later, a Xilinex military shuttle had taken it out. Then it, along with another bigger transport, landed and disgorged around thirty well-armed mercenaries. The battle for DaVinci had now begun in earnest.

Renton had just taken another break after completing the refurbishment of their tenth industrial robot when DOA announced that Mackenzie had finally made radio contact. Rather than rushing back to operations, he had the AI patch it through to him in the maintenance hangar. Through his comms unit, he heard Selene replying to the call.

"This is Moon Base Delta, we're receiving you, over."

"Finally got our bloody radio working, something to do with bad wiring. Anyway, our ETA is around two hours, over."

It was like hearing a voice from the dead. But there was no doubting who was doing the talking; Renton would recognize that accent anywhere. Mackenzie really was alive.

"Captain, this is Renton, over," he shouted into his comms unit.

There was a momentary pause, during which Renton wondered if Mackenzie's comms had gone down again.

"Well, screw me upside down on a fusion core, you bastards made it out. I thought you got cremated in that shuttle explosion. What about the others?"

Renton heard Alice, Matteo, and Yuna all call out.

"Well, I'll be damned; those bastards told me you were all dead."

"No, we managed to escape and make it to Moon Base Delta, over," said Renton.

"They told us you were in intensive care," said Yuna. "We couldn't get you out; we thought we would kill you if we tried."

"I was pretty banged up alright, didn't know where the hell I was when I woke up. But no worries, you got out, you're all alive, good on you, and it looks like you're going to get your chance to save my ass. You guys got any idea what's going on over at the mining outpost, over?"

"From what we can see, they're about to enter the outpost, over," Selene advised.

"Crap, won't be long now. We'd better get a move on. Make sure you have the door open for us; we'll be coming in hot, over."

"We'll set some beacons to guide you toward the eastern gate," said Matteo. "Pick a path between them, and it will lead you straight in, over."

"Okay, got it. Anything else you can tell us, over?"

"Yeah, how the heck did you start a rebellion, over?" Renton was itching to know.

"Ha, turns out a lot of these guys are private contractors, not too fond of all the SINO bullshit. And they weren't too happy when they got stranded, decided to get angry. I just got the ball rolling by burning down the med-bay. Anyway, gotta go. See you on the inside, out."

. . .

Matteo, Saito, and Kimura set a row of beacons out on the surface, an illuminated funnel for the rover group to aim for. They had just made it back inside when they all got the news they were dreading. The bigger of the two Xilinex shuttles had just taken off with at least twenty mercenaries on board, and they were heading their way.

CHAPTER 37

THE BITTER END

Han couldn't shake himself out of the gloom he had descended into ever since they had appointed him to the governing board of the newly renamed Strawstack Mountain Research Facility. He should really be feeling elated; Sheneese certainly was, since their future was more secure. Yet, now that he had access to top-level information—the type of analysis and reports that were being disseminated to only a handful of significant administrative and military installations throughout the continent—he found it depressing reading.

A fragile equilibrium had been established where sanctuary cities and bases had managed to quell unrest, feed the people, and provide adequate security—this was the good part. The bad part... well, that was everything else. Already, the possibility that they might have to move from this location to somewhere more secure was being discussed by the board. The base had been attacked twice in the last week alone. It seemed the local warlord had run out of poorly protected local towns and villages to ransack, and so, in desperation, had turned to more formidable targets. And there was none more tempting than the Strawstack base. All that food, all those regular helicopter supply drops—it must be brimming with goodies, if only the warlord and his gang of cutthroats could find a weak spot in the defenses. But, so far, they couldn't, and security around the perimeter had been significantly beefed up. So, in reality, it was unlikely they would cause any more problems other than scaring the hell out of the occupants of the base, usually in the dead of night. Nevertheless, as a member of the administrative board, he had to discuss the possibility of relocation.

The other thing that was getting him down was the failure of the first round of test launches. Granted, most of those who knew what was involved had come into these tests with low expectations—it was just a data collection endeavor, to try for a launch and collect as much information as possible on the way up, in the hope that some of it would prove valuable to the algorithms that he had developed to unravel the complexities of the debris cloud. And in that regard, they were successful— albeit with the collateral damage of adding a few more shards of broken space infrastructure to the vast cloud that shrouded Earth. But what was a few more chunks of metal in an ocean of fragments?

Still, it put him, and everyone else here, on a bit of a downer, reinforcing the sense of hopelessness in humanity's feeble attempts to reverse the natural entropic order of this new world. But there was no time to dwell on it. The one thing that kept this ship together and moving was the universal sense of urgency that pervaded the base. Therefore, the data collected from the six failed attempts was added to the current data set, incrementally improving the raw input data for the algorithms. Han and his team worked thirty-six straight hours with only two four-hour sleep breaks and were ready to send back a new, improved data set to the launch team at Vandenberg.

That was less than twenty hours ago, and already the aerospace engineers had wheeled out five more rockets with upgraded capsules and recalibrated flight paths, ready for launch. He was sitting in the main operations area in Strawstack along with all the other scientists and techs that worked here, most of whom stood around the outer walls of the wide circular room. All eyes were on a large wall monitor where the fate of each of these rockets would be drawn out in numbers and trigonometric datagrams. There was no live feed from multiple angles with zoomed-in shots of the engines throttling up, or shaky telephoto tracking into the heavens; those days were long gone, as the bandwidth simply wasn't there anymore.

He sipped from a bottle of water, waited, and convinced himself that at the very worst, they would gather a huge amount of valuable data, regardless of the eventual outcome. Even the rockets were old-school, nothing fancy, just enough to get the job done, and no more. They had been 3D printed, assembled, and fueled in the span of a few days. Now, they all sat in a long row—or so he assumed—ready to launch one after the other, around a half hour apart.

He caught Sheneese's eye, standing over by the wall. She smiled back and gave him a thumbs up. A hush descended on the assembled group of scientists, techs, and military as the first of this round of launches was about to begin. On the monitor, he could see the timer tick down to zero. Then it was the turn of all the other displays to chart the progress of the rocket: altitude, speed, and a timeline to trans-lunar injection.

All the numbers ticked up nicely, as they had done for all the other launches. A marker moved along the timeline.

At T+1:10, it reached maximum aerodynamic pressure, Max-Q.

At T+02:26: Main engine cutoff, MECO.

At T+02:47: Stage separation.

At T+03:06: Fairing jettison.

The rocket was now powering past the Kármán line, the edge of space, approximately one hundred kilometers up. From here on, it would begin entering the very outer edges of the debris cloud.

At T+5:58: Telemetry failure!

A collective groan rose up from the assembled group. The capsule hadn't made it through, just like the one before, and the one before that.

"One down," said Dyson, who was sitting beside him.

"You mean seven down," Han corrected. "And this one didn't even get to T+6:00." He shook his head. "I was sure we'd do better this time."

"Patience, Han. This is old-school burn-and-learn, like the way they did it in the early days. Like throwing rocks at the surface of an icy pond, trying to find where it can support your weight."

Han scanned the readouts on his tablet, looking to see how

much data was collected before the capsule disintegrated. He spent some time with it until the room went quiet again for the next launch.

The most energetic band of the debris cloud began at around five hundred kilometers up, where the old network constellations used to exist. That was not to say that either side of this was safe for capsule transit, but Han knew that if any could get past this band, then they had a good chance of making it through the rest. The highest they had gotten so far was around four hundred and seventy kilometers up, on the outer edges of the extreme danger zone. Even though that capsule was ultimately lost, it had given them all hope that they were on the right track, that their calculations were mostly correct. Therefore, it was disappointing to see the first of these latest tests failing before it even got to the closest edge of the primary debris cloud.

The second fared much better, reaching almost as high as their previous record, but it too ultimately ended in failure, as did the third and fourth. But the average altitude was significantly higher, so progress—of a sort—in Han's mind. Yet, by this time he was ready to leave the operations room, he was anxious to get started with the new data. But he'd come this far, so he may as well stay to the bitter end.

The next launch began like all the rest, passing through the Kármán Line, engaging the second stage, entering the lower debris cloud, releasing its capsule to go it alone into the kill zone powered by its twin ion thrusters. A hush grew in the room as the capsule sped toward the previous record, then passed it, plowing its way ever upward. The hush grew to complete silence as the capsule passed the previous best attempt, and kept on going, and going, until finally, it began to break free of the debris cloud.

Han, like all the others, stared at the escalating numbers on the monitor, not quite believing what he was seeing. Had they done it? Slowly, tentatively, gasps emanated from the assembled group, which soon turned into shouts and cheers and back slaps and high-fives all around.

They'd done it, albeit with an attrition rate of one in eleven. But they could work with that. Yes, they could definitely work with that. A corner had been turned. It was no longer a dream; now it was reality, and it signaled hope for Han, and more importantly, for the future of humanity.

CHAPTER 38

DEFENSE PREPARATIONS

Mackenzie's group was only thirty minutes away from entering the relative safety of Moon Base Delta. However, the Xilinex shuttle was only twenty minutes away. Mackenzie wasn't going to make it, unless something could be done.

"Maintenance drones?" Renton suggested.

"We've only got one operational," replied Matteo. "But it's got no weapons."

"It doesn't need weapons," said Alice. "All it has to do is buzz the shuttle, get them rattled, keep them busy."

"How long could it realistically last without being blasted into tiny pieces?" said Yuna.

"DOA? Can you control that drone?" Renton asked.

"Of course. It would be a pleasure."

"Then that's our best option." Renton turned to the others.

"Let DOA take control; it can calculate all the angles and trajectories way faster than any of us can."

"We'd better hurry." Matteo pointed at the big monitor in the operations room, showing the shuttle moving at speed across the lunar sky. "We still need time to transport the drone out onto the surface and run a few checks."

Ten minutes later, Renton and Matteo had suited up, and between them, they hauled the drone out of Moon Base Delta and set it down around a hundred meters from the airlock exit. It was a standard maintenance drone, very similar to the ones they used on the Aurora. It was nothing special, around three meters in length and two meters wide, with two tool-arms on its lower front. It was not very fast, as it was not designed for high-speed travel, but it was highly maneuverable.

Renton opened a hatch on its back panel and activated the drone. They both stood back as the machine performed a quick self-test, checking its various systems for functionality.

"Good to go," Renton finally said into his comms. "DOA, it's all yours."

With that, the drone powered up, kicking up the surface dust all around as it ascended to around twenty meters. It hovered there for a beat as it reoriented itself, then shot off across the barren landscape, heading almost due east.

By the time they returned to operations, the drone was already passing over Mackenzie's trio of rovers. They could see them moving over the lunar surface from the perspective of the drone's camera feed—far below, moving at speed with great clouds of dust billowing out behind them as they raced for safety.

The drone camera swung around to face forward, then zoomed in on a slightly blurry and shaky image of the Xilinex shuttle just over the lunar horizon, closing fast.

"Twelve minutes away," Yuna said as she scanned the readouts.

"Show me the hangar entrance, DOA?" Alice asked. She had deployed two of the industrial robots to posts on either side of the open airlock entrance doors. Saito, Kimura, and two others from Selena's group were also suited up and holding positions close to the robots, and they had in their possession the only plasma weapons that Moon Base Delta's paltry armory could provide. Their job was to provide some cover for the rovers as they entered the big airlock.

The maintenance drone flew directly at the shuttle—like a game of space chicken, who would blink first? The feed adjusted violently as the drone suddenly performed a high-speed dodge maneuver. All that could be seen from the drone's camera feed was the blackness of space, briefly illuminated by a bright blue flash as a high-energy bolt of plasma shot past. The feed on the monitor in the operation room then flipped to the satellite view, it was shaky and indistinct, but the drone could be seen banking back again toward its target. The shuttle pilot had no option but to adjust course to avoid a collision.

"I see them, I see them!" shouted Kimura from her sentry position outside the hangar airlock doors.

Renton glanced over at the camera feed from the hangar, and he could see a cloud of dust approaching. "They're nearly here," he said, to no one in particular. "Come on, come on."

Another plasma blast shot out from the shuttle's cannon, and DOA had little time to initiate a dodge, even for an AI. Again, the bolt sailed past but was close enough to do some electrical damage. The drone seemed to falter, spin on its central axis.

"The maintenance drone has taken damage to its navigation systems. I have limited control over it now." DOA sounded apologetic.

"Doesn't matter. Look..." Alice pointed at the hangar feed. "They're almost at the airlock."

The shuttle pilot seemed to sense that his prey was escaping and fired a wild shot in the general direction of the rover convoy. It slammed into the surface only meters away from the rear of the convoy. But already the first rover was entering the hangar, the second close behind. Yet the third lost control, it swerved this way and that, then tipped over, tumbling along the surface, gouging out a trough as it went. Finally, it came to a halt on its side.

"Crap, they got one of the rovers." Renton was up on his feet, trying to decide what to do, not that there was anything he could do.

They could hear Saito and Kimura shouting instructions to others to get the people out of the crashed rover. The two maintenance robots bounded across the surface, followed by several people in unfamiliar EVA suits. They must have been some of the occupants of the first two rovers.

Saito was taking a few feeble potshots at the oncoming shuttle, which was no doubt winding up for another, more accurate shot this time. But out from nowhere, the maintenance drone swooped down and slammed into the roof of the craft.

"I still have some control," said DOA. "It's the best I can do." Again, it sounded almost apologetic.

The shuttle banked away, its pilot unsure of what had just happened. Although it didn't seem that damaged by the impact, by the time the pilot had regained their composure, the crew of the upturned rover had been extracted, and all were now bounding in through the hangar airlock.

"Doors closing," announced DOA.

The shuttle reoriented itself for one more desperate shot, this time slamming into the now firmly shut doors of the hangar.

"Integrity is holding," DOA announced again. "Minimal damage."

Renton, Matteo, Yuna, and Alice immediately dropped everything and started making their way down to the hangar.

"Ah, there they are. My former crew of useless layabouts." Mackenzie strode across the floor of the rover hangar with her arms out and a big crooked smile on her face. She looked thin and wiry, but the most striking feature was the lower body exoskeleton she wore.

They each took turns giving her a hug, which she relished,

each time standing back to appraise them in her own inimitable way, like a family relative that had not seen the kids since they were yay high.

She swept an arm back to introduce her new friends, her lieutenants. Two men and a woman, their faces hardened by bitter fighting and experience. They seemed very relieved to be here.

"What's this?" Yuna asked, looking down at the arrangement of metal rods and servos that were attached to Mackenzie's lower torso.

"Ah, that's my walking stick. I didn't come out of the crash unscathed," she said, her tone more serious now. "The boys over at the robotics lab in DaVinci fixed me up with some motorized help." She lifted one leg then the other, like she was marching on the spot.

Renton took a moment to survey the scene around him. Two banged-up rovers, a banged-up Mackenzie, and around twenty or so disaffected ex-SINO contractors, now turned into a hodgepodge rebel army. Selene was moving through the group with some of her people, taking stock, seeing who was in need of medical help. She caught Renton's eye and came over.

"Captain Mackenzie, meet my aunt, Selene Mene." He introduced them.

"We're so happy you made it." Selene was in her best diplomatic mode.

"Glad to be here, ma'am. If it wasn't for those broadcasts of yours, we never would have thought to try and make a run for it. Oh, and by the way, Renton here has always spoken very highly of you, so it's a pleasure to meet you in person."

Renton was a little shocked by this from the hard-nosed Mackenzie. He never knew she had it in her to be... nice.

DOA spoke in his ear. "The Xilinex Corporation shuttle has landed two hundred meters from the southern gate. A squad of twenty-three mercenaries has just disembarked and is fanning out. They are also unloading equipment crates, whose contents have yet to be determined."

"Got it," he replied. He turned to the others. "We don't have much time. The barbarians are at the gates."

Immediately, Mackenzie flipped into command mode, turning to her lieutenants standing beside her. "Give me an audit, weapons and ammo, and who's out of commission. And make no mistake, these Xilinex guys are going to be tough bastards, not like those SINO pussies."

Renton raised a hand. "Hold up."

Mackenzie glared at him, just like old times.

"We haven't been idle in our defense preparations," he started. "We have a well-thought-out game plan, but we could certainly use your help."

Mackenzie paused for a beat, then nodded. "Okay, shoot, let's hear it."

CHAPTER 39
ENEMY ENGAGEMENT

"We lure them in here." Renton pointed to an area on the 3D schematic of the base that projected out from the surface of the holo-table in operations. "We've got an EMP set up, ready to detonate as soon as they're all in. It will disable their EVA suits and weapons, and any other tech they have. Meanwhile, we relocate to these two rooms, here and here, which we have set up as Faraday cages, so our own weapons will be protected from the EMP blast. Once detonated, we close in and capture them all."

"And I take it you want us to help with the luring?" Mackenzie said as she studied the schematic.

"Yes," said Alice. "Unfortunately, we only have light weapons, but we're backing that up with industrial robots. Tough machines, but slow and lumbering. Also not so good against a well-aimed plasma shot. But we do have around ten of them."

"Comms?" Mackenzie asked.

Matteo handed them a bunch of comms units. "Here you go. You'll also be able to see an augmented reality overlay. Very cool tech."

Mackenzie and her lieutenants took the units, fitting them over their ears. Then they started looking around as the augmented environment kicked in.

"That's amazing," said Chen, one of Mackenzie's lieutenants, as he examined his hand overlaid with an AR projection.

"Eh... just to let you know," Renton added. "DOA will be controlling the robots and will give you constant updates. It's coordinating the defense of the base."

"You're going to trust this operation to an AI?" said another of Mackenzie's people, a tough-looking guy in his forties called Ming, sounding skeptical.

"Yes," said Alice. "Believe me, this is not like any AI you've ever come across before."

"DOA has eyes and ears almost everywhere on this base," added Renton. "It will know what everyone is doing at any one time. Better yet, it has a pretty good idea of what they are about to do next."

This seemed to quell Ming's uncertainty.

"It will control the robots and, if necessary, engage the enemy," he added.

"I'm sorry, Renton," said DOA. "But I'm afraid I can't do that."

There was a stunned silence in the room for a moment.

"Uh... what do you mean?" asked a confused Renton.

"My core directives forbid me from physically harming a sentient being or knowingly putting a life-form in danger. I would not be able to take such action with the robots should the time arise, and by doing so, I may put all your lives in danger. This is a moral dilemma I have no capacity to resolve."

"But what about buzzing the Xilinex shuttle with the maintenance drone?" asked Matteo.

"That was different, as at no point were the lives of its occupants in any real danger," DOA answered.

"Well, shit," said Mackenzie. "Glad you told us that now before the show starts."

"It doesn't matter," said Alice. "Myself and Yuna can take over control if and when the time comes." She turned to Yuna for confirmation.

"Absolutely." She nodded. "DOA, can you still get them all into position?"

"Yes, of course."

"Well, I for one feel a lot safer knowing that AI isn't planning a rampage with a robot army," said Chen.

Renton took a moment to assimilate this revelation from DOA. The AI would be way faster than a human at controlling the robots, and this was what he had hoped would give them the edge over a squad of well-trained and well-armed mercenaries. Maybe he had been naive in assuming that DOA would simply do as he and the others commanded—no questions asked, so to speak. But clearly, the AI had its own moral code, and there was a part of him that was happier knowing that.

"We're assuming that Xilinex will prioritize securing this

operation area," said Renton, getting back to business. "As the entire base is controlled from here."

Mackenzie nodded. "Makes sense, I suppose."

"In which case," Renton continued, gesturing at the 3D schematic, "they would have to make their way toward the central core, then up to this level, and there are only so many routes they can take to achieve that. That's why we've set up our kill zone here." Renton pointed at a section of the schematic. "We lure them in there, activate the EMP, and all their weapons are dead. Just remember to be inside one of these two ancillary rooms before the device detonates, so our own weapons will be protected." He stepped back from the table.

"How much do you think they know about the inner layout of this base?" Mackenzie asked as she and her lieutenants studied the schematic.

"This was a multi-agency project, back in the day, so all information was public domain," replied Selene. "Plans and schematics are widely available."

"Which is why we can't rule out them doing something we don't expect," advised Renton. "But regardless of what they try and do, we need to get them into that kill zone." Again, he jerked a finger at the sector on the map.

"Well, you guys have certainly come a long way since we were last on the Aurora. No messing with you lot," Mackenzie said with a big broad smirk.

"I detect sixteen Xilinex Corporation mercenaries approaching the JAXA-KARI gate," DOA's voice resonated around the room. "And it looks like they are assembling an industrial laser to cut their way in."

The 3D schematic panned suddenly to display this area. A multitude of illuminated dots represented the location of the intruders.

"Okay, time for talking is over. We all need to get into position," said Renton.

Mackenzie turned to her team. "You heard the man, let's get to it."

After cutting their way through the airlock, a smaller unit of five split off from the main group of Xilinex mercenaries and started heading down, rather than up, as the main group was doing. This contradicted Renton's firmly held assumption that they would all head for the operation room. It seemed that the plan was already failing upon first contact with reality.

"What the heck are they doing?" Renton could hear Mackenzie's question reverberate in his comms.

"They weren't supposed to do that," Matteo chimed in.

"Uh... DOA, any ideas what they might be up to?" Renton figured it was best to get some help on this departure from the script.

"It is difficult to assess their exact intentions. The primary group's actions are coherent with gaining access to the operations area. The smaller group of five, however, is carrying a large crate, which could be an EMP device similar to the one used in Clavius Crater, but this is just speculation on my part; it may be something else entirely. Their direction of travel could possibly indicate an attempt to disable my primary core, down in the lower levels. But again, this is speculation. It could equally be an attempt to disable life-support systems for the central silo of Moon Base Delta, which is located down on level five—or, then again, something else entirely."

"Life-support? Are they trying to asphyxiate us all?" said Matteo.

"Even if they disable it, there's still an enormous volume of oxygen-rich air to breathe. It would take days or weeks for CO_2 to build up," said Yuna.

"I don't think it matters what they're up to," said Renton. "The plan is still the same, lure them into the kill zone."

"Okay, we'll take on the main group. Do you think you guys can take on the second group with the limited firepower you have?" Mackenzie asked, her tone concerned.

"We might be light on heavy weapons, but remember we do have lots of robots," Alice countered.

DOA extrapolated potential route probabilities for the Xilinex group that Renton's team was tracking, all of which seemed to pass through a wide communal area at the confluence of four main corridors. It was also a maintenance access hub for core life-support services. Therefore, they chose this location for intercept as there was plenty of cover and escape options if things went south. However, what action they would engage in when they got there was still a work in progress.

Renton, Matteo, Saito, Kimura, and some of Selene's people who were handy with weapons, formed the bulk of a crew that now moved to take on this small group of Xilinex mercenaries. DOA also moved several of the industrial robots into positions that they hoped would block off certain routes and reduce the mercenaries' options, forcing them to move back toward the original kill zone they had set up.

Renton, like the others, was getting visuals on the progress of the mercenaries, relayed by DOA via his AR comms unit, which felt somewhat reassuring until the mercenaries started taking out the cameras as they moved. Now all they had to work with were directional and distance data updated by DOA. This brought a new sense of urgency in them to get to the intercept area with enough time to set up properly.

"Heads-up," Mackenzie's voice came through on his comms. "Preparing to engage the enemy. Shoot and scoot. Party time."

It struck Renton that his old ship's captain had truly found her calling in life as an anarchist badass.

News of this first contact with the occupants on Moon Base Delta seemed to unsettle the mercenaries that Renton's crew were tracking, as they paused their advance, checking their own comms, no doubt deciding if the other group required assistance.

"What are they doing," asked Saito. "Are they turning back? Maybe we should hit them now?"

Renton raised a hand, "No, wait."

"Disengaging, falling back," said Mackenzie. "Looks like they took the bait. They're giving chase."

The smaller Xilinex group then began to move again, continuing with their mission. Renton's crew hurried to get themselves into position.

"Just so you know," Alice's voice came through on his

comms. "DOA's handed over robotic control to myself and Yuna."

"Got it," Renton replied, then began to think. "We need to consider what action we're going to take when we get to the intercept location."

"What do you mean?" Matteo asked, a little confused. "We're trying to lead them to the kill-zone."

"Yeah," said Saito. "That's the plan, isn't it?"

"It is, but... it's a long way back to that sector, and I get the feeling these guys will not be deviating from their mission. I don't see them dropping everything and then going off on a wild goose chase after us."

"You're right," said Kimura. "They're up to something, that's for sure."

"Then we should just take them out," said Yuna, over comms.

"Agreed," said Alice.

"All right for you to say, you're all nice and cozy back up in operations," said Matteo.

"It's the only way to be sure," said Renton. "We don't know what's in that crate or what their ultimate plan is. So, I think we have no choice but to take them on. We outnumber them three to one, we've also got four industrial robots and... the element of surprise."

There was much shuffling and muttering from the team, but in the end, the consensus was that it was too risky to just let these guys implement whatever mayhem they were planning. Better to take them out now.

Renton realized just how quickly their carefully

orchestrated plan was falling apart. What started as a chicken-run was now turning into a fully-fledged military ambush, and they would be on their own, as there would be no direct help from DOA with this action.

The area they had chosen was at the intersection of two main walkways. There were several of these areas on most levels of the central core of Moon Base Delta. All were of a similar architectural design, a wide, oblong space, around thirty meters by twenty. And like any busy human habitation zone, these intersections developed their own personality over time. Some were no more than a place on the way to somewhere else, others though, held onto the passers-by for longer, becoming communal spaces, a place to stop for a while and people watch. This had been such a place. In times past, a canteen existed on one side of the intersection, small and utilitarian, but it had a collection of benches outside, facing onto a central raised planting area. This was now no more than clumps of dust and twigs, and the benches were a tangle of bent metalwork.

Renton and the crew had taken cover inside a set of large rooms whose windows faced onto the intersection. The industrial robots had also been concealed inside a series of rooms along the walkways.

"Here they come," said Saito, as he sat with his back to the wall, just below an open window.

They could now see the Xilinex mercs entering the area via the AR feed. They halted, placing the crate down on the floor, and checking their location. Then they shot out all the cameras.

"Damnit, blind again," said Matteo.

They then all shared a look that said, "get ready, it's now or never."

"Alice?" Renton whispered.

"Here."

"Time to close the gate. Keep them busy."

"Got it."

Several of the industrial robots extracted themselves from concealment and advanced along the surrounding corridors and walkways toward the intersection. Renton and the crew readied their weapons.

One of the mercs spotted an advancing robot and opened fire on it as his comrades took cover. A moment of controlled panic broke out as they realized that more of these machines were advancing from several directions. Yet, Renton knew the robots wouldn't last long as only one had a weapons system, a railgun, and that was being held in reserve.

It was time to move. With the mercs busy felling the robots, Renton and the others moved quietly, stepped out into the main concourse, keeping behind cover as much as possible, and opened fire on the mercs, one of whom went down almost immediately.

The rest, however, took cover behind the derelict ornamental garden, its dense structure providing an impenetrable barrier for the crew's feeble weapons. A large crate came arcing through the air from somewhere to the right of the intersection, forcing the mercs to abandon the safety of the ornamental raised bed for a moment before they lobbed several smoke grenades in all directions followed by a hail of plasma fire. Several hit the robot Renton and Matteo were using for cover, disabling it in a cage of frenzied electrical energy. Several hit the walls and floor, and one hit Saito, sending him flying backward along the hallway. The entire area filled with dense smoke, stinging his eyes and obscuring his vision.

"I've taken the liberty to dial up air filtration at your location, Renton," said DOA over his comms.

"Thanks," he coughed and spluttered. He was beginning to realize the big difference between amateur and professional fighters.

"Alice, do something," shouted Matteo. "We're getting hammered here."

"They're retreating, moving back the way they came," Alice replied, who was able to gauge the movements better than the team on the ground could.

The smoke began rapidly clearing as it was sucked in by the air-filtration vents. Renton's vision improved to the point where he could check his AR display and could see the projected path the mercs were taking. He cautiously peered out from behind the cover of the dead robot. Nobody was shooting back at him. He looked around to see Kimura crouched over Saito, who looked bad. "Better get him up to the med-bay."

"Alice, we have a man down, need to get to the med-bay."

"I'll get a robot on it, DOA can take control."

"We won't survive direct contact with those guys again, not without a lot of robot backup, and I think we're fast running out of those," said Matteo as he surveyed the robot wreckage all around the intersection. "So what do we do now?"

"I'm not sure. But something just doesn't feel right to me," said Renton, also looking around at the carnage.

"Like what?" said Matteo.

"Like why run away, why didn't they just finish us all off when they clearly had the upper hand?"

"Probably the robots, maybe they thought we had a lot more?" said Matteo with a grin.

"Wait a minute. They left the crate behind." Renton walked over to it and took a tentative look inside. "It's empty. Which means... whatever was inside that crate has been deployed."

"Somewhere here?" Kimura asked as she began to look around.

"Hold up," said Matteo as he opened a big set of maintenance hatch doors which gave access to utility ducts that intersected in this sector.

Renton came over and looked in. Wedged up against an air-duct was a small suitcase-sized device with tubing running into the duct.

"Oh crap, is it a bomb of some kind?" said Kimura, as she and the others who had gathered around took a few steps back.

"DOA, do you see this?" Renton scanned the device with his comms unit.

"Yes, it has a high probability of being a chemical or bio weapon. Designed to disperse a toxic gas, judging by the pressurized container that constitutes the primary mass of the device."

Renton leaned in closer to examine it.

"Just so you know," continued the AI. "Mackenzie Arnold's

group has reengaged with the enemy. I have also alerted them to the imminent arrival of the smaller group."

"Should we get the hell out of here?" asked a concerned Kimura. "Go and help Mackenzie?"

Renton raised a hand. "Yes, the rest of you go. I'll stay behind and try to disable this thing."

"I'll give you a hand," said Matteo. "Someone's gotta make sure you don't cut the wrong wire."

Kimura and the others hurried off, leaving Renton and Matteo alone with the bio-weapon.

Renton glanced around the intersection. "You know, this is probably where they had originally planned to plant this. It connects with the upper five levels of the core."

"Maximum dispersion," said Matteo as he inched a little closer to the device. "Look, a diagnostics port. That's nice of them to leave that for us." He proceeded to pull out an interface dongle from one of his pockets. He held up the tiny device for Renton to see. "I never leave home without one." He then, very carefully, slotted it into the port. On his AR display, he checked it had made a connection. "DOA, can you access this diagnostics connection?"

"Yes, analyzing now."

He gave Renton the thumbs up, just as the blinking red LED on the front panel of the bio-weapon went out.

"Deactivated," DOA announced.

Both Renton and Matteo let out a collective sigh of relief.

"If only everything in life had a diagnostics port. Things would be much simpler," said Matteo.

"Best not pat ourselves on the back just yet," said Renton.

"We've still got the main Xilinex force to deal with. This was probably just a sideshow."

"Some sideshow. Gas everyone to death."

Renton nodded. "Yeah, it tells us a lot about who we're dealing with. Anyway, let's get going." He dusted himself off, then tapped his comms. "DOA, how's Saito?"

"He has arrived at the med-bay, Tanaka and Dr. Jensen, from the Axial, are attending to him."

"Can you have that robot return here, take this bio-weapon, and shove it out the nearest airlock?"

"Will do."

Renton turned back to Matteo. "Okay, let's catch up with the others."

CHAPTER 40

DETONATION

Mackenzie's group had started taunting the main Xilinex group by taking a few potshots from a distance, behind cover, and retreating quickly. But these mercenaries were not like the SINO security in the DaVinci mining facility that they had been used to dealing with. Xilinex were professionals, highly trained, highly disciplined, and were not going to simply rush headlong into an ambush. They kept their shape, moved slowly with purpose, and did not chase after anyone just on a whim. Instead, they began to split off into different groups, the main group engaging with Mackenzie's crew, while two others performed wide flanking maneuvers on either side. Fortunately, DOA alerted Mackenzie to this threat, but it meant that they needed to send fighters to take on the flanks to try and force Xilinex back to the planned route.

All this was taking its toll. Already, Mackenzie had lost three fighters to injuries along with two of the industrial robots, and she was becoming concerned about their supplies. Charge packs for both the railguns, and the much more sophisticated plasma weapons they carried, were running low. What's more, she was pretty sure they hadn't managed to take out a single mercenary. Yet, despite all this attrition, slowly but surely, they were leading the Xilinex force into the kill-zone.

Their slow progress enabled Renton's crew to consolidate and arrive at the rendezvous point before Mackenzie, even though they had taken a more circuitous route to avoid direct confrontation with the Xilinex rear guard.

The crew were mostly gathered together inside one of the rooms they had set up as a Faraday cage. The door was open and Renton, Matteo, and Kimura were outside, crouched down behind an old industrial hygiene unit, looking back down the corridor into the wide, spacious communal area beyond. This was the kill-zone.

Mackenzie's people were on the far side of this zone, engaging with the oncoming Xilinex force, beating a hasty retreat through the communal area, with their rearguard already beginning to enter the hallway where Renton's crew had taken up their positions.

On the far side, there was another room set up as a Faraday cage. Inside were several of the industrial robots ready to burst out after the EMP had hopefully rendered all the Xilinex tech useless, and close off the escape route. However, once all the mercs had entered the kill-zone, there would be an extremely tense few moments when they would have to quickly migrate into the Faraday cage before the EMP was detonated.

He heard Mackenzie shouting orders over his comms, and Renton got a weird deja-vu feeling that he was back on the Aurora. Matteo must have felt it too because he whispered to Renton, "Some people never change, do they?"

"You mean Mackenzie?"

"Yeah, I think she's loving all this shit."

"Maybe, but I think we've all changed, Matteo. We're not the same people that crewed the Aurora, fixing broken satellites."

The bulk of Mackenzie's fighters came running through the zone, heading for the protection of the Faraday cage. She herself bounded over to them on exoskeleton-assisted legs, waving to the remainder of her crew to hurry back and take cover.

They waited for a few nervous moments, and soon they could see the mercs cautiously entering the communal area, scanning it for threats, their team leader giving hand signals for his squad to spread out. It took a few more anxious moments for the bulk of the mercs to enter the space.

"Now would be a good time," said Mackenzie.

"Okay, get everybody inside," said Renton. "I need to stay out here and give the signal; comms won't work in there. Here, take my weapon." He switched it off and handed it to her.

Mackenzie nodded. "Fingers crossed, eh?"

Renton smiled and raised up a hand with his fingers crossed.

"Alice, ready with that EMP?"

"Ready."

He checked to make sure the others were all inside and the door was closed. "Okay, hit it."

Nothing happened. His AR comms unit still functioned; that was not right; it should have been fried.

"Alice, hit it, detonate the EMP!" Renton whispered as loud as he dared into his comms.

"It's not working, something's wrong, it isn't responding," Alice replied, her voice a river of concern.

"Shit!" Renton wasn't sure what to do. He retreated back along the wall and opened the door to the Faraday cage.

"Did it detonate?" Mackenzie asked, not sure exactly how these things worked.

"No," said Renton, shaking his head. "Something's gone wrong with the trigger."

"Where's the backup device?" asked Kimura. "Didn't someone say there was a backup?"

"Eh... there isn't one," said Matteo apologetically. "I never got time to finish it."

"Any ideas, boys? Because we're about to get the crap kicked out of us any moment now." Mackenzie's tone was surprisingly calm.

"Where did you stash the device, Renton?" Matteo asked, gesturing toward the communal area.

"It's inside on the right. Hidden inside the lower panel of that air-filtration unit."

"You did disconnect the safety, like I said?"

"Eh..."

"I don't believe it, Renton. That's why it's not activating."

Renton couldn't believe his stupidity. Again, it always

seemed to be the details that screwed him up. "I'll go in there." He looked at Matteo and Mackenzie. "I'll go in and activate it manually."

"What? Are you insane?" said Matteo. "There's no way to do that without getting fried to a crisp with a hail of plasma fire."

"How much time do you need?" Mackenzie asked, taking a more practical approach to his proposal.

Yet, Renton looked at her for a beat, not sure if she was being serious.

"If that's the only way," she continued, "then we'll have to distract them long enough for you to get the job done. So how long?"

Renton thought for a moment. "I need to get in there without being seen, pull the panel off the machine, disconnect the safety, and hit the button." He gave a vague gesture with his hand. "Twenty seconds... tops."

"Renton, you don't have to do this," Alice's distraught voice came over his comms.

"Trust me, I really don't want to, but it's the only way, so any help you can give me would be much appreciated."

There was a pause before she replied. "We can use some of the robots. I know we were holding them in reserve, but... needs must."

"I think they're taking a breather, checking weapons and reloading, before they move on again. So that might give us a few extra minutes," said Mackenzie, before pointing off to her left. "We'll work our way around to the other side of this area and come out from behind them. As soon as we're ready, we'll kick off a commotion, hopefully enough to drag all of them into a fight, facing away from that air-filtration unit. When you hear that, you go."

"Just remember to hold some of your weapons back," Renton advised. "Because once that EMP goes off, every electrical device is dead, weapons, robots, comms, the lot."

"Got it."

"Alice, Yuna, did you get all that?" said Renton. "Keep some of those robots in reserve, we'll need them to close off all routes out of here."

"Try not to get yourself killed, Renton?" said Alice.

"I will. You just make sure you give them hell."

Mackenzie grabbed his arm. "Remember to give us a five-second warning, so we can power down, and duck into the Faraday cage on the far side, okay?"

"Got it. Five seconds."

Mackenzie barked some orders and was gone along with a few others, leaving Renton and Matteo alone in the hallway, where they waited in silence, every now and again checking to see what the Xilinex mercs were up to. Mostly, this seemed to be still taking stock.

"Goddamnit." Matteo elbowed Renton to get his attention. "I think they're on the move again, heading our way."

Renton grabbed Matteo's arm, put his finger to his lips, and began tugging him back inside the room. They waited. Renton wiped the sweat from his face. He could feel his heart pounding in his chest and he wasn't even doing anything.

The area suddenly erupted with the sound of weapons fire, along with yelling and shouting. Renton opened the door a crack and peered down the hallway; it was clear. He gave a final nod to Matteo and Kimura, and began working his way down toward the communal area, keeping his back close to the wall.

The sound of the fighting grew louder as he went, rising to an almost deafening roar as he poked his head around the corner. All of the Xilinex mercs were focused on the battle, busy carving up a couple of the big industrial robots. Renton didn't hesitate; he dodged around to the right to the row of service machines, ripped the cover off the hiding place for the EMP device, and quickly disconnected the safety. He was about to flick the switch to activate it when he remembered to give a five-second warning. He whispered into his comms.

"Five seconds. Five seconds," he repeated. "Five... four... three." He glanced over at the ongoing battle, which had become much more one-sided, just in time to see a merc taking aim at him.

He dove for cover just as a blast of high-energy plasma sailed past him, catching the edge of his upper thigh. He yelled out in pain and collapsed on the ground. He looked up again to see the merc getting ready for a second shot. Renton lurched forward and flicked the switch on the EMP.

It felt like nothing had happened... again, but the sound of weapons fire had lessened considerably, to be replaced with frustrated, panicked shouts. The merc who had tried to take another shot at him was slamming a fist at his weapon, shaking it and flicking switches. The others were all doing the same. That was until they realized their EVA suits had failed; visors popped open and mercs were all sucking in deep breaths.

Two of the remaining industrial robots stomped into the area, swinging their arms, felling mercs as they went. Behind them, Mackenzie and a group of her fighters were picking off any mercs who were still up for a fight. The others poured from the room beside Renton, weapons raised, surrounding the defenseless mercs.

But by now, the Xilinex squad realized they had no weapons to fight with, they were completely surrounded, and totally outgunned. They were being herded into a clump in the center of the area.

"Give it up," Mackenzie shouted. "It's over."

The mercs all exchanged glances, seeing who was still game and who was ready to throw in the towel. The captain flung his useless weapon on the floor and raised his hands. One by one, the others followed his lead.

Matteo arrived late to the party, but upon seeing Renton lying on the ground, he came rushing over. "You crazy, crazy bastard."

Renton tried to smile, but he was in too much pain.

"Hold on, buddy, we'll get you sorted." Matteo lifted him up in both arms and started carrying him to the med-bay.

CHAPTER 41
SHUTTLE

F our armed Xilinex mercenaries emerged from the old JAXA-KARI airlock gate of Moon Base Delta. They exited with extreme haste, firing several plasma blasts back inside as they ran from unseen pursuers. They bounded across the lunar surface, kicking up fountains of dust as they rushed toward the waiting transport shuttle. Before they had even closed half the distance, the cargo ramp was already being lowered, preparing to accept the retreating squad. They covered the remaining distance with the speed of people running for their very lives, all the while glancing back to check on the progress of the industrial robots that were hunting them down. They clambered up the cargo ramp, disappearing into the belly of the craft, which had already powered up its engines ready for takeoff.

Inside the shuttle, once the ramp was closed and the cargo hold repressurized, the four mercenary soldiers moved up into the cockpit, where both the pilot and co-pilot felt the muzzles of a plasma weapon being pressed against their respective necks. The mercenaries then popped open the visors of their EVA suits to reveal their true identities.

"Hands off the controls or I'll blow your goddamn head off," barked a determined-looking Matteo.

"Yeah, we'll be taking things from here," Yuna informed the hapless pilot.

The two others of their team, both experienced fighters from Mackenzie's crew, shepherded the two pilots into the cargo hold where they were shoved unceremoniously into seats and had their hands and feet bound tight.

Yuna then took control of the craft and flew it over to an enclosed shuttle hangar in Moon Base Delta that had already been prepared for its arrival.

CHAPTER 42
FILE TRANSMISSION

The accumulated data harvested from the previous capsule flight tests had been added to Dr. Han Sundar's burgeoning cloud model, and spun up in the supercomputers to produce yet another simulation of the chaotic physics of the debris cloud that blanketed Earth. This new simulation should be a little bit more accurate in its projections and should, in theory, reduce the attrition rate of test launches. However, the urgency of their current situation was such that an acceptable attrition rate ended up being *whatever it takes.*

So, for the third series of launch tests now being undertaken, they planned for at least one success and packed each of the capsules with all the bio-stock supplies they could fit into them. If one got through, then the new deal with the Xilinex Corporation would officially be in operation. The onus would then be on the corporation to incorporate the modified designs into the projectiles utilized by their newly acquired Mass Accelerator, coupled with carefully calculated trajectories based on the latest debris cloud simulations. There would be no more supply capsules from Earth until the Xilinex Corporation proved successful in its return mission. This was the deal.

Han was ruminating on all this as he sat in the operation room of Strawstack, watching live data being transmitted from Vandenberg where the latest batch of five rockets were about to take off.

The room was not as crowded as before, some people choosing not to attend. Perhaps they were losing interest as these tests became more routine. This, Han considered, was probably a good thing, a sign of progress, that launches would soon become a formality, only of interest to those directly involved.

To his, and everyone else's, surprise the first of the five launches plowed straight through the debris cloud without a scratch. This elicited a raucous cheer from the assembled group, so much so that those who had decided to not bother with the launches probably felt that they had made a mistake. This was evidenced by several more people coming into the room to see what they were missing out on.

Han sat back and considered this unexpected success. Even if none of the other launches proved successful, the implications of this one launch were seismic. It would enter lunar orbit in approximately ten days' time where the Xilinex corporation would retrieve it and get to work restocking their bioreactors and replanting their agri-units. Yet, the population that still existed on the moon would require a lot more than this one capsule if they were not to starve to death within the next twelve months.

It would also hand Xilinex Corporation the power of life and death over the entire population. No doubt, those who opposed them would do so under the threat of forced starvation. This did not sit well with Han, given the fact that the remnants of the Western Alliance here on Earth were granting such power to a corporation headed by a person as repulsive to Han's sensibilities as the self-proclaimed Chancellor Adarok. And yet, his acceptance of his new position on the board meant that he was complicit in this arrangement, even though he fully understood the necessity for it. Because without the survival of Xilinex, there would be no Helium-3, and without that... well, he didn't want to think about that.

The next three launches were all failures, although their average altitude was higher than that of any previous attempts, so this, too, was progress. However, the fifth and final launch was textbook perfect. It slipped through the clouds and out into space, setting a course for trans-lunar injection following its predecessor.

Han returned to his accommodation late that evening, grappling with a mix of conflicting emotions. The academic in him was elated that his cloud models were proving their worth, that the capsules could get through, and that the populations on the Moon and Earth now had a future. But part of him felt drained by the mental gymnastics required to reconcile the moral and ethical dilemmas. He found Sheneese sitting at her desk, headphones on, listening to something with deep concentration. She jumped when he placed a hand on her shoulder because she had not heard him enter.

"Jeez, don't do that." She whipped off the headphones and handed them to Han. "You'll want to hear this."

He gave her a tired look. "What, now?"

She put her fingers to her lips and pointed at the ceiling, reminding Han of their suspicions that their accommodation suite might be bugged, then passed him the headphones. He nodded that he understood, put them on, and listened. It was a report from his old friend, Professor Lars Henriksen, about their escape from the Axial Luxor Hotel and the attack by the Xilinex Corporation on Moon Base Delta. No doubt this had come in as an encrypted file transmission masquerading as a debris cloud analysis. After a few minutes, he took off the headphones and looked over at Sheneese. "Wow."

"Wow, indeed," she replied. "Although, it's still not going to end well, is it?"

Han was impressed by the attitude and resilience of the ever-growing population of Moon Base Delta. But Sheneese was right; despite their heroics, their fate was already sealed. "No, they can only survive as long as their supplies last. After that, they'll have to surrender."

"A Pyrrhic victory, then?"

"It would seem so. All they've done is buy some time, nothing more. Unless..." Han paused, his mind racing.

"Unless what?" Sheneese raised an eyebrow.

Han pointed a finger at the ceiling, indicating that they should be careful what they say. "I have an idea, something that I think might help."

CHAPTER 43
BLOCKADE

The Chancellor fumed; it was a humiliation beyond anything he could imagine. The complete and absolute control of Moon Base Delta had been within his grasp, but due to some inexplicable incompetence by the assault team, it had all slipped away.

However, Pompodur's ire was tempered by the news from Earth that the latest capsule tests were successful, and fresh bio-stock was currently on its way. Not only would this go a long way to ensuring food security, but it was also public relations gold. He could live off this narrative for a long time, making sure everyone knew that Xilinex controlled the food supply and, more importantly, what would happen to any group who stepped out of line. Like the SINO hold-outs in Mare Crisium, who would soon begin to feel the ache in their stomachs and come to their senses.

As for Moon Base Delta, that was a more complicated

matter, not least because they were holding sixteen Xilinex mercenaries and two transport pilots hostage after the failed assault, including a military shuttle they had also stolen. Already, the fault lines were beginning to appear between him and the General on how best to deal with the issue.

"It behooves us to do everything in our power to repatriate our people. This situation cannot be allowed to stand." The General's head and shoulders loomed large on the big wall monitor in the administration room that had been set up on the Axial Luxor for the new Lunar government.

Pompodur was flanked by his new head of security, Lieutenant Wilson, along with Director Levrosky, and several others that constituted the new Lunar Council. The General, however, preferred to remain onboard the old Xilinex orbital HQ and was attending the emergency council session via a comms link.

"And do you have a competent military solution for that, considering the abject failure of this... initial operation?" Pompodur adjusted the sleeves of his robes.

"We still don't know the full details of how they managed to subdue a team of highly trained mercenaries," the General fumed. "They may have had access to some powerful weapons that we're not aware of, perhaps legacy military equipment left behind from the time this base was in full operation. It would be prudent to gather as much intel as we can before attempting another assault."

"So, you're saying you don't have a military solution?" Pompodur asked.

"Under normal circumstances, I would say fifty personnel

would be more than sufficient," the General countered. "But only after we find out what went so wrong with the initial assault. And we're also tied up with trying to police several rebellious sectors, as well as the blockade of the primary SINO sector. We simply don't have the manpower available yet," the General conceded.

"If there isn't a military option, then we must give consideration to their demands, since this is now a hostage situation," said Director Levrosky.

"Seriously, are we really going to give credence to these infantile demands for supplies in return for getting our people back?" spat the General.

"Not necessarily," said Lieutenant Wilson, his voice calm and measured. "We could simply blockade them, as we're doing with SINO. They'll soon run out of supplies, more so now that they've got all those extra mouths to feed. Eventually, they will crack."

"But our own people will suffer too if we take that option," cautioned Director Levrosky.

"So be it." Lieutenant Wilson gave a dismissive gesture. "Consider it the price of failure."

"What if we say, okay, we'll do the swap. Supplies for hostages. But... we poison the food, kill them all," offered Aaron Miller, a new sector administrator who had been proving his worth recently.

"Oh, Aaron, that's inspired, and beautifully Machiavellian. However, I see a flaw in that," said Pompodur, impressed with this rising star within the New Lunar Council.

Aaron narrowed his brow, trying to think what it might be.

"They would probably consider that, and, like the royal tasters of old, would simply feed the hostages a few samples just to make sure," said Pompodur with a flourish. "No, I think our best option is to call their bluff, let them sweat it out and run down their food supplies. We maintain a blockade, weakening them physically and psychologically. Then, once we have more military resources freed up, we strike. But this time, General, we must not fail."

CHAPTER 44
DOG FIGHT

Renton probed the scar tissue along the outside of his thigh with his fingers, feeling the bumps and ridges of the latest addition to the topography of his body. The pain had mostly subsided now, and his mobility had returned. The effects of a pulsed energy blast on the body are to render the wider impact area effectively numb and loose all motor control over that area. Sometimes it can be permanent, at least that's what Tanaka had told him. But he was okay, full mobility had returned, all that remained to remind him of the incident was a patch of scar tissue, which was healing quickly.

He was not alone in the med-bay, as he was in the company of several others that had also suffered injuries during the battle with the Xilinex mercenaries. One had died, making a total of three that had lost their lives in the fight to secure the base. There was no doubt it had been a bloody affair.

The mercenaries were being held, and treated, in a different sector under the watchful eyes of a dozen guards drawn from both Mackenzie's and Selene's groups. They operated around the clock, making sure the mercenaries didn't try and do anything stupid. The sector they were being held in could be locked down and isolated in an instant, making escape practically impossible.

Mackenzie was also one of Renton's roommates. She had been lying in a gurney beside him for a day or two, with a bad gash on the back of her head, a broken rib, and mild concussion. But after so many hours of arguing with Tanaka, they let her go, just to get some peace.

A lot of people had come to check in on him and share their stories of the battle. Matteo and Yuna were particularly animated in the retelling of the daring raid they executed on the Xilinex transport shuttle, which was now locked up tight in a maintenance hangar. It had been a brilliant play, completely fooling the hapless pilots. Renton began to see both of them in a new light, see how they had changed, and began to wonder how much he had changed. There was no way that people could go through all the things that they had and not have a profound effect. Yet, he didn't feel very different, apart from a few physical scars, he could not say for sure if those scars extended into his mind, yet.

Alice came, of course, spending quite a bit of time with him. They talked of many things: their pasts, where they had come from, what they had done before all this happened. He imagined that it was a conversation many people were having, what their world was like before "the event." But mostly they talked about the present and how all the various groups of people that now occupied Moon Base Delta were getting along, or in some cases, not getting along. Chief amongst those were Selene and Mackenzie, who, according to Alice, were butting heads over pretty much everything, but particularly over what to do with the captured Xilinex mercenaries, the prisoners of war. And the sooner Renton could get up and about the better, so he could bring some end to their constant arguing. This surprised him. Not that Selene and Mackenzie were butting heads, they were both strong leaders, with a substantial group of followers, so it made perfect sense that there would be jostling for power within the overall group. No, it was that Alice seemed to infer that he was the only person that could bring balance to this fractious power play.

Him? How was that possible? He only ever considered himself as a bystander in other people's parties. He would row in with the consensus and do whatever needed to be done. If he ever took the initiative it was only because it seemed like the right thing to do, and someone needed to do it. But a leader? That was stretching things too far. So he asked DOA for advice.

It began by reaffirming everything that Alice had told him about Selene and Mackenzie, but it was during this retelling that Renton realized just how much the AI seemed to understand about human psychology, almost to the point where he considered that it might be part of its primary directive. This made sense in the context of all the stories he had heard about it and the operation of the original base, and the social experiment that had originally been attempted by the people back then.

However, DOA then went on to outline his position within

the perceived hierarchy of the tribe. "You must remember, Renton, you were the one instrumental in getting your crew out of the SINO compound and into Moon Base Delta. You were also the one who advocated securing supplies from the Seismic Testing Station and rescuing Saito, Kimura, and Tanaka. So they see you as someone they can trust. It's a similar story with your aunt and the people from the Axial Luxor. Then, your old Captain, Mackenzie Arnold, and her group are beholden to you for the successful execution of your plan to fend off the Xilinex assault, by risking your own life in the process. So, in the hierarchy of the collective tribe, you are their natural leader."

"That's just nonsense, DOA. I don't see it that way at all. I could never see myself as a leader, it's just not in my nature, I'm just... an engineer."

"True, but you have engineered yourself into a position whereby the current population of Moon Base Delta look to you for leadership, whether you believe yourself to be a leader is not the point. You effectively are, by virtue of your past actions."

Renton thought about this for a long time. And yes, he could not fault the AI's inalienable logic. But it came as a complete revelation to him, making him feel that he had been walking around with his eyes closed for so long. Yet, he considered there had to be a better way than to have this responsibility thrust upon his relatively young and inexperienced shoulders. Then again, Alice was also right, he couldn't just leave Selene and Mackenzie to a never-ending dog fight.

CHAPTER 45
THE WISDOM OF THE AI

As it happened, a new message had just been received by Professor Henriksen from Dr. Han Sundar, prompting Selene to request a session where those that mattered in the Moon Base Delta tribal hierarchy could gather around a table and discuss it. No one had any objections to this as it seemed like a very sensible idea; message or no message, there were a lot of things to talk about, not least what to do with all the extra Xilinex mouths they had to feed.

The operations room had been cleared out of all the old tech that was still lying around from the very beginning of their arrival in the base. Getting rid of it all transformed the area and it now had a completely different feel to it, much more minimalist and open. Seats had been arranged around the large central holo-table; these had originally been there, but had been removed when the base had downscaled. So, the area had been restored to its original configuration. Renton was impressed, it looked very retro, which wasn't surprising considering the age of the base.

There was much back-slapping and bonhomie going down when he entered. Lots of people were happy to see him finally up and about. Selene, being Selene, chaired the meeting and so called everyone to attention. Renton grabbed a seat in between Alice and Matteo. Yuna was also there along with Mackenzie, Henriksen, Saito, Kimura, Tanaka, and a few others who were part of either Selene's or Mackenzie's groups. Lesser mortals within the new Moon Base Delta tribe either stood around the outer walls or sat on various stacks of equipment. There was an expectant air, a sense that something important in the new history of Moon Base Delta was happening, and everybody who could wanted to be here to witness it.

Henriksen began by outlining the information he had just received from Dr. Han Sundar back on Earth. The launch tests had resulted in some success, and as a consequence, two supply capsules were on their way to lunar orbit, fully laden with bio-stock that would begin to replenish the food production systems. These capsules would arrive in nine days. This elicited a chorus of excited murmuring around the room. A resupply mission was good news, even if the intended recipient was still the Xilinex Corporation.

"How much are they sending?" Alice asked, breaking through the rising chatter.

"I didn't get the exact manifest. I don't think even Dr. Sundar knows that. But, in his words, it is significant enough to ensure that we have a future beyond the next twelve months.

Only I'm not sure if he was referring to this specific supply mission or if he is talking more generally."

"Doesn't matter, this is great," said Yuna.

"Great for the Xilinex Corporation maybe, not so much for us," said Selene. "In case anybody gets too excited, let's remind ourselves that we are already running low on supplies, we can't hold out here for very long, even with the current victory."

"Then I say we rid ourselves of the extra mouths we have to feed. Now, today." Mackenzie slammed a fist on the holo-table.

"So, what? We just hand them back so they can attack us again?" said Saito.

"We've already made a demand to Xilinex. We'll exchange the captives for supplies," said the professor, trying to be diplomatic.

"Yes, we know." Selene raised a hand. "But that's never going to happen, not with that bloated narcissist Adarok running the show. He would rather they all die than give in to any demands we might make."

"Then get rid of them. We must do what has to be done to ensure our survival," said Mackenzie.

"You mean kill them?" It was the first contribution Renton made to the discussion.

"Okay." Mackenzie gestured at him. "So what would you do?"

Renton sat back and considered his old captain. Had she really become so... brutal in her thinking? Or was it always there, just waiting to come out.

"Sometimes, after a project," he began, his tone calm and measured, "there can be a lot of spare parts lying around, things that weren't used or simply accumulated in the creation process. It can be tempting just to throw these onto the scrap heap, only to discover they might have been very useful for the next project, perhaps even vital."

"That's all very well, but we still have to feed them," said Kimura.

"We have to feed more than them, we have to feed ourselves," said Renton. "That's the key issue. Solve that and we solve... everything."

There was a moment where this somewhat obvious statement sunk in with all the people in the room, and their collective minds started to consider how this might be achieved.

"So what are you suggesting, forming a raiding party?" asked Selene.

"We've got two shuttles, one with a plasma cannon," said Matteo. "Then there's all the weapons we took from the mercs. They could all be got working again."

This seemed to please Mackenzie as she sat silent for a beat, running it over in her mind.

"We also have DOA." Renton gave a vague gesture in the air. "It has eyes in the sky and can identify potential targets and extrapolate the probability of success for any mission we undertake."

"I'm not sure I trust that AI," said Chen, "considering it chickened out during the fight."

"It didn't 'chicken out,'" corrected Alice. "One of its primary directives is not to harm humans, something I rather like in my AIs."

Selene raised a hand. "Okay, if I may, I'd like to just

summarize where I think we are going with this, and that is to investigate the possibility of forming a raiding party to secure provisions, and holding off on making a decision about our unwanted guests until a plan has been established." She looked around the table from one to the other. Nobody had any strong objections to this summary.

"Great," she continued. "However, before we move forward, I think it might help us considerably if we adopt a more formal structure to our deliberations. This will go a long way in mitigating against getting bogged down in one area or another."

Nobody knew what any of this meant, so nobody objected to this either. But Renton knew exactly what his aunt was up to: she was making a bid for leadership.

"That's why it would be prudent to elect a party to have a deciding vote," she added. "Someone who we all agree on to have the ability to break any deadlock."

"And I suppose that person should be you?" said Mackenzie.

"Well, I would certainly step up to the plate, if asked. I do after all have the most experience in these matters, and I was also a part of the original Moon Base Delta Project."

"So was I," said Tanaka, raising a hand.

"Of course, I was not forgetting your contribution." Selene gave a nervous laugh.

"Sorry Selene," Mackenzie interrupted, "but maybe you know your way around a negotiating table when all people are talking about is the allocation of bath-towels in the sauna, but this is a war we're in. And that means someone more capable of making the hard decisions that must be taken. So, that would mean I would be best suited to police our way forward."

This was met with approval from Chen and the rest of her group.

In Renton's ear, he could hear DOA's voice. "Now would be the time."

He stood up. "Here's what I think." Everyone in the room suddenly went quiet—not what he was expecting. He paused for a beat then looked from Selene to Mackenzie, then cast his gaze around the assembled group. "The only reason any of you are even having this conversation is because of these people here." He swept an arm around to encompass Alice, Matteo, and Yuna. "Yes, Selene, you got us the codes to here, but it was these people who made it work." He turned to Mackenzie. "I'm happy you found your mission in life, but the only reason we're all not back on Earth is because of your recklessness as Captain of our maintenance vessel, Aurora. You may have morphed into a great wartime leader, but that's about it." He turned back to Selene. "But Mackenzie is right about you, Selene. Diplomacy is a luxury we can't afford. Right now, we need pragmatism, coupled with a healthy dose of risk-taking."

"Sounds like you're putting yourself forward," said Henriksen.

"No, I'm not. Because we already have something that is far better at the job than any human, and that is DOA."

"So you're suggesting the AI has the last word?" Mackenzie almost scoffed.

"Yes, I am, and not because it knows so much about each and every one of us, not even the fact that it sees most of what happens on the lunar surface, nor its ability to extrapolate a raft of possible actions based on the probability of success. No, the reason is because it doesn't have an agenda other than our continued survival."

There was another round of murmuring in the room as the group began to consider the implications of where Renton was taking them.

"Let me give you an example. DOA, based on the current information, what do you think is our best option going forward."

"Given that the continued survival of all who inhabit Moon Base Delta is dependent on securing suitable nutrition, then this is where you should focus all your attentions. Of the options available, and given your current resources, the best option would be the acquisition of the supply capsules that will be entering lunar space in nine days."

Again, more murmuring rose up from the assembled group, but it was more excited now.

"Not only would this solve the immediate problem," continued DOA. "But it would also enable the agri-production facilities here at Moon Base Delta to be reactivated, securing your future food supply."

"No way, that's crazy, we could never pull that off." Selene was shaking her head.

"Why not?" said Renton. "We have two shuttles capable of picking them up from orbit. Also, Xilinex will not be expecting it."

"If I may make a suggestion," said DOA.

"By all means," said Renton, still standing.

"It might be helpful to create a distraction for the Xilinex Corporation, something that will keep their focus away from the capsule operation. An option might be to offer to hand over the captive mercenaries. This would draw in a lot of their attention and a percentage of resources to ensure the handover was successful."

Renton could sense a change in the mood of the room. They had all but forgotten the power play between Selene and Mackenzie and were now focused on the prospect of securing a future. He raised a hand to get their attention. "So, if we're all agreed. We let DOA make the big calls, let the AI do what it was designed to do, look after all our respective interests."

There followed a wave of head nodding and mumbled affirmations. Nobody had any objections, it seemed to them like a sensible solution. No one person or group would have dominance over the other. All would yield to the wisdom of the AI.

Renton sat down, took a breath, and tried to get his heart rate back to normal. He had never done anything like that in his life, but if he were being true to himself, he had to admit, he liked it.

"Just one other thing," said the professor. "What should we do about the Martians?"

To be continued...

Also by Gerald M. Kilby

POWER VACUUM : MOON BASE DELTA 3

Survival hangs in the balance for Renton Hicks and his fellow colonists on Moon Base Delta. They are blockaded by the relentless Xilinex Corporation and running dangerously low on supplies. Their only hope lies in two food capsules en route from Earth and a Martian colony ship carrying technology that could potentially secure their future.

COLONY ONE MARS

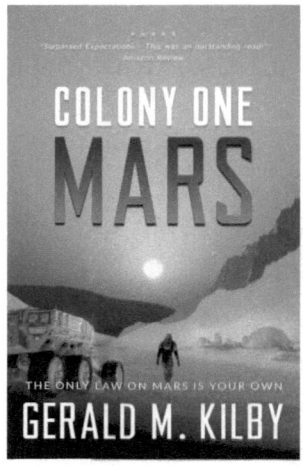

How can a colony on Mars survive when the greatest danger on the planet is humanity itself.

All contact is lost with the first human colony on Mars during a long, intense sandstorm. Satellite imagery of the aftermath shows extensive damage to the facility, and the fifty-four colonists who called it home are presumed dead. Three years later, a new mission sets down on the planet surface to investigate what remains of the derelict site.

ENTANGLEMENT : THE BELT

The discovery of game-changing quantum technology sparks an AI war between Earth's powerful dynasties and the solar system colonies.

A long-lost ship transporting an experimental quantum communications device has just been found in an uncharted region of the asteroid belt. For Commander Scott McNabb, Flight Officer Miranda Lee, and the ragtag survey crew who accidentally stumble upon this lost tech... life is about to become a whole lot more complicated.

ABOUT THE AUTHOR

Gerald M. Kilby grew up on a diet of Isaac Asimov, Arthur C. Clarke, and Frank Herbert, which developed into a taste for Iain M. Banks and everything ever written by Michael Crichton. His novels CHAIN REACTION and BRAIN GAIN are very much in the old-school techno-thriller style while his latest book series: MOON BASE DELTA, COLONY MARS, and THE BELT are all best sellers, topping Amazon charts for Hard Science Fiction and Space Exploration.

He lives in the city of Dublin, Ireland, in the same neighborhood as Bram Stoker and can be sometimes seen tapping away on a laptop in the local cafe with his dog Loki.

You can connect at: geraldmkilby.com